DOWN the ROAD
ROAD
on THE LAST DAY

written by
Bowie V. Ibarra

cover art by
Raymond Reyes

edited and designed by
Travis Adkins

Permuted Press
The formula has been changed...
Shifted... Altered... *Twisted.*
www.permutedpress.com

©*2006 Bowie Ibarra. All Rights Reserved.*

ISBN-13: 978-0-9789707-2-7
ISBN-10: 0-9789707-2-1

Down the Road: On the Last Day

*For Lazy, Pain, and everyone
who bought my first book
and supported my work*

*And especially Bo Woodman:
friend, fellow artist, and
disciple of Mad Max*

Frank Garza Makes A Choice

"We have to kill her," said Frank Garza, sitting on the couch in his charming south Texas living room. A crocheted blanket was draped over the couch, darkened a bit by age, but still nice.

He held a .38 in his hand.

"We can't," said his wife, Dolores, who was standing, gazing through a hole in a boarded-up window.

The afternoon was pretty. A spring day was dawning. Birds flew from tree to tree. A butterfly fluttered in the wind. A soft breeze caused tall grass on the side of a distant road to wave gently.

And a zombie shambled across a yard two blocks away.

"Please don't shoot Alyssa, Daddy," said Blanca Garza, weeping. "Please don't."

Alyssa was Blanca's best friend. They first met in kindergarten, fighting over a young boy they both thought was cute. Their animosity turned to friendship, and they spent the past eight years having fun and getting into some trouble along the way.

One night during their first year of junior high school, Alyssa snuck out of her house to meet a cute boy while Blanca was sleeping over. When Alyssa's mom came to check on the girls, Blanca stalled for time and stuffed Alyssa's bed with some blankets and a pillow. Blanca answered the door and—making sure the lights stayed off—

1

told Alyssa's mom that they were asleep. Politely and quietly, Alyssa's mom apologized and closed the door.

Things were all fun and games for the two girls.

Then the plague hit.

Three days ago, when the world began to fall apart, Frank had to shoot Alyssa's father dead outside of his own home.

* * * * *

Alyssa had called Blanca's dad for help. So Frank ran down the street to their house. Alyssa was in the yard, hiding under the porch.

"What's wrong?" asked Frank.

"It's my dad," she said, rocking back and forth. "My *dad*."

Frank entered the house through the front door and went straight into the living room. He saw Larry Munoz on his knees by the sanguine corpse of his wife, Nina. He had torn open her stomach and was eating her bloody innards, soaking their patterned carpet in blood. The red liquid and goo caked around his mouth as he chewed on a long cord of intestine. A struggle must have occurred, as the house was a total mess.

On the television in front of them, a commercial for *Spray-n-Clean* illuminated their bodies. Despite the national emergency, sponsors were still shilling their products.

"New Spray 'n Clean Double Power combines two powerful stain fighters to clean more stains better than Attention and OxiWash."

Had Frank not regurgitated his breakfast in disgust, Larry might not have noticed him, as he was concentrating intently on his meal. The vomit splattered onto a large area rug by the door. A lion resting on the African savannah was now covered in what started Frank's day that morning: chorizo and eggs.

"Take the Stain Challenge and get an unbeatable clean versus most leading detergents!"

Frank could remember how Larry haggled over the price of the carpet in a Mercado in Mexico. Larry always claimed he could get a good price on anything.

After the first round of vomit, Frank darted back out the screen door, spitting up again on the porch.

Alyssa stood on the front lawn nearby and watched Frank puke. Soon she was spitting up on the lawn as well. Some specks of brown bile speckled across her white and red shoes.

Frank came off the porch and stood near her on the lawn. "Go to our house, Alyssa."

Before Alyssa could start running, her dad, Larry, threw open the screen door and stumbled onto the porch. An intestine was still in his hand, slowly dripping dark brown slime.

Frank was stunned for a moment. Larry's eyes met with Frank's. A second passed before Larry began to smile and extend his hands toward Frank.

"Get to the house now, Alyssa!" Frank yelled as he raised his gun at Larry.

Alyssa quickly began to scurry down the road to the Garza's house. She was crying in disbelief.

Frank aimed directly at Larry's head as Larry tumbled down the stairs. He hit the pavement of the concrete walkway hard, busting his head open.

Frank had spent the past four days learning about the plague from news reports, but he never expected it to come to Beeville. And certainly not to his neighborhood.

But small outbreaks were occurring in town the past two days. Local law enforcement were able to contain the spread in the town and quarantine the city, but the past several hours had seen a rise in problems. Not only was the infection a problem, but word came that the police numbers were depleting. Some dying. Some running. Some hiding. The remainder was defending the city from anyone trying to enter through major inlets.

A rumor started two days before that kids returning from San Antonio on school-related activities had started the problem in town. Band students and the track team all fell ill with high fevers after returning from a track meet at MacArthur High.

Larry was a bus driver for the band on their trip to S.A. Good old bus 26. He had driven it for close to fifteen years. Larry knew where every child that got on his bus was let off, and parents depended on him for that.

And now he was rising from the pavement. Blood trickled from his now broken nose and split head. Frank raised his gun again.

But before he could get off a shot, an adolescent boy grabbed his arm. Instinct and quick thinking caused Frank to jerk away, stumbling back and falling down. The kid fell awkwardly to the ground, and judging from the way the boy growled, Frank knew the kid with the blonde mullet and white Poison t-shirt featuring C.C. DeVille and Bret Michaels, stained with blood, was infected.

Larry was already just a few feet away. So Frank, still on his back, brought the gun up and popped off two rounds. One cut into Larry's shoulder just above his embroidered initials on his blue polo shirt. The other hit square on the forehead, creating a small entrance wound in front and a large exit wound out the back. Blood, skull pieces and brain matter sprinkled across the lawn before Larry fell flat on his back.

The boy was quickly crawling towards Frank. Frank rose to a knee and let off one shot, splitting the kid's jaw in two and severing the spine. The blonde hair on the back of his head, (the proverbial *party in the back,*) flew up for a moment as the bullet exited from his neck. The young boy fell to the ground and started to twitch. Nerves were trying to regain control in a noble yet futile effort as the brain was still feverishly sending commands to disconnected extremities.

A scream resounded through Frank's ears. Standing, he noticed an elderly neighbor had exited her house next door and was holding her hands to her face. Her bright green and orange flowered muumuu stunned Frank for a moment. It was atrocious.

"Get back in your house!" Frank yelled. "It's not safe out here!"

Several people in the neighborhood joined the old lady on their respective porches. Though the town had been secured for the most part, Mayor Hickland encouraged all people to stay in their homes and fortify them as they saw fit. They were encouraged to stay there as well, even though a large area of downtown near the courthouse was secured if anyone wanted to go there.

Or, if things got worse before they got better.

Frank put the gun in his belt and ran home.

* * * * *

Now Alyssa was gone. She had become one of the creatures.

She had been almost inconsolable during her stay. But she was also showing signs of infection. The day before, she had become very lethargic. She had a high fever and her skin began to lose its dark brown color, turning paler and more sickly by the hour. Frank and Dolores figured she was on her last leg.

So moments after she closed her eyes, Frank and Dolores duct-taped her to a metal folding chair in the guest bedroom. Within three minutes, (only mere moments after she was secured to the chair,) her eyes opened. Her eyes, once a pretty shade of brown, had become clouded with goo, an effect of the infection.

Minutes after putting Alyssa in bonds, the family knew things were probably going to get worse before they got better. So Frank asked his wife and daughter to go to the shed and get the wooden boards and anything else they might be able to nail to the walls to secure the windows and doors. It was two hours into their work when the mayor issued the edict via recorded phone message for citizens to stay in their homes and secure their property.

Before nightfall, Frank's family had secured every door and window of their house.

But Alyssa's screams and groans throughout the day had echoed through the walls, slowly driving the Garzas bananas. After repeatedly listening to the television advising people to shoot any creatures in the head, Frank presented the idea to his family.

And so there they sat, on the couch they bought only last month. It was brand new, but Dolores insisted on keeping the embroidered throw blanket on it. It was part of their home, she said. Her mother had made it ten years ago, and everyone who had seen it raved about it. The skill. The colors. The time sacrificed.

When her mother died two years after making the blanket, the throw became a comforting reminder of Dolores' mom. Dolores became very protective of the blanket, mending it when it would unravel and even going so far as to insist Frank didn't fart on it.

As the years passed, the blanket lost its luster. Stains from drinks, snacks, and general use had tarnished it. Yet it remained in place. Frank and Blanca knew how important it was to Dolores. So did all the same people who raved about it for so many years.

But the memory of Frank's *suegra* was the furthest thing from his mind as the family contemplated taking Alyssa's life.

—Or *afterlife*, whatever the case may be.

"Please don't kill her daddy," pleaded Blanca. She was a blooming thirteen year old girl with all the worries, desires, and tensions of a girl that age. Boys. Looks. Stars like Orlando Bloom and Johnny Depp plastered her wall.

She was having a tough time, too. She hadn't heard from any of her friends the past two days. And spending this time with Alyssa made her fear the worst. For a girl who spent several hours a day on the phone with friends, she was suffering a kind of smoker's with-drawal: tummy aches accompanied with headaches. Fortunately, there was no weight gain.

But it was clear to the Garza family that the isolation that Beeville once enjoyed was being invaded by the plague the T.V. made out to be a big city problem.

Blanca's beautiful tan face was stained with tears. Her long black hair was beginning to tangle. It rolled down the back of her faded blue American Eagle brand shirt. Her off-white cargo capris were dirty from wiping her hands from the lumber used to fortify the house. White *chanclas* held fast to her feet, the white strap secure between her red painted big and second toe.

Frank stared at the votive hands forever sculpted in prayer on the coffee table by the issue of TV Guide. Kelly Clarkson's Texas smile graced the cover, promoting her scheduled guest appearance on *Dawson's Creek* tomorrow. Pre-empting the show with the government-sponsored news reports of the terror across the nation was highly probable.

"What are we going to do with her, 'Lores?" asked Frank to his wife. "Just keep her in there? Huh?"

Dolores knew Frank was right, but only responded with silence. The zombie outside, many yards away, stood still for a moment.

"*Mi hijita*," Frank began, "Having her in here puts all of us in danger. You've heard the news. Their bites are infecting people. Making them sick and turning them into one of them."

Blanca, sitting on her knees on the floor, put her face in her hands and wept.

For several minutes, everyone stood in their places: Dolores watching the zombie down the way, Frank thinking, Blanca weeping. Clear snot clogged her nose.

Frank continued to sit silent, the votive hands on the coffee table reminding him to pray.

Pray for protection.

Pray for his family.

Pray for forgiveness.

Frank rose and strode to the room Alyssa was tied up in. He took the gun off safety.

Dolores and Blanca were so focused on their thoughts that it took them a moment to realize Frank had left.

Frank opened the door.

Blanca rose from her knees and screamed, dashing to the back room.

Dolores awoke from her daydream and followed Blanca, yelling, "Frank, no!"

Alyssa was still tied to the chair, and her black hair was still tied in a *chongo* on the back of her head. A plain red shirt was moist with saliva. She still had on her very short blue shorts. Solid black Jordan's were still on her feet. Her dark brown skin was pale, her cheeks sunken.

Frank raised his gun.

Blanca pushed her father aside and stood between him and Alyssa. Frank immediately raised the gun away from his daughter.

"*Mija,* get out of the way!" he yelled.

"Please, Dad! Don't!" screamed Blanca.

"Move now, Blanca! I'm not playing!"

"No!" she yelled. "I won't! Look! I can show you she still has a chance!"

Blanca turned to Alyssa and gazed into her glazed eyes.

"Alyssa," began Blanca, calming down, "Alyssa, it's me, Blanca."

Alyssa looked into Blanca's eyes. She groaned a phlemy response and opened her mouth. She seemed to smile.

"You remember me, right?"

Alyssa began to wiggle in her chair. She vocalized awkwardly again. She tilted her head to the side and smiled.

"You remember when we were at the mall? At Claire's? You bought me this bracelet there, remember?" she said, indicating her simple bracelet. Alyssa smiled again, a bigger grin, with teeth. Her eyes squinted a bit, a sign of a true smile.

Blanca turned back to her dad.

"You see! You see! She remembers!"

Alyssa's smile quickly faded and she looked toward Blanca. In a surprise move, Alyssa yanked free from her bonds, grabbed Blanca by the arm, and bit. Blanca screamed in terror as a piece of her warm flesh and blood found a new home in Alyssa's living dead mouth. The bite was precise and efficient.

Frank grabbed Blanca by the shirt and threw her behind him into the hallway, out of the room. The powerful yank caused the flesh on her arm to tear clean off, the strength of a father trying to protect his daughter. A modest arc of blood flew through the air in the empty space of Blanca's flight pattern. Blanca crashed into her mother, and both hit the wall and tumbled clumsily to the floor. Frank and Dolores' wedding picture fell from the wall and busted open.

Alyssa slowly chewed on Blanca's flesh. Blood oozed messily from her lips. She gazed at Frank, who was already pointing the gun at her. She had no chance to grab at him as the bullet was already flying to her face down the well-oiled barrel of Frank's .38. It exploded her nose as it traveled through the nasal cavity and viciously cut through the R-complex above the spine. Red blood splashed against a bookshelf behind her, covering her YM magazines in red as she fell to the floor.

Frank immediately spun around and answered the cry of pain from his own daughter. She was already being treated by Dolores, who had wrapped a towel around her bite. The real magic of motherhood.

Frank embraced Blanca, who was now crying in pain. Dolores joined them. They all knew what was about to happen. With emergency help out of the question, her fate was sealed.

Blanca looked into her father's eyes.

"I love you, Daddy."

"I love you, too, *mi hija.*"

* * * * *

The next three hours were difficult at first, but warm in the final minutes. They all recalled happy stories from the past. About family. About trips. About life and love.

"You remember," Blanca began, short of breath and tired, rivulets of sweat flowing down her face. "You remember... when Tío Manuel's ... pants fell down... at the river?"

Frank and Dolores smiled and giggled, sadly. "Yes, *mi hija.* I remember."

As Dolores and Frank strapped Blanca into a chair when she continued to become progressively lethargic and racked with fever, it was her love for Frank and Dolores that she professed.

After a Lord's Prayer and a Hail Mary, they made the sign of the cross as a family. Frank and Dolores kissed their daughter. Both began to weep.

"Don't leave me, Mom. Don't leave me, Dad," mumbled Blanca, barely coherent.

They didn't.

Frank and Dolores held her cold hands until her eyes closed.

Then Dolores left the room, shaking and crying.

Moments later, Blanca's eyes slowly opened again.

Foggy.

Sad.

Frank discharged an aimed bullet from his gun, dropped it, and searched for his wife.

They both cried themselves to sleep, embracing each other on the new couch, comforted by the faithful old blanket.

Bowie V. Ibarra

Gary Chapman and Wayne Crocker

I need a reload here! Pass the ammo! Pass the ammo!" yelled Wayne Crocker to his buddy Gary Chapman.

"We haven't shot anything yet, dumbass," said Gary as Wayne put the camouflaged Suburban in park and turned off the ignition.

"I've always wanted to say that," said Wayne with a smile.

"You're a dumbass. You know that?"

The old hunting vehicle sputtered to a halt as the two looked across the abandoned parking lot of the Coastal Bend College dorms. Smoke from burnt oil burped forth from the tailpipe and caressed the hot pavement, then drifted off into the ether.

Gary and Wayne were attempting to go above and beyond the edict set down by the mayor two days before. Mayor Hickland had issued a recorded order over the local phone lines to all residents in town: All able-bodied men were to join with what few police remained and secure six different sections of the city.

And within days, the sections were secured.

But the college campus was not part of the assigned areas. The college itself was a distance away from City Hall and the plaza. It was not given importance.

The day Hickland set down the declaration, many residents showed up, armed and ready. No police official really cared whether the guns were registered or not, just that the men were armed and

11

had plenty of ammo.

But once Beeville was relatively secured, Gary and Wayne volunteered to check out the college grounds and dorms. Mayor Hickland gave them his blessing, and they were to report back with what they saw. Gary and Wayne figured the dorms could offer a shelter for people who were sneaking into town through the back roads, but they had to be secured first.

"You know, more and more, I'm thinking this was a bad idea," said Wayne as he exited the tacky black, brown, and green hunting machine.

"C'mon, Wayne," said Gary, who was already out of the vehicle and shouldering his bolt action, aiming for a shot, "Don't wuss out on me now." Gary fired off a round. It blasted open the head of a male creature in the distance. Blood spewed forth on its yellow and purple letterman jacket as it fell to the sidewalk near the theatre building, away from the dorms.

"Nice shot."

"Thanks," said Gary, putting the rifle on safety and slinging it over his shoulder. The parking lot, dorms, and campus looked relatively abandoned, with the creatures scattered in the far off distance posing no immediate threat.

"But how do you know it was one of *them*, huh? Maybe you shot someone looking for help," teased Wayne.

Gary paused for a moment. An awkward silence ensued.

"Well, let's go look," said Gary, taking out a .45. It was an alternate weapon in case things got a little tight.

"All right," agreed Wayne.

They walked toward the theatre building and further away from their vehicle.

Gary Chapman looked older than fifty-six. Service in Vietnam had been unkind to him. He never rose higher than Corporal, but fought like a Sergeant. Twice he was promoted to the leader of his squad when their chief was shot dead by the Viet Cong. He did not want to shoulder the responsibility either time, but valiantly led his friends, (or "battle buddies," as he called them,) into the breach to accomplish their mission.

Their first mission was to find and secure a VC tunnel entrance along a portion of the Mekong Delta. The entrance had been identified and located by Army Intelligence. Along the way—mere moments after starting their journey through the jungles of southeast Asia—they were ambushed. The point man was shredded to ribbons as they had stumbled upon a makeshift pillbox hidden in the green foliage. The heavy machine gunner was blasting through the ranks of Gary's squad, sending bolts of fear to his heart. Not even two minutes had passed when their squad leader, Sgt. Jack Kellner, took two to the face and three to the body. The medic immediately went to assist, but it was no use. His head was mincemeat.

Being the next highest rank in the squad, Gary immediately rallied those who were out of range of the machine gun nest. Together they devised a simple plan that centered around securing positions for their heavy machine gunner, and that plan was executed efficiently without any losses on their end. Ultimately, they were lucky to meet so little resistance, as they figured more VC were out in the jungle somewhere.

The other mission was to recapture (for the third time) Hill #296. The hill was in the center of enemy territory. Gary knew there was no strategic value for the hill, but the military claimed otherwise. His squad leader stepped on a landmine, handing him the duty of completing the mission, which he did.

Three days later, Gary learned the hill was recaptured by the enemy.

Gary made many friends during his tour of duty, but seemed to lose just as many on a daily basis in the jungles of Southeast Asia.

War is never fun, but it was an absolute nightmare for Gary. Thirty years later his nights were still filled with horrific images of combat: dead women, maimed children, pieces of friends.

Though the war was quite unkind, the families of the men who died under his command were far worse. Gary spent two years in jail for assaulting and beating down the brother of Private Lance O'Connell, who died at the third battle of Hill #296.

When he was released from prison, finding a job was nearly impossible. For several years, Gary hit the bottle like a champ, drinking himself into oblivion. Daily, he would hold a sign on the corner begging for beer money.

It took kind hearts and lots of time in an alcohol rehab clinic to heal his pain, forgive his faults, and regain his pride. With help from rehab, he got a job washing dishes at a Mexican restaurant called *Mi Familia* in Beeville. He was even able to rent an apartment and get an Associates Degree in History from Bee County College, the very campus he was now securing.

"Ten dollars says it wasn't," teased Wayne.

"That shit ain't funny, man," said Gary. A long black moustache rolled from above his lips down to his chin. It was very gray, a contrast to his dark black skin. White snow-like hair curled around the side of his head. His bald pate gleamed in the afternoon April sun. Today he wore black combat boots, faded blue Levi's, and a gray Beeville Spartans high school football shirt. Patches of sweat darkened the area around his armpits.

"Fine, a beer," said Wayne.

"Now we're talkin'," said Gary, still unappreciative of the joke. They walked toward the body lying still on the concrete sidewalk.

Wayne Crocker was a forty-five year old mechanic and football fanatic. He was a rabid Dallas Cowboys fan—one of the really obnoxious ones who liked to throw the Cowboy's dynasty in the face of anybody who was fond of other teams. To Wayne, Jimmie Johnson was God, Jerry Jones was stupid to fire him, Barry Switzer didn't know what was going on, and Ken Norton was the best defensive player the Cowboys ever had. Wayne felt Norton was even better than Randy "The Man-ster" White.

Though Wayne was kind of a jackass when it came to football, he was still a good friend to Gary. Wayne had been taking Gary to Texas Stadium in Arlington for the past fifteen years to watch the Eagles versus Cowboys and the Redskins versus Cowboys. Gary wasn't really much for football, but admired the courage of Emmitt Smith and Troy Aikman, although Gary secretly liked division rival Philadelphia Eagles. Gary was a closet fan of Reggie White and Jerome Brown before he died.

Wayne was rather plain. His hair was usually unkempt and he always wore a blue or white Dallas Cowboys t-shirt, regardless of its condition. Lonely, Wayne watched a lot of porno, with his favorite porn star being Amber Lynn. Apart from Gary and very few friends at work, Wayne kept to himself. He usually only communicated with others on Cowboy message boards and fan sites. Not really a computer geek, Wayne knew just enough to be an overly obnoxious smack-talking Cowboy superfan.

They approached the body.

"Well?" Gary asked.

"Well, shit, man. I can't tell. He's got no head. That was a good shot."

"I can tell you he was a creature," Gary said with certainty, scanning the area for danger.

"How?" Wayne replied, who was still trying to figure out the body's previous condition. Large chunks of brain, skull, and flesh sat like hamburger meat on the pavement. Dark black blood continued to pour gently from the head.

"Because he wasn't walking, he was stumbling along."

"What if he was drunk?" Wayne asked, kicking at the corpse. A pair of dice fell out of the blue and yellow letterman jacket.

"He wasn't drunk, man. He was dead," said Gary, looking back down at the corpse. He picked up the dice, then put them in his pocket.

"Fine. I owe you a beer," Wayne groaned, putting his double barreled shotgun to his shoulder. "So now what?"

"Let's secure the theatre building first, then work to the—"

"—Why not just check the dorms, then the theatre? We could camp out on the roof of the theatre building. Make it our headquarters." Wayne was talking like an excited kid going to Six Flags, Fiesta Texas in San Antonio.

"Huh?"

"Yeah," Wayne said, his blue eyes widening. "We can go get some mattresses from the dorm and camp out on the roof of the building!"

"Are you kidding?" Gary said. "We'd roast up there." The Texas sun was already drawing sweat from their pores.

"Well, shit. I don't know."

They thought for a moment. The funk from the executed zombie began to drift to their noses. They both gagged and took a step away.

"He's dead all right," Gary said, chuckling.

"Maybe we can get a canopy or a table with an umbrella above it and put it up there?" Wayne suggested, still shaking his head to escape the funk stuck in his nose.

"Still too hot, you dummy."

"Well, it *is* a good place to keep an eye on *one-eighty* if people try to come into town." (The Highway 180 exit was about a half mile away from the school and secured by the police.) "It would make a good point to watch the road in and report to the mayor if we see stuff. We could even take our time and clear other buildings if we want to later on. Or, shit, a *dorm room*." Wayne gave a silly double thumbs up.

Gary stood silent for a moment, scanning the area again.

"Aw, hell. Why not," he responded. "Not like anyone's waiting for us back in town. Okay, let's do the dorms first, then we'll figure it all out."

"Wait," Wayne said, shouldering his shotgun. He was aiming at a creature stumbling out of the dorms. "I can get it."

"What are you thinking, fool?" Gary asked. "You don't have any range with that."

"What do you mean? I'm using slugs," came the reply.

The creature heard their bickering and turned toward them.

"Yeah, but it's—like—forty yards away!"

"You can hit something with slugs forty yards away."

The creature stumbled closer.

"Maybe the body, but not a clean headshot."

"Yeah, you can."

"No, you can't."

The creature was drawing closer, about twenty yards away now. It was moving at a good clip.

"Yes you can, Gary. Watch." Wayne shouldered the double barrel gun and aimed.

"Use the center line of the barrels."

"I know. Look, just shut up."

"I'm just sayin'." Gary backed away and watched.

The creature was now between ten and fifteen yards away. Wayne squeezed off both barrels. A huge portion of the creature's head burst off, spreading blood all over its vintage beer shirt. It stumbled forward and fell to the ground.

"See. I told you so," Wayne said, clicking open the shotgun and shucking the used shells from the barrels. They tapped across the pavement. The hollow plastic and metal of the shells sang a short farewell on the ground. Gentle smoke emanated from the barrels like the smoke of a neglected cigarette in an ashtray.

"Yeah, but he was only, like, ten yards away."

"*What*?! That's, like, twenty yards."

A gurgling howl took them by surprise.

"What's that?" Wayne asked.

Another creature came from the dorms from the same passage as the now headless beast.

"I got it," Gary said, putting the .45 away and raising his bolt action and squeezing off another shot, sending the ghoul to the ground with deadly efficiency.

But three more came out. Then four. Then seven. Then four more. All shuffling in their direction.

The men stood stunned for a moment.

Then Wayne broke the silence: "What do you say we tell the mayor the college is hopelessly occupied?"

"Fine by me," said Gary.

They turned back to their truck, only to find it surrounded by several creatures, with more shambling in from the main campus area.

They both yelped, "Oh shit!"

Pulling out their pistols, they let the monsters have it. Guns blazed and zombies fell as they tried to secure the vehicle.

A bullet from Gary busted a window in the rear of the Suburban. Wayne slouched, grimaced, and grumbled, "*Aw, man.*"

"Sorry, Wayne," Gary said, cleaning a path to the driver-side door. He pulled at the handle.

It was locked. Force of habit.

"Shit! Keys!" Gary yelled, sending another two zombies to the ground. More were closing in.

"You've got them, man," Wayne said as he arrived at the passenger side door. Two were threateningly close to him.

"Damn!" Gary reached into his pocket and found the keys. He then promptly dropped them.

Wayne let off two separate blasts from his shotgun, leveling two creatures with unpleasant gut shots. A ring of red was forming in the parking lot around the vehicle. Three more zombies were yards away from Wayne. He couldn't help but notice one of the creatures he shot begin to twitch on the ground. Innards splashed out of the ripped stomach as the nerves convulsed the body. The other beast, on the other hand, was rising again, spilling its intestines all over the parking lot.

Three more were also uncomfortably close to Gary as an empty magazine fell from his pistol. He had not had a chance to get the key yet.

Committing to action, Gary removed his rifle from his shoulder. Though several creatures were mere yards away, he methodically blasted the zombies in the face and head. Glorious sprays of crimson and bone splashed through the air like fireworks.

Never before had Gary valued the marksman training gained in the Marines so many years ago. There was an exercise in which Gary had to shoot an entire clip on a bolt action rifle in the quickest time possible and still hit the target dead on. After successfully performing from the sitting, standing, and prone position, Gary received a second place marksman award.

"Let's go, Gary!" yelled Wayne in utter fear. He was in survival mode as he clicked his shotgun shut again, and blasted two more creatures who were close by. Entrails fell from the backs of the ghouls as the slugs severed the spines. The two creatures fell to the ground, their upper bodies trying to rise again, their legs paralyzed.

Gary picked up the keys, fumbled for the proper one, then unlocked the door. Before he entered, he flicked the power lock and called to Wayne, "Get in!"

Wayne opened the door and sat down as the engine of the hunting Suburban engine turned.

"Let's get out of here," Gary said, throwing the vehicle in reverse.

"You said it," Wayne agreed, shivering.

The vehicle moved swiftly backwards, knocking a creature down. Gary then shifted to drive. The vehicle drove over the bodies they had leveled, rocking the two men to and fro for several moments accompanied by an audible, "*Whoa...*"

They headed back to town.

"So, tell the mayor the college is occupied, right?" Wayne asked.

"Right," Gary said with assurance.

The remaining creatures began pursuit of the camouflaged Suburban as a ring of bodies were marinating in blood on the asphalt of the Coastal Bend College dorm parking lot, simmering in the warm Texas sun.

Monsignor

A cool breeze caressed the vibrant green countryside. A relaxing blue color could be seen at erratic intervals in a sky congested with puffy white clouds. A robin flew to its nest, while a cardinal cracked a nut from a bush.

A flock of sheep grazed on the countryside. The shepherd held aloft his staff and the animals responded by moving in a gentle wave across the field. The shepherd smiled.

Yet behind the shepherd was darkness. It was slowly enveloping the land. Lightning danced across the growing wasteland, setting fire to trees and buildings. An army of zombies was marching steadily toward the shepherd and his flock.

The shepherd turned to the encroaching darkness and struck the land with his staff. A bolt of lightning fell from the sky, striking the staff and delivering a burst of energy into the army of ghouls. A large mass of creatures fell, but rose again.

Again the shepherd sent a blast against the beasts, only to find them rising again.

The shepherd turned to his flock. To his horror, they were being consumed by a gang of zombies. The sheep released sad cries that were soon snuffed out by the rotting cadavers who were thrusting their hands into the bellies of the sheep and eating their red entrails.

Above the shepherd, an alabaster altar was floating in the sky, which was now becoming dark. A crimson angel stood over a helpless lamb strapped to the altar. It raised a blade above its head, ready to strike the lamb.

The shepherd turned away, only to come face-to-face with the army of zombies.

They lunged at him...

Monsignor O'Leary woke from his dream with a yelp. Stunned, he took an inventory of his surroundings. After a short moment of taking in his bedroom and realizing he was safe in his rectory domicile, he took a deep breath. With a sigh, he brought his penitent hands to his head in prayer before returning his head to the pillow.

* * * * *

The long crack in the mirror, stretching all the way from the top to the bottom, subtly split Monsignor Ralph O'Leary's image in two as he buckled his white collar around his neck. He cringed for a moment as he attempted to button the sacred garment, which was fitting very tight. His finger was digging into his throat, trying to relieve the suffocation. After a few tries, the button clicked into place.

The crack in the mirror began below a carved crucifix at the top of the elaborate dresser in his living quarters in the Parish auxiliary. It extended to the bottom, near an old, haggard Bible on top of the dresser. There was nothing else on top of the dresser except for cufflinks—nary a speck of dust. Monsignor O'Leary was a bit on the fanatical side when it came to cleaning.

As O'Leary took a cufflink off the immaculate dresser, he looked at his hands. Brown liver spots and thick veins lined them. A broken index finger on his right hand had shifted the finger subtly to the right.

It was a reminder of that glorious youthful day in Ireland, years before his family moved to America. He was playing on a local football team. The coach had put him in as a striker in the final moments of a game when their star striker—*and his personal rival*—Emory MacDuff, was ejected after an obvious two-handed penalty. The star defender of the opposing team had goaded MacDuff into making a bad choice, costing him an early visit to the showers.

Moments after Emory left the field, O'Leary struck with a header into the goal, giving his team a point advantage and, ultimately, the victory.

As his teammates charged at him with joy, a wayward high five caught his finger wrong and caused the hand he still carried to this day.

He buckled his cufflinks and gazed into the cracked mirror. His white hair wrapped kindly around his head. His bald spot was speckled with freckles. A large nose stood nobly under two large, bushy white eyebrows. He was relatively tall, and a bit stout. His daily runs that only recently turned to walks around the block kept him healthy.

But he did have a secret vice, and as he walked to the door on his way to Saturday confession, he partook of a shot of Johnny Walker.

Generally, O'Leary consumed one shot an hour before bed to calm his nerves from the stresses of dealing with the parish business, as well as ease the repression of his earthly desires. As a Catholic priest, he was expected to follow a very rigid code of conduct, foregoing all selfish desires. The needs of the physical being was one particularly strong force that required intense focus and meditation to repress.

So apart from the daily shot, O'Leary was never abusive of alcohol. However, the past two weeks had been trying on his soul. Watching in horror as the world fell apart on the TV screens shook O'Leary's very being. Witnessing in true sadness and impotence the world being literally consumed by these Satanic monsters. Monsters who, from all accounts, are the recently dead rising. Rising and attacking. Attacking and consuming the living. It was an unbelievable abomination, but it was all true.

The dead were rising.

The very thing he celebrated every Sunday at *Our Lady of Perpetual Forgiveness*, the glory of the risen Lord, Jesus Christ, and the wish of every Parishioner was now occurring, but on a perverted basis. It was a gross defilement, almost spiteful corruption of the promised gift of resurrection and to all of Monsignor O'Leary's life work in Catholicism.

Philosophically, O'Leary was stuck between the sanctity of life and survival.

When the plague struck, his first instinct was to call his family in New York. His older brother, Ewan, didn't answer. Neither did his sister, Leela. He tried several times a day for several days with no success.

Three days into the global plague, an edict was issued by the Vatican. O'Leary and the world watched closely on the television as the Pope spoke from a pulpit within the walls of the sacred temple.

"My brothers and sisters, we must not lose faith in the plan our Lord has set down for us. We must continue to treat each other with love and respect, and treat our brothers and sisters affected by this malevolent curse with dignity and respect... But make no mistake: These beasts—these living, walking dead creatures—are not children of God, but atrocities of Satan. Therefore, they must be destroyed."

Monsignor thought to himself how nice it was to have a German Pope in this trying time, one who would not pull punches. One who would speak the harsh truth. One accused of being influenced by his younger days in the failed Hitler Youth program in the final days of the second world war.

Monsignor O'Leary postponed mass the second week of the outbreak while the City of Beeville regained control of their territories, sans federal help. Once the problem was contained within the city limits, O'Leary continued his daily masses, though Sunday was reduced to only two masses, one in Spanish and one in English.

Most of the big cities in the United states were still experiencing the worst in the veritable deathgrip of the plague. But Beeville, once secured, was fortunate enough to go about its business. Hence, O'Leary leaving his room to bestow his regular duties of delivering the holy sacrament of confession within the church walls.

Sheriff
Sam McMurtry

T he doors of Beeville City Hall were thrown wide open. Papers swished and swirled in the air, then floated back to the floor as Sheriff Sam McMurtry closed the door. Very few artificial lights were on in the building, but natural light was basking the hallway in a pleasing radiance, forcing shadows to disappear.

City Hall was a great stone structure that doubled as the courthouse. The wooden interior was desperately in need of more renovation, (as it was the same material used in the construction close to a century ago,) but the grant from the state to restore the building went to the copper dome and the statue of Lady Justice standing on top. The Hall stood in the middle of the plaza in the center of town. After the outbreak, the building was all but abandoned.

There had been a bit of a ruckus the first couple of days when the outbreak hit Beeville hard. There were still blood stains on the floor even though all the bodies were removed several days ago. The mayor had decided to use City Hall as a natural central command for the re-securing of the city, and that is who Sheriff McMurtry planned to visit.

He opened the door to the mayor's office. It was a spacious room with couches, a table, and several desks. The centerpiece was the receptionist's desk, and sitting behind the desk was the mayor's personal secretary, Stephanie Zapata.

"Hi Stephanie."

"Hello Sam."

Before the Sheriff could make a request, Stephanie chimed, "So what have you heard?"

McMurtry was expecting the question. He answered, "Good news all around, ma'am."

Even though McMurtry was about twenty-five years her senior, he could not help but notice her young, tan Latin body. Thin glasses sat on the tip of her dainty nose. A tight and revealing red top housed her young yet generous breasts and tight stomach.

"Well, that's great to hear," she responded. Stephanie behaved as if it was an ordinary day, seemingly ignoring the danger that had been repelled, yet still loomed like a dark specter around the city. "I'll tell the mayor you're here." A manicured finger pressed a button on a desk phone. "Sheriff McMurtry here to see you."

"*Send him in*," came the reply.

"You can go in," said Stephanie to a stunned McMurtry. He had been staring at her youthful cleavage and the black brassiere peeking not-so-subtly around the edges of her blouse.

"Huh? Oh, yeah," he responded. Embarrassed. Caught.

She grinned and gave him a wink as he entered the office, her smile revealing one snaggletooth among an otherwise perfect set of teeth.

Mayor Hickland rose from behind his desk and walked around to greet the sheriff with a firm handshake.

"Sheriff McMurtry, how are you?"

"Just fine, mayor. And yourself?"

"I'm pretty fine myself," he said. Hickland wore navy blue suspenders holding up his navy blue pants. A plain white shirt was buttoned up almost all the way and a paisley maroon tie hung loose under his collar. He asked, "So what's the news?" as he guided McMurtry to a table near the desk. A large map of the county lay unrolled on top, defaced with large red marks and squares.

"Well," the Sheriff said, "the men holding down the three main roads into town have encountered low to moderate resistance from traffic on the highways. At your direction, we have denied all entry into the city. For the most part, traffic has decreased significantly day by day."

"Any confrontations?"

"Five of real consequence over the past week."

"Fatalities?"

"Two. None taken on our end."

"And the monsters?"

"Little to none. Close to a dozen might be seen daily by all three sections near blockades along the roads. But they're easily taken out. There are multiple sightings daily within the city limits, but most are quickly neutralized by our established militia."

"Sounds like our city is secure," said the mayor with confidence.

Abruptly, McMurtry's CB radio went off. A static voice said, *"Dispatch to McMurtry. Do you copy?"*

As it fell silent again, McMurtry excused himself from the table, took a few steps away from the desk, and answered back.

"This is McMurtry. Over."

The static voice replied. *"We have a situation at the Highway Two-Ten post. Deputy Ferguson needs you to advise."*

"Patch me in to Deputy Ferguson, please."

After a moment, Ferguson's voice called out. There were screaming voices in the back. *"Ferguson. Over."*

"This is McMurtry. What's going on? Over?"

Stephanie walked in with a file and approached the mayor.

"We have a large group of over twenty. They're insisting we let them in. Over."

"You heard the mayor. No one is to enter the town. Over."

"Roger," came the response. The CB fell silent.

McMurtry replaced it on his collar, then turned to see the mayor and Stephanie whispering quietly, very close to each other. McMurtry stood for a moment, wondering how to share the news when Stephanie walked toward the door and back to her desk. She cast a glance at the sheriff and grinned.

The mayor asked, "What's the news?"

"Situation at post three. Told them to follow your order."

"Good man," Hickland replied, adjusting himself.

Awkwardly, McMurtry went on, "I'm going to head out there and lend some assistance."

"Thanks for the update, Sheriff. Take it easy," replied Hickland with insincerity.

McMurtry walked out of the office. He closed the door behind him.

"Have a nice day," said Stephanie, covering every word with honey.

"You, too, ma'am," said McMurtry chivalrously. He strolled to the door. Once again, papers took to the air as the door opened, then closed again.

City Hall fell silent.

Stephanie clicked on the intercom button.

"You're so powerful," she said in her low voice, colored by her years of smoking. "A whole city secured by your command. That's *hot*."

After a moment, the mayor replied, "That's enough, Stephanie. You know my wife wouldn't appreciate this."

Stephanie grinned deviously as she replied through the phone intercom, "Aw, c'mon. It's the end of the world. Besides, you never cared before." Every word was laced with sexual intent.

It was not that he never cared, but more that his sex life had been much different with his wife the past seven months. Since he found out Evelyn was pregnant, the sex had been different. Gentler. Loving. Not that the husband and wife were not capable of it, but he enjoyed more energetic engagements.

And Stephanie provided that.

He pressed the reply button. "Come on in."

* * * * *

Sheriff McMurtry drove down the road to Deputy Ferguson's position at the intersection of IH-37 and Highway 210.

The Beeville police force had been decimated the past few weeks. They had lost about sixty percent of their force, reducing them to about one hundred men. These men had been assigned by Mayor Hickland to secure the entrances to the City of Beeville against the mass exodus from San Antonio and surrounding towns. Resistance had been minimal, with only several skirmishes with travelers putting the men at risk. No one from the force up to this point had died.

Mayor Hickland had commanded his police force to set up three

26

blockades at major entrances to the city: Two at the business exits into Beeville at 181 and Highway 210, the other at the west end of town at the intersection of IH-37 and Highway 59. They had a one-hundred percent success rate, preventing any and all refugees from getting into town. Locals, though, did bring in friends and family through farm road 799 and 796.

The blockades were set up three days after the epidemic began, creating a primitive quarantine of Beeville. Mayor Hickland encouraged all people to eliminate any threat within the city. Lawlessness did arise in several sections of town, but were soon checked and eliminated by the more responsible members of the city. Several days of skirmishes within the city limits eventually put not only the creatures, but the looters too, in check. By the time the city was considered secure, bodies lined many streets. An effort to remove the bodies was underway, but to no real effect. Law enforcement put the bodies in bags and stuffed them in the back of eighteen-wheelers. Mostly, people within secured neighborhoods managed the bodies they were responsible for in their own way, either through cremation or stacking them in sections of the neighborhoods that were abandoned.

Though it was a challenging battle, the city was officially secured, with infections revealing themselves sporadically. As tough as things had been lately, Sheriff McMurtry was thankful for his job.

Five years had yet to fill the emptiness in his heart for his wife of twenty years. Lydia Jane McMurtry bravely fought a noble battle with cancer, and not a day passed when Sheriff McMurtry did not remember the final month. It was a month filled with the moments families should spend together without knowing one of them was dying. With their only child, Edgar Lane, in tow, they traveled across Texas. They went shopping at the RiverCenter Mall in San Antonio. They went to Dallas to watch a Dallas Maverick's game. Lydia always liked looking at basketball players. Sam never did mind so much. He was a fan of the sport, lettering in basketball for the Beeville Spartans his sophomore year. They even had some thrills and laughs watching the Texas Rollergirls revive the sport of roller derby in Austin.

Sam and Edgar were fortunate in a way as Lydia Jane crossed over to the other side in her sleep. Sam immediately knew she had gone, as she was always an early riser. He called his son Edgar at his apartment in Austin and consoled him. Edgar immediately drove home for the funeral.

After a proper burial and time off for mourning, Sam and Edgar moved on with their lives. Edgar graduated with a law enforcement degree and joined the Army, just like his father had. As a college graduate, Edgar was able to enlist as an officer, but insisted on being a part of basic training like all the others. The last time Sam heard from Edgar, he was stationed in Kuwait, fighting the good fight against terror—The same terror Cable News Channel was blaming on the plague unleashed around the world.

At Sam McMurtry's side, next to his can of pepper spray, was his cell phone. Every ringtone was set to the standard Nokia tone, except for one. That one in particular had been programmed to play the theme song from *Sanford and Son* when a specific caller was on the other end: His son, Edgar. Watching the show became a bit of a ritual for the two McMurtry boys during Edgar's college days. When Edgar would drive back into town from school, they would both stay up late to have some laughs together, thanks to TV Land. It was a moment for father and son to bond.

The last time Sam heard the theme song blare from his phone was two weeks before the world fell apart. His son had not called since.

Though the job had kept his mind focused on other things, it was not easy. Sam got the feeling this moment at the I-37 blockade would be no exception.

* * * * *

"You assholes!" screamed Katy Russell to the remnants of the Beeville police department lined up behind the five-car barricade. "Let us in!"

Large orange and white roadblocks were set about twenty yards from the police cars in the middle of the road and even off into the ditches beside the road. Every police officer, (which numbered only twenty-five,) had their weapons drawn and aimed at the small group of refugees. All the officers in the column wore flakjackets and black helmets. A time traveler from the 1940's or a fan of the History Channel might mistake them for Nazis.

Deputy Ferguson was speaking over a megaphone to the group of nomads who had packed into two large trucks.

"*You need to go somewhere else. Beeville is not allowing anyone into their city. Mathis, Pettus, and George West have all set up for letting people in. Not us. They have rescue stations.*"

"Are they FEMA centers?" a voice called out.

"*No. They are not official FEMA centers, as government agencies have yet to come this far.*"

Sheriff McMurtry pulled up behind the barrier, turned off the vehicle, and stepped out.

Katy Russell continued her aggressive plea for compassion. "I've told you, we need to get to a hospital! We have several people who have been bit by those things!" She was wearing tight blue jeans and a thin blue belly shirt. Her blonde hair was cut just above her shoulders. A plastic barrette sat in the middle of her head, keeping her hair back away from her face. She was twenty-eight years old and very fit, and could usually get her way by simply looking the way she did. She was dismayed that it wasn't working this time.

"*And I told you they're already dead!*" replied Ferguson with cold assurance. "*You'd better kill them now before they infect others in your group!*"

Deputy Armstrong walked up and stood by Ferguson. He was holding a small pair of binoculars.

"We have spotted and confirmed four bite victims. They all look like they're done for."

McMurtry walked up.

"Gentlemen," he said.

"Sir," both men formally replied.

"What do we got?" he asked, taking the binoculars from Armstrong.

"A group of thirty, confirmed. Four confirmed to have infection. All are refusing to leave."

"Give me the megaphone," said McMurtry. He exchanged the binoculars for the bullhorn. He put it close to his mouth and declared, "*Attention! Attention! You need to leave this roadblock now. You will not be granted admission into Beeville. The police will use force if you do not leave and take your infected counterparts with you.*"

A cacophony of boos, catcalls, and colorful metaphors filled the

29

air as the tension rose. Several of the cops, positioned behind the cars, cast nervous glances at each other. Several Adam's apples rose and fell in anxious dismay, the anxiety of facing a new and brutal moment of truth.

The raucous crowd was a group of survivors from Three Rivers. The plague had reached their town a day after the outbreak, but hit with a vengeance. People within the community had family in San Antonio, Laredo, and Corpus Christi. By returning home to Three Rivers to be with their families, people brought along the infection.

It started at night. Though the town was aware of the national threat, no plan of action was taken to prevent it from penetrating the borders. And the town was small enough for most everyone to think that the big city problem would certainly not reach their own doorstep.

But it literally did.

* * * * *

Laura Espinoza was going to school at U.T. Brownsville. Its claim to fame was that it was the southernmost university in the United States. It was literally on the Texas/Mexico border. The bridge into Mexico—*Matamoros*, specifically—was only a block away from the university.

It was no surprise that Laura Espinoza and her friends spent many Saturday nights crossing over into Matamoros for the Mexican bar scene. Twenty dollar "drink and drowns" were commonplace, and the clubs made it very easy for anyone 18 and up to find their way inside. Buses and vans owned by club owners would wait at the border near the bridge to take prospective customers straight to their bars. It was a smart way to make money.

Laura kept her grades up enough that her parents did not mind her enjoying herself every once in a while.

The day before the first reports of the plague, Laura had attended a concert at a local arena. It was part of a national event called "Songs for Life: Music against Terrorism" sponsored by Halliburton, the Rockafeller Foundation, and the Carlyle Group. The three organizations, interestingly enough, had made quite a profit from the war on terror and wanted to put a more compassionate face to their name by pledging to send part of the proceeds to all nations affected by the war. And they made sure to maximize their profits.

Knowing that staging a large event at one location would miss out on a large segment of the U.S. population (which also translates to a loss of potential profits,) they chose to have performances in every state in the continental United States. The lone star state of Texas had seven shows alone: Dallas, Houston, San Antonio, El Paso, Austin, Lubbock, and Harlingen.

Laura enjoyed the Harlingen show. The headliners featured Micheal Salgado, Axe Bahia, and Thalia. Local bands opened the show, but Laura didn't pay too much attention to them. Instead, she got to know Alfredo, a guy from her Tuesday and Thursday College Algebra class. They spent the evening together, and after a few beers got to know how much space was really available in the back of her '97 Toyota Corolla.

The following morning, Laura awoke with a peculiar cold and immediately the guilt set in. She knew for sure she must have caught a venereal disease.

As the television began to reveal early moments of the world falling apart at the hands of the bizarre plague, Laura couldn't shake the thought of what she might have caught. She immediately called Alfredo as the first reports of the dead rising began to flood the media.

The gurgling digital ringing of a phone diligently attempting to connect sounded twice before Alfredo picked up.

"Hello?"

"Alfredo?"

"Who is this?"

"It's Laura."

"Who?"

Laura was a bit taken aback at the comment. For the past two months she had had a huge crush on Alfredo. Last night was the lucky culmination of her lustful desires. But being forgotten after sharing herself mere hours before cut to the core.

She dismissed any dignity she might have had and replied meekly, "Laura from last night."

"Oh, shit. *Laura*," said Alfredo, embarrassment lacing every syllable. "Are you okay?"

She decided to be blunt after the inconsiderate remark. "Are you clean?"

"What?"

"Are you *clean*?"

"I bathed when I got home."

What a dumbass, she thought. She bluntly asked, "Do you have VD?"

"No!" exclaimed Alfredo, suddenly understanding the first euphamism she used. "No, I'm totally clean. I got checked three months ago."

"And have you fucked anyone since?"

Alfredo seemed distant, and his response revealed that his attention was on something else. "Have you seen the news?"

"Yeah, why?" She turned to look at the television, which was now onto regular programming featuring four female celebrity news reporters gossiping behind a large desk.

"They're now saying people who are dying are returning to life."

"Shut the fuck up," said Laura in disbelief. "You're full of shit."

"I'm serious." Alfredo coughed into the phone.

"Hey, *Mister Manners*, thanks," replied Laura with obvious sarcasm. She grabbed her remote and found a 24-hour news channel.

"*...confirm that bodies of the dead are rising. There are unconfirmed reports that those people are also attacking the living....*"

Laura took a moment for the comment to sink in.

"Laura, are you there?"

"Hey, let me talk to you later," she said and hung up the phone on Alfredo before he could say goodbye.

Regular programming did continue on most of the stations as the morning gave way to the afternoon, with interruptions and updates coming in at the top and bottom of the hour.

As reports continued to convey more information, Laura got a little scared. But she prepared for class anyway and walked out the door like she would any other day.

It took her a half hour to walk to class and back to her dorm room. Word spread quick about all classes being cancelled for the day. She noticed many of her fellow campus students scattering to their vehicles. Classes returning to normal schedule the next day was now suspect, and Laura decided it was time to take action as she was noticing signs of a fever rising in her body. If she caught some sort of sexually transmitted disease, she would need someone to nurse her back to health in this crisis. Her mom would be willing, as always.

She never suspected she might be coming down with the epidemic that was sweeping the nation.

So Laura packed some of her things and walked to her car to return home to Three Rivers. As she started the engine to her Corolla, she opened the bottle of *Robitusson Severe Cold and Flu Formula* and took a long swig. When she was finished she placed the bottle in the cup holder by her seat and hit the road.

She turned on the radio.

"*... you are near the border, do not attempt to cross over into Mexico. Homeland Security has closed all bridges into Mexico. Americans on the Mexican side of the border will be detained there indefinitely. Any attempt to cross back into America by either United States citizens or Mexican nationals will be met with lethal force and shot...*"

Laura couldn't believe her ears or her eyes as she pulled out into the street from the university. A line of cars were stacked up against each other, pointlessly waiting to reenter Mexico, coughing up invisible exhaust into the air, filling the air with a choking gas. Traffic going the other way was also horrendous. It reminded her of a hurricane evacuation that took place the year before. And this day would prove no different. Movement was slow and erratic, with Laura finally reaching Highway 77 within an hour.

After spending the afternoon in a long line of cars moving out of the city, Laura finally turned off onto a back road that would take her to Three Rivers. She was curious how the border patrol checkpoint was going to handle all the people on the roads.

She was surprised to find the post abandoned. Blood stained the walls and ground around the checkpoint and bodies littered the road. It was her first up-close and personal view that things were wrong in the world.

She was fortunate to have gassed up her vehicle before the show the night before, as the hours on the road made her car drink the fuel inefficiently. As day turned into night, Laura was close to home, finally reaching IH-37 from Highway 77 at around six o'clock. Her health was quickly fading. Thinking it was a combination of the cold and the noxious fumes from the vehicles all around her most of the day, she soon realized her failing health might be something more than a cold or fever. Her brown skin turning pale was a big indicator, as well as her round face sinking at her cheeks.

When she finally turned into her home in Three Rivers, she was in great pain. Her body had become almost totally stiff and she had just enough energy to open her car door, take one step out, and fall to the ground.

The headlights on the Corolla were set to high beam, shining through the curtains in the window of her adolescent sister's bedroom in the dark, waxing minutes of the twelve o'clock hour.

Bright lights reflecting strongly off the mirror in the bedroom, Danielle awoke and looked out the window. She recognized Laura's car, but could not see her on the ground beside it due to the bright lights. Danielle moved from her bed and went to her parents room.

She knocked on the door.

"Mom?"

No answer.

She knocked again.

"Mom."

"*What*?" came a muffled reply.

"I think Laura's home."

Danielle waited about a minute before her mom, Lynette, opened the door. Lynette was wearing her pink slippers and bathrobe. Her hair was up in curlers. Without a word, she walked through the hall into the living room and towards the front door. Danielle followed close behind.

As the two set foot in the living room, they both stopped in their tracks as an ominous knock emanated from the front door. The three knocks in slow succession held the two frozen, like two store mannequins displaying sleepwear in a shop window. The sound of the still-running car's engine clicking outside in the driveway hummed a mechanized song in the stillness, suspended in park.

Lynette was the first to move, walking toward the window near the front door. She pulled back the white lace curtain and looked outside.

"Who is it?" asked Danielle.

"I can't see."

Lynette walked to the front door and flicked on the porch light. It lit for a second before the filament broke, flashing brightly before it popped into darkness.

"You're kidding me," whispered Lynette. "Danielle, get the living room light."

Danielle instinctively found her way to the illuminated hallway and flicked the living room light switch on. Danielle and Lynette squinted, giving their eyes a moment to adjust.

Lynette looked out the window again.

"It's Laura," she said and scrambled to the door.

Unlocking the bolt lock and unhitching the chain lock, Lynette opened the door.

The light from the living room cut into the darkness of the porch and illuminated an emaciated and pale Laura, who was swaying slowly.

"Laura?" said Lynette. She almost moved forward to embrace her, but hesitated. Something was wrong. Though the family was aware of the national crisis, it didn't click that Laura might be one of the new statistics.

It was in that moment that Laura lunged forward and grabbed her mother. Under normal circumstances, it could have been considered an embrace. But as Laura bit into her mother's neck with Lynette screaming in pain and surprise, it was clear to all that this was not the homecoming they were expecting.

A struggle ensued as Lynette tried to release herself from the literal death grip of her living dead daughter. Blood covered Laura's arms as Lynette tried to pull away to no avail. Danielle screamed in terror. In a spontaneous show of courage, Danielle came to the aid of her mother. Delivering several sloppy but intense punches to her big sister's stomach and ribs, Danielle made Laura loosen her grip on their mother, who pushed her matricidal dead daughter stumbling back onto the porch.

As Laura fell backward, she grabbed Danielle by her curly brown hair. They both lurched out the door onto the illuminated portion of the porch.

Startled from his slumber, Leo Espinoza stumbled through the hallway and into the living room. He rubbed his eyes and tried to come to his senses as he was shocked awake from the middle of a ninety minute sleep cycle. It was hard for him not to think that he was in the middle of a horrific dream, still sleeping in bed. His wife was bleeding profusely against the wall by the front door, trying to stop the bleeding by applying direct pressure. Blood dripped around a hand already layered in crimson. She was hyperventilating and whimpering like a frightened dog. Leo's two daughters were struggling on the porch. Danielle was unloading punches to Laura's body and face in an untrained assault.

Leo dashed to his wife.

"Save Danielle," she gurgled. Her entire chest was a slick red river.

Danielle was now screaming as Leo ran to the porch.

Still not quite understanding what was happening, Leo yelled at Danielle, "*Danielle, stop!*"

He grabbed her around her neck and pulled her off.

"Dad, no!" yelled Danielle.

"What the hell is going on here?!"

He was answered by Laura, who grabbed his arm and bit into his forearm. He yelled in pain and disbelief, punching his dead daughter in the nose. She let loose and stumbled back onto the porch.

"No!" yelled Danielle.

Lights from the neighboring houses began to illuminate once dark rooms as the hubbub was waking up other households.

Leo stumbled back into the house, gripping his forearm. Danielle, possessed by anger, returned to assault her sister, clobbering her with punches. But it left her vulnerable to a bite, and Laura pulled Danielle down to her by her pajama shirt and bit her shoulder. Danielle screamed in terror and pain as she pulled away from her sister, losing blood fast, dripping from her shoulder onto her nighty. She bounced against the outside wall and looked at her wound.

Laura would not be denied. As if looking for revenge, she steadily returned to her feet and approached Danielle. When Danielle tried to get to her feet, Laura pounced and bit again, this time in her neck. With the first bite seemingly taking the fight out of Danielle, Laura began the chore of consuming her sister alive. Danielle screamed in terror.

Leo had fallen near his wife. She was sitting still in a pool of blood, her hands at her side. Blood had ceased pumping from her neck.

"Lynette? Lynette?"

Her eyes were open, but vacant.

It was then he remembered the news and truly realized the national plague they had watched unfold on television that day had penetrated their small town.

Leo began to weep as flesh was torn from bone just outside on the porch. He reached for the face of his wife, touching her eyes, caressing her cheek.

Lynette's eyes moved, different somehow. Cloudy. She looked at Leo and slowly began to smile. Leo returned a smile. Lynette slowly reached for his hand and gripped it. Her skin was cold.

"I'm sorry, Lynette."

Lynette bit into his hand, removing a chunk of flesh from between his thumb and index finger.

Leo screamed and struggled with his wife as she bit again, deep into his arm, hitting an artery.

Within moments, the Espinoza family of 163 Indian Paintbrush were the first victims of the plague in Three Rivers.

After freeing himself from the grip of his wife, Leo ran to the porch. Laura was disemboweling Danielle, tearing vital organs from her sister's belly. It was as if Laura was making sure everything was out from the corpse before she continued to eat, spreading still-pulsating organs all around the porch. Blood, filth, and bile fouled the porch as Leo dashed past the carnage and scrambled to a neighbor's house for help, bleeding and dying. He was totally oblivious to the fact that he was about to seal the fate of Three Rivers. The neighbors were unaware as well.

Leo passed the plague along to his neighbors, who were only so willing to help.

Lynette, Laura, and even the disemboweled Danielle rose and walked to the houses in their neighborhood. Danielle's walk was a crouching nightmare, as there was no support for her heavy upper body. Her abdominal muscles had been torn apart, but her legs still worked. Each girl walked to a different house, as if aware of what they needed to do to spread the plague. They easily passed it on with a swift and unexpected bite to the neighbors that had watched them grow up—Neighbors that only wanted to help.

As the night turned to dawn, Three Rivers was facing a crisis. Just like the Espinozas, family and friends were returning to town from the big cities. And just like the Espinozas, families were being infected. As dawn turned to day, the city was in a panic. With limited law enforcement available, things could not be contained in the small south Texas town.

When day turned to dusk, people were scrambling to get out of town or securing their homestead. When dusk turned to night, fights to survive erupted around town. As night turned to day again, the final survivors fled the city amid a rising tide of dead, dying, and of fellow citizens returned to life as abominations.

*   *   *   *   *

And so they stood, frightened, scared, and angry. The last remaining survivors of Three Rivers, Texas, were staring down a living wall of boys in blue, guns prepared to fire on them, denying them safe entry into Beeville.

"You fuckin' assholes!" came a shout from the refugees.

"What do we do, sir?" asked Ferguson.

"The men have their pepper spray, right?"

"Yes, sir."

"Do we have any tear gas?"

"Yes, sir. About thirty canisters," Ferguson said, indicating the city's only SWAT van.

"Good. I need you to—"

But before McMurtry could finish, the refugees began to disperse, screaming in terror and scattering like spooked cattle. They ran in all directions. Out of the back of one of the trucks, a creature stood up. It was an old man. Another in the back of the same truck, a man dressed like a mechanic, had grabbed a fellow passenger, securing their arm and biting.

A gun was fired, from where or by who no one knew. The bullet traveled through the standing creature's head. Another shot was fired.

"Hold your—!" yelled McMurtry before stopping mid-sentence.

It was too late. The mystery gunshot startled the police. The tension was too much and what was left of the Beeville Police Department opened fire on the last remaining citizens of Three

Rivers.

"Stop! Cease Fire!" yelled McMurtry.

The people running to the police barricade for help were cut down first, followed by the people running on the highway. The very few who got away, including Katy Russell, headed into the brush on the opposite side of the road. Rusty barbed wire on the fence line along the road tore at their clothes, but they ignored the scratches and ran into the brush.

"*Goddammit*," grumbled McMurtry, walking back to his vehicle in disgust. He threw open the door, climbed inside and turned the ignition, then sped off.

Ferguson heard tires squealing for several seconds until the car McMurtry was driving disappeared down the road. The gunshots around him began to subside, like a belt of firecrackers that had been lit all together and ending their explosive volley.

"This is bullshit," came a voice from the line.

Standing before them on the highway, the vehicles, and the ditch beside the road, was a sea of dead bodies. Men, women, and children were mowed down by the police. Blood was dripping from their wounds. Groans could be heard in the distance. The people of Three Rivers had been massacred by the Beeville police. Within moments, they would rise.

Armstrong approached Ferguson. "Shall I send someone out to confirm neutralization?" he asked, grimly doing his duty. Confirming neutralization was the process of sending out a policeman to shoot all the bodies in the head, confirming death.

"I'll do it," Ferguson said with shame. He grabbed an automatic weapon and an extra magazine and headed into the murdered mass.

Arguments were breaking out among the men as Ferguson crossed the barricade to confirm neutralization.

A woman was lying face down near the barricade. Ferguson put a hole in the back of her head. Hair and flesh quickly readjusted near the entrance of the bullet. A man was on his back, four holes in his chest. Another bullet found a new home.

Another.

Then another.

Yet another.

Ferguson had neutralized close to thirty bodies before he made it to the truck that contained the creatures that started it all. As he stepped closer to the vehicle, angry voices from the police barricade indicated arguments were reaching a fever pitch.

In the back of the truck was one of the creatures that initiated the riot, chomping on a portion of arm. It seemingly ignored Ferguson, greedily tearing flesh and gristle away from the bone with its teeth.

As Ferguson aimed his machine gun, he wondered, *Who was this person? A father? A son, sure. A husband?* He realized at this point it did not matter anymore.

The creature continued to ignore Ferguson, devouring the arm like a hungry school kid at lunch on hamburger day. It hardly flinched as Ferguson sighted down on the weapon, aiming for the head.

Ferguson blinked as he squeezed the trigger, unleashing a bullet that removed a significant portion of the creature's head. Brain matter splattered across the rear window of the truck. Specks of blood spread on his weapons and arms. He looked down at it in disgust. The creature slumped to the side of the truck, dead. Its hands fell across its chest, covering the shirt of perhaps its college alma mater, *Rio Grande College.*

Ferguson stood near the truck for a moment, staring blankly at the truck's interior as fuming voices spewed vulgar insults and degrading remarks at each other back at the barricade. His eyes registered a CD case. He couldn't help but notice a *New Order* CD, like the one that he had at his house in the CD carrier. The synthesizer of the new wave band began to play in his head, blending with the gunfire that suddenly erupted behind him. Several short blasts from automatic weapons discharged their deadly lead payload. The sound danced through Ferguson's ear and out the other as he recalled his favorite song, still standing and staring into the beautiful blue Texas sky. Vultures circled above the asphalt a mile down the road. It was a song that brought a moment of comfort to the unreal pressure he was feeling.

A body crawled to him.

"Please... help me... please... help me..."

It was a middle-aged woman, wearing what was once a pretty sequined light blue shirt that was now stained with blood. Streaks of blood stained her gray hair. Two bullet holes in her chest dripped scarlet over a sequined sun.

"Please... help me..."

He had a chance to help, to make a difference in this woman's life—what was left of it. But instead he erred on the side of caution and put the woman down with a shot square in the head.

A bullet from somewhere around the barricade grazed Ferguson's own head and he flinched, taking cover behind the truck. Another shot rang out and Ferguson heard a body fall to the ground near the barricade.

A car engine revved and sped away as Ferguson cautiously raised his head from behind the truck, shaken from his daydream of days gone by. Safer days. Peaceful days.

He looked back to see Armstrong, gun drawn but pointing upwards, signaling him to walk back to the barrier.

As he reached the police position, he could not help but notice six of his men lying dead on the ground. His first instinct was to reload his gun and neutralize them, but he had had enough of that.

Instead, he delegated the duty to Deputy Tomasi, who was standing near Armstrong.

As Tomasi began to empty his service pistol into the heads of his fallen comrades, Ferguson turned to the remaining four policemen. Pointing at the barriers, Ferguson stoically commanded, "Hold this line."

Pierre "Red" LaRue and Alexander Rich

South Loop 410 in San Antonio, Texas, looked like the infamous "Highway to Hell" massacre from the first Gulf War: dead bodies on the road, roasted bodies in cars, and wrecked and burned vehicles dented, crashed, or charred black littering the once bustling highway. But this was not the result of a ruthless air strike, but a veritable picture of the national living dead crisis.

Rain gently began to pour over the land, caressing the souped-up blue/black 1985 Ford F-150 that was ruling the trail of ruin. Large tires splashed in newborn puddles of water, washing the undercarriage with muddy water. Large chrome floodlights stood above the cab on a thick iron rollbar. A large white metal guard on the front of the truck also housed two more floodlights. Water dripped and rested in several small pockets of rust along the rear bumper, safely engaging in its process of oxidation, slowly eroding away the steel bumper. A *Gilley's* sticker warded off fading on the left side of the truck's bumper.

Pierre "Red" LaRue maneuvered through the silent and still traffic of Loop 410 with his companion in this apocalypse, Alexander Rich. The classic Ford was a roaring blue transport searching for life in a sea of death, hoping to find safety and solace somewhere down the road.

"Red" LaRue was wearing a black and worn Night Ranger concert t-shirt and blue jeans. Black boots housed his feet, and a bandana was making a valiant effort to contain his wild curly red hair. Rain began to gather on his pale arm.

Alex Rich was wearing a worn white t-shirt with the words "*Listen to Richard Wagner*" printed in black on the front. The shirt fit tight around his stout barrel chest. His blue jeans were stained with dirt and blood. Alex also wore black boots. His hair was thinning, and his hairline was receding. His face was stern, but was cringing in frustration.

Red took notice.

"So are you gonna say something, or do I turn on the radio?" Red asked. He looked at Alex and judged by his facial features and demeanor that he was sulking over something. The re-upholstered blue seat was holding him in a comfortable slouch.

"All right, all right. Just leave me alone for a minute, all right?" replied Alex, staring out the open passenger side window. Raindrops had soaked his sleeve, but he didn't care.

"Dude, you're acting like you were queer for George or something," said Red, goading Alex with humor, trying to break the funky spell he was under. George Zaragosa was a man they had met in San Antonio who had stumbled into a safe house they were a part of. They both swayed for a moment as Red maneuvered around a wreck.

"Man, you go to hell," said Alex, bugged by the homosexual reference. "It's just hard for me to accept what he's going through right now, you know?" They both had a suspicion that their newfound friend from Austin had had his card punched by the global sickness.

"Man," said Red, "Live and let die, dude. Live and let die." Though Red wasn't necessarily a hippie in the classical American sense, his attitude tended to reflect that hedonistic impulse.

"Red, do you have to associate everything with the Beatles?"

"What?" asked Red in feigned disbelief. "The Beatles are one of the greatest rock bands ever."

"Dude, for the past ten minutes you've been singing *Octopus' Garden*."

"Well, I'd rather be under the sea in an octopus' garden in the shade."

"But for twenty fuckin' minutes? The song isn't even that

goddamn long, man. I mean, c'mon!" Alex watched a zombie emerge from the wreckage and try to pursue the vehicle.

"Well, what do you want me to sing?"

"I don't want you to sing shit. Just drive."

"What do you have against the Beatles, man?"

"I don't have anything against the Beatles. It's just annoying to sit in a vehicle in the middle of a goddamn global apocalypse with a guy singing *Octopus' Garden* for twenty fuckin' minutes."

Red was hurt. "Fine. Then turn on the radio, then."

"I will."

"Fine."

"Fine."

Red thought it amusing that even though they had only known each other for the better part of a week, they were bickering like brothers.

Alex switched on the radio. The same announcement from FEMA, the Federal Emergency Management Agency, sang the same tune.

"*...person's found to have firearms in their possession will be subject to interrogation and incarceration...*"

"Incarceration, my ass," said Red. "Did you know that in a national crisis, all prisoners in prisons are released?"

"I thought it was if war broke out within the U.S.?"

"No, man. It's a national emergency in the area."

"Interesting," said Alex, not totally convinced.

Though the two did not see too many things eye-to-eye, their political beliefs were more or less in line with the standard conspiracy hallmarks.

"Yeah. Crazy, huh?"

"Well, yeah."

The radio rambled on.

"*...nearest FEMA center near you...*" Then an artificial break cut off the message from the government. "*...In San Antonio, the Alamodome, the SBC Center. All High School football stadiums and gymnasiums...*"

"You know," said Red, nonchalantly running over a zombie with the tires, "That's easily one of the stupidest things to do."

"What is?"

"Put your faith in the federal government."

"Amen."

Both Red and Alex held a common distrust of the government, specifically the voluminous codes set down by the maritime government and all of the people running it. From mayors allowing eminent domain seizures of family lands passed from generation to generation, to governors working towards double taxation through toll roads—and do not even get them *started* on the President of the United States.

"If what George Zaragosa said is any indication of what could happen in a camp, no one should search out those damn FEMA places."

"They're probably all done for by now anyway."

Alex pursed his lips, knowing he was right. He thought about George.

"Is that Highway Thirty-Seven?" asked Red, squinting at a sign in the distance. He was a bit nearsighted, but not enough for him to buy glasses.

"Read the sign," said Alex, knowing the answer.

"Dude, I can't see it from here," said Red.

"Yes, it's thirty-seven, man," said Alex. "That's the one that takes us to Highway One-Eighty-One to Poth, right?"

"Read the sign," said Red, getting Alex back. Alex smirked.

The sign read: *IH-37, Floresville, Poth.* Floresville was thirty miles away. Poth was forty.

They had heard word that Poth had fortified the city and they wanted to join them.

"Exit here," said Alex.

"I know," said Red.

Pierre "Red" LaRue was born and raised in Universal City, a subdivision of the San Antonio metroplex. He was an artist at heart, and his red hair and curls always set him apart from the other kids— That, and his constant scribblings, drawings, and rants he would enter into his sketchbook.

Over time, he grew to accept how others looked at him and actually relished being different. If he found that a large group of people, even his friends, supported a particular sports team or political figure, Red would support the opponents. He always loved the underdog. Feeling the glory from a victory by an underdog was always more satisfying than the victory of a proven and dominant winner.

Red was also quite the sporting kind. He had played second string outside linebacker for his high school football team and also had an affinity for the *other* football—*soccer*—though he never played it formally in school. Mainly, he was a special teams standout in football that liked to hit people.

Red became wary of the government during the Clinton Administration. Hours after the Oklahoma City bombing, Red became confused as news reports began to change their stories as that fateful day moved forward. In the first few hours, reports were that there were several undetonated bombs in the building. There were even live reports saying that the bombs that did not go off were being deactivated by local officials.

However, by the next day, the official line had eliminated the previous day's reports of multiple bombs on site and changed the entire event to a lone bomber. Red knew something was wrong. It was here that he began to scribble notes in his sketchbooks, eventually keeping the two separate. His art sketchbooks were blue. His notes on global events were in red. Both would have a little art or writing in them as the inspiration found him.

Red tended to be a straight arrow when it came to behavior, but had moments where his artistic libertine would be released, usually around women. It was especially hard for him working at a Blockbuster Video near the St. Edwards campus in San Antonio. Young college coeds frequented the video store. Not a week went by when Red did not join one of his female customers on a Friday or Saturday night and watch a movie—*watch*, of course, being used very loosely.

"So you think Poth is still secured?" Red asked.

"I certainly hope so," Alex said.

Alexander Jackson Rich was a bit of an aristocrat, but separated himself from his lower high class status. Born and raised in Houston, Texas, Alex had had the best of everything available to him. He was not of "old money" like most of the oil families in Houston were. His father, Hector, was a dentist and invested wisely during the dot-com boom, wisely pulling out before the bubble burst. He then invested that money in a land deal that brought the money in. Though they had plenty of cash, they still lived a modest life. In high school, Alex drove a simple Chevy Cavalier—but it was brand new, of course.

Alex graduated from St. Mary's University in San Antonio with a Bachelor's in Mass Communication. He was working at a local TV station as a cameraman for the news. At around this time, he recalled a report about alleged Delta Force training in urban warfare. The report was about how the city Police Chief did not allow the Delta Force to engage in their training activities, as they would be using live ammunition in populated areas.

Alex then did a little more research outside of work and found a conspiratorial superpatriot in Austin named Alex James had also found out about the report and dug up more information with a formal interview with the San Antonio Police Chief. Alex was so impressed by the work of the man that shared his first name that he began to follow his work. Before long, Alex Rich was spouting some of the best conspiratorial hallmarks and was officially an info warrior against the so-called "New World Order" when the plague hit. Somehow, the whole thing sounded like a globalist plot. But the jury was still out for him. Right now, he was more concerned about survival.

"Poth: twenty-nine miles. How's that sound?" Red asked, reading the sign.

"Fine by me," Alex replied.

The rain was falling faster as the afternoon was taking its sweet time working towards the evening.

When the plague hit San Antonio, it came with a vengeance. Alex had chosen to drive to his girlfriends house on the south side of town near Luther Burbank High. The highways proved to be hard to maneuver through on loop 410 and traffic had come to a grinding halt. Along the freeway, Alex noticed some vehicles being attacked by creatures, so he decided to take his chances outside of his vehicle. Below the area where he first started his journey was a very familiar tourist location in San Antonio. Alex decided to take his chances there.

—*The Mercado.*

Alex took a risk and jumped from the freeway to an elevated parking lot below. He hit the jump with success. As he got his bearings, he noticed two creatures walking up a ramp toward the elevated parking lot. A fervent advocate of the second amendment of the United States Constitution, Alex pulled his gun from the holster strapped around his shoulder and popped off two precise shots to the heads of the creatures. Blood and brains burst out of the back of the monsters' heads and splattered on the pavement in almost identical patterns as the bodies fell. Alex sprinted toward the Mercado.

It was there that he met Red. Within the same afternoon that Alex arrived, a large group of people chose to secure the Mercado. For several days, Alex and Red remained with the group of shady, but amicable, refugees and held out with the people until the "Zaragosa Incident," which brought them here today.

"Put a tape in," said Red.

"What?" Alex asked, surprised.

"Put a tape in," Red repeated, indicating with his thumb a storage box behind the middle seat. Alex lowered it down, and after finding the latch to release the cover, clicked the case open. Alex looked at the selection. There were many worn cassettes. Plenty of Beatles. Some Pink Floyd. Some jazz. Some country. But Alex saw something else that caught his eye.

"Donna Summers?"

"What?"

"You like disco, too?" asked Alex with a smirk.

"What's wrong with disco?" asked Red.

"Nothing, I guess, if you're..."

"I'm not a fag, man!"

"Who said anything about being a fag?"

"You were implying I'm a fag because I listen to disco."

"I said no such thing."

"You implied it."

"I didn't imply a thing."

Red slowed the vehicle down to a stop. Until now they had been driving down a four lane road out of the city. To their right was railroad tracks.

"*Get out*," said Red.

"I'm not getting out, dude," said Alex. He was confused at the remark.

"Get out of my vehicle, now!" Red yelled.

"Dude, I take it back," Alex said.

"I don't care, get out!" Red yelled.

A low rumbling emanated across the countryside as the iron railroad tracks began to vibrate and rattle with kinetic energy.

Alex was getting concerned. He had never seen Red so angry. Granted, he had only known him for about a week, and that was certainly not enough time to truly get to know someone.

"C'mon, man," Alex pleaded.

A railroad crossing post began to blink its lights and lower its gate. A metal clapper began its mechanized and consistent warning, banging against the metal bell housed near the blinking lights.

Red pulled out a gun on Alex and pointed it at his head.

For a moment neither said a word. The rumbling grew louder. Small rocks shifted back and forth below the sturdy rails. The bells rang clear and loud.

Perhaps it was stress or frustration. Perhaps it was a bit of neurosis setting in at witnessing the carnage of the past few days, especially witnessing the climax of the Zaragosa incident. Alex was speculating, trying to figure out if Red was for real.

Red ended the awkward pause between the two.

"Get out, Alex."

The mighty iron engines began to pass slowly by the road and the two refugees.

Alex decided Red was bluffing.

"Red, calm down."

Red cocked the hammer.

Alex then decided playing his hand against this life or death bluff was not a good option. The stakes were too high to try to call.

"All right, all right," said Alex, opening the door and slowly exiting. He made sure to not only keep his hands in the air, but to keep his eyes glued on Red. "Red, reconsider. I'm sorry for—"

Alex stopped talking as he noticed Red gazing at something just behind him. Red slowly repositioned the hammer on the gun and lowered it. Alex slowly turned around to see what Red was seeing.

It was the train.

The passenger cars were passing by. In the windows were gruesome red strokes of vicious carnage. Blood caked various windows. People—or *things*—could be seen walking inside as the carriages passed like a traveling mausoleum. One window of a carriage was smashed. A body dangled out of it. Another car was smeared and splashed with blood. And another. Yet another. Another window was smashed, and another body hung out. But this one was being devoured by two creatures.

Alex and Red were paralyzed and dumbfounded.

Several more bloody passenger cars passed as the bells and lights of the railroad crossing resounded and flashed. The final carriage passed and several seconds elapsed before the bells and lights of the crossing blockade near the road stopped. The final bell echoed across the road as the gates lifted. As the echo faded, the train clicked across the steel tracks in the distance, like the metal heartbeat of an iron robot. The clicking soon faded, then was swallowed by the horizon.

Red and Alex stared into the distance. A gentle wind blew as a flock of birds flew across the blue spring sky.

Alex broke the silence.

"Sorry about the fag thing."

"Yeah."

"Let's get to Poth."

"Yeah."

"How 'bout some *Village People*?"

"Yeah."

Captain Phillip Carson, U.N. Peacekeeping Mission Leader for Central Texas

Line the insurgents up against the wall!" called out the tall man in blue camouflage and baby blue beret. His name was Captain Phillip Carson, and he was in control.

Total control.

Captain Phillip Carson had been born in Leeds, England, and into a long line of military heroes. His grandfather fought the Nazis in France during World War II. His father had fought in the Faulkland Island conflict. And Phillip earned his stripes in the Royal Air Force.

With his record in combat, he had been invited to lead a company of soldiers for the United Nations. The United Nations had a global reputation as peacekeepers and saviors. Like any influential organization, there were many people with sincere dedication to helping the poor, the starving, and the helpless around the world. The most positive efforts always received more than enough publicity by the global press to paint a pleasant picture of peace.

But like most influential organizations, there were also people at the top who were out to serve their own agendas and line their own pockets. And it did not stop there. There were many in the trenches whose purpose was to take advantage and abuse. Every incident that would tarnish their reputation was quickly swept under the carpet.

The United Nations certainly did not have a clean slate, and Phillip Carson did not, either. Serving and obeying commands without flinching in Bosnia, Sierra Leone, and other African countries solidified his reputation as a strong military leader. So much so, that his name was erased from any reference to the genocide in Rwanda, in which Carson had had a hand in the decision to remove soldiers from a U.N. sponsored refugee camp. Within minutes of the soldiers leaving, the camp was attacked by enemies of the refugees. The entire camp of Tsutsi's had been massacred by the Hutu's, hacked to pieces by machetes.

After several more sterling performances in resolving global conflict through peacekeeping efforts, Phillip Carson's dream of moving through the ranks was stymied by infighting, peacekeeping politics, and his bad attitude. The glory his uncanny leadership skills brought him began to go to his head. In his mind, he was feeling as if he was much better than his superiors. His newfound arrogance did not go unnoticed by his military colleagues. He was passed over for promotion three times.

Then the plague hit.

As the plague began to consume the world, the U.N. was mobilizing in underground bases in Europe and America. Carson never questioned the almost precognitive preparation the United Nations peacekeeping forces showed the day reports first started coming in. Within hours, large units were mobilized and en route to their destinations. Many of them were headed to the United States, and Phillip Carson was on one of those airlifts.

It was decided among the world powers cooped up in underground bases, (also with an eerie precision and timing,) that a good way to begin to retake European and North and South American cities was to begin at both active and inactive military bases. Russia, China, and North Korea chose to nuke several of their own cities. America had yet to use the nuclear option. Many wondered why a crippled America was not attacked, and North Korea and China had offered their assistance, which was met with stern American disapproval.

As the plague began to overtake America, local law enforcement, in conjunction with the soldiers of Homeland Security and FEMA, were failing miserably at containing the threat and protecting the citizens from the domestic terror of the walking dead. So an Executive Order was implemented that put Homeland Security, FEMA, and local law enforcement under the control of the United Nations. As expected, there were several mutinies among remaining military officials and soldiers, who broke off and formed rogue squads of mercenaries within the United States. The ones that stayed had decided there was really no place to run, so they followed orders as programmed.

So the plan was to secure and activate military bases in the United States as bases of operations for further military action. In Captain Carson's case, he was assigned to refortify and secure Kelly Air Force Base in San Antonio. After Carson arrived, it took only a single afternoon for his company to secure the entire base, then a full day to get it fully operational again. All remaining soldiers in the base were under U.N. control.

He had had to have six of the American soldiers shot for mutiny, and three U.N. soldiers from France were happy to execute the order.

His confidence high, Carson initiated a plan with his superiors to retake south Texas and give the U.N. Peacekeeping forces a port city for a naval assault. Deciding on Corpus Christi over Houston, Carson planned to retake and secure every city to Corpus along IH-37. It was audacious. But the desperate times called for desperate measures, and Carson's superiors admired his daring strategy and decisiveness.

They gave him the green light and even gave him all available resources he might need, including airlifting soldiers, equipment, and military vehicles when needed. The officers were going to use his idea, if successful, as a template for future strategies.

So Carson began his journey down the road two days after securing the base. His soldiers blazed a trail south, securing a small section of San Antonio, mainly along the highway leading to the coast.

The commands from Carson's officials was set into several categories.

1. *Exterminate all infected Americans.*
2. *Exterminate all Americans suspected of infection.*
3. *Disarm the populace.*
4. *Send all survivors to either FEMA camps or U.N. refugee*

camps.

5. Neutralize all insurgents. (With "insurgent" being defined as anyone refusing to disarm and/or unwilling to be sent to a FEMA or U.N. refugee camp.)

The first few towns had been fully infected. No survivors, at least in their eyes. With the number of the walking dead being 100 times more than any living, Carson had the entire city torched through six coordinated air strikes with white phosphorus and napalm.

But Pleasanton had been different. After securing the city of creatures, it was found that two of the areas of town had been secured by locals. After liberating the city, Carson had insisted on the civilians exiting their fortifications and traveling to a camp.

When the civilians refused, wanting to return to their homes and properties instead, Carson attacked their positions with explosives, armor, and a coordinated assault by infantry. It quickly became a bloodbath for the untrained civilians. From each of the two fortified civilian positions, the remaining survivors surrendered. Carson was cruel, but he had a streak of honor running through him. He gave them a last meal of bread and water before lining the insurgents against a wall at the H.E.B. The survivors were zip-tied and waiting to be neutralized. A line of four U.N. soldiers stood, guns poised and ready to execute the insurgents.

"You can't do this, asshole!" yelled a young man no older than twenty-five. "This is America!"

"This *was* America," muttered Carson.

Six soldiers walked up to Carson. Carson nodded his head, as if approving some sort of secret agreement. The men grinned and walked toward the insurgents. At gunpoint, the soldiers took the four women in the group and marched them into the store. One was in her forties. Two were in their late twenties. One could not have been more than ten years old.

Looking at the remaining thirteen men, Carson gave an order. "Sergeant Cortez, *shoot them.*"

Cortez yelled "Fire!" and the soldiers opened up. One man was completely mowed down. Bullets tore open his chest and back. Bloody bullets busted bricks as the man was joined in execution by six others who were critically wounded. Lungs burst, hearts tore, and heads cracked as one by one the Americans were killed.

But six made a break for it. Four were tackled by the baby blue peacekeepers and executed with a shot to the head.

Two made it through the group of blue men and dashed toward the alleys of the various buildings in downtown Pleasanton. Carson sent six men after them. Two white Hummers quickly revved up and pursued their prey.

"What if we can't find them, sir?" asked Corporal Daniel Kuffour.

"They'll only need to find one," Carson replied smugly, raising his AK-47.

Though not known for its accuracy, Carson was still able to squeeze off a shot from the AK that brought one of the free men to the pavement. The man tried to hold his now torn and shattered right leg together through his Wrangler blue jeans. Blood began to cake around the denim in a black abstract painting of pain and anguish. He howled in agony. Tears of fear and torment laced his cheeks as Carson shouldered his weapon and aimed again. With maniacally masochistic merriment, Carson watched the man drown in his misery for a few moments. The metal sight danced around the trembling body, as if poking and prodding him to dance his wounded dance. Then Carson popped off another round, striking the man in the neck. Blood shot in all directions and stained the pavement. The man was neutralized.

To Carson's surprise, two creatures emerged from a nearby building. He quickly shot them both, crippling the creatures before they could reach the body. He wanted to make sure the body was not infected.

"Corporal Kuffour, go neutralize those creatures and bring the body of the insurgent to me."

"Yes, sir." Kuffour dutifully responded by running in the direction of the body and the crippled creatures.

Cortez approached Carson. "Sir, why do you want the body?"

"*You know*," Carson began, hocking up a loogie into his mouth, "there's a tradition here in Texas." He spit out the thick green secretion. "Something hunters do when they've shot a deer." He paused and watched Kuffour plug the creatures, and then the body of the insurgent. "Cortez, *when in Rome, do as the Romans do.*"

Meanwhile, the surviving insurgent—perhaps the last person alive from Pleasanton—ran into an alleyway. He swiftly placed

57

himself behind a dumpster, just out of view of the alley entrance. Breathing heavy, he tried to figure out what to do next. Two walls stood on either side of him, but straight ahead was a door that was possibly an opening to another alley.

The Hummer revved into the alley, and the rebel made a break for the door.

The truck chased after the survivor. It knocked the dumpster into a wall, spilling trash everywhere. The man felt the truck getting closer, but the door was almost within reach.

Slamming into the metal door, he turned the knob. To his joy, it opened—but to his dismay, it unleashed a small pack of zombies. Screaming in terror, he turned to face the soldiers.

The soldiers opened fire on the creatures and the rebel, peppering the bodies with lead until they all fell to the ground.

Laughing and speaking in foreign tongues, the men put the Hummer in reverse and backed out of the alley.

The McCann Street Girls

T he people running this damn country are a bunch of douchebags," said Audrey Garner, taking a drag off a half-smoked cigarette. Her husband, an old school punk-rocker named Eric, just sat beside her on the porch of their house and grunted in the affirmative. They lived on McCann Street, a simple street with simple houses in the simple city of Beeville.

McCann Street ran parallel to Main Street and was considered an alternate road by the people of Beeville. While the lights of Main Street sometimes ran long, McCann Street only had stop signs every few blocks. McCann Street eventually fed into Main Street a block away from Beeville City Hall.

"You know, you put together an organization that's supposed to handle emergencies and they can't get their shit together enough to bail out the country they're supposed to protect."

"Fuck them," grumbled Eric. The heat of the Texas sun made his greased-back hair a little warm around his head. Sweat and oil ran down his neck.

Audrey was wearing black pants tucked into black and worn combat boots and a garage mechanic shirt with her name written in cursive on a white patch above the breast pocket. Her subtle bosoms were contrasted by her feminine hips and thick legs. Black and blonde hair fell over an over-powdered face. Dark eyes were complemented by pink eyeshadow. Painted red lips kissed the filter of the cigarette, blessing it with affection with each puff.

Audrey thought about their time in Beeville. She was still working on her qualifications to become a librarian when she met Eric at a punk rock club in Dallas. It was love at first sight. When Audrey got her certification, she accepted an opening at the Beeville Library and the couple moved to the south Texas city. Though the humidity was tough to handle at first, the two adjusted to life in the small town, eventually having a son named Billy Joe. Billy Joe was smart, but a bit of a slacker—a natural result of his parents' punk rock mentality. He kept his grades up, but could sometimes be trouble when authority overstepped their bounds and Billy called them on it. It was tough for the High School faculty and administration to do anything to him as he was also the star linebacker for the Beeville Spartans. His charm did not hurt him either, and he often used it to his advantage.

The two watched vultures circling around the sky above.

"You think this thing will blow over?" Audrey asked, pulling herself away from the criticism and thinking about the future.

Eric just grumbled something incoherent. Audrey shook her head.

Audrey, Eric, and their son Billy Joe had joined with their neighborhood watch members and secured their neighborhood when the plague became a problem in Beeville. Now, they were guardians of McCann Street, the alternate route to Main Street. They were formally assigned to protect McCann Street by the mayor, who also assigned the same duties to others in town who were happy to help.

Though the city had been secured, no one was really sure how many families were hiding their relatives who might have been infected. It was not uncommon to see creatures still shambling around town, even though they were eventually gunned down within hours. Most people chose to stay holed up in their houses, boarding up their windows and doors and only leaving when necessary. So any creature that might be out could usually walk around without harassment.

But not on McCann Street.

Picking herself up off the porch, Audrey stood and said, "I'm going in for a minute. Want a beer?"

Eric just mumbled. Audrey had known him long enough to know that he said *no*.

"All right." She stood and looked around. "Where's Billy Joe?"

*   *   *   *   *

"Oh, God! Oh, God! Oh, God!"

Lucy St. Claire stretched the final '*Oh, God*' for several seconds, drifting into a sustained cry of passion as she reached that sacred cosmic connection, that trembling and resonating spiritual gift of the corporeal being that motivates the whole of humanity. Yes, Lucy St. Claire was having sex—and a pretty intense orgasm, as female orgasms go. Yes, *sex*. That special, fun and vital piece of humanity that drives reproduction and guarantees the continued existence of the species.

The kitchen table rocked back and forth. A ceramic napkin holder depicting a pastoral scene shifted on the table several times, almost falling over.

Behind Lucy St. Claire, thrusting his youthful energy into her in a measured and steady rhythm was Billy Joe Garner. Their slapping bodies resonated around the kitchen, disguised only by the country music compilation CD playing Alan Jackson on the budget boom box over her sink on the windowsill. Dark brown curls danced around her tan face as Billy Joe worked himself almost into a trance. Billy Joe had not even taken off his striped Polo shirt, as Lucy's sexual appetite was absolutely ravenous.

Lucy St. Claire was a thirty-five year old divorcee with two children (who, fortunately, were not in the house.) Her skin was dark and her eyes seemed stuck in a perpetual high, halfway open or closed, depending on your personality type. Her heritage suggested Hispanic, but she could pass as Polynesian. She had a five year old girl and a seven year old boy who the court had actually awarded to the father. Lucy had well-documented run-ins with the law and trips to drug rehab in San Antonio that did not endear her too well with the judge.

The shrinks said her problem originated with her father, who divorced her mother when she was only five. As Lucy got older, she blossomed into a gorgeous young girl. Her mother, Grace, was loving, nurturing, and caring, but had a sordid past. It was for this reason that at one point she wondered if her daddy was truly her father. She would learn the truth later.

Once a month, when she visited her so-called father for the weekend, it was pure hell. Her father and her uncle would get drunk, watch porno, then go to her room in the middle of the night and play "Juice the Hot Dog." When she reached her fourteenth birthday, it turned into full-blown rape.

Finding within herself the courage to speak up, she secretly video-taped one of the rapes and showed it to her mom, who promptly called Child Protective Services. Within days, arrests were made, and—though the lawyer tried futilely to paint her as a manipulative young girl—her father and uncle were sent to jail for ten years each.

But the weekends of rape had destroyed any kind of self-esteem she may have possessed. Doctors hooked her on anti-depressants, but the bad crowd she started hanging out with at school had even better drugs. Her mother tried to help, but it was tough to do when she was working two jobs. Lucy did enough to keep her grades passing, out of respect to the mother who she dearly loved. But she still tried to fill the hole drilled in her heart with alcohol, drugs, and promiscuous sex.

After High School, she tried her best to pull herself together. Putting away the black clothes, makeup, and jewelry, Lucy went for a more preppie look. Working towards a professional certification at Bee County College was her first start to a new self-image. While completing her certification at a Beeville beauty school, she met her future husband, Lawrence St. Claire. He was a kind-hearted and God fearing man who looked past Lucy's disreputable and sad past and saw the beauty that had been lost so many years ago. After several months of dating, Lawrence popped the question and proposed marriage. Lucy accepted, and Lawrence gave her the world.

For several years, everything was fantastic. Lawrence's job with city management offered her a happy living, even allowing her to stay home with their two children who they were blessed with shortly after their marriage.

But as the picture perfect marriage continued, the ugly specter of her past came creeping back. A letter arrived from the state penitentiary. It was from her father. His letter was a cruel revelation.

"Dear Lucy: I'd like to say I hope you're doing good, but I don't.

Thanks to you, I've learned what happens to what people call 'child rapists' in prison. Thanks. Thanks a lot.

"*I don't deserve any of this, Lucy. It was all your fault. You were a little whore and you know it. You remember my cock? I still remember your young pussy and how good it felt. I can still hear you moaning. You liked it and you know it, slut.*

"*You're probably wondering why I'm writing this and telling you these things. You were a good fuck because I'm not really your father. That's right. Your mom's a filthy whore, just like you. That's why I never felt guilty fucking you. And why you liked it.*

"*So, anyway, I hope you're doing horrible right now. Hopefully with VD or taking drugs again. You always were a stupid and worthless bitch.*

"*Don't worry about writing back, and thanks for my stay in prison.*"

He didn't bother to sign it.

Slowly, Lucy began to feel like she did not deserve her perfect life anymore, like she wasn't worthy for what she had. She was not a good person, but a little whore, just like her 'dad' had said in the letter—the same things he said so many years ago.

Like an ocean's tide slowly creeping onto shore, the drugs entered back into her life. After a noble effort to regain the ground he had gained in her recovery, Lawrence's notoriety in town forced him to choose. He went with his job, and took the kids with him.

Audrey and Eric Garner were kind enough to retain their friendship as she tried to pick up the pieces of her life. But they had no idea their son was learning the literal ins and outs of sex at her knowledgeable hands.

"*Oh, Mizz St. Claire,*" moaned Billy Joe, living the teenage dream of many young boys. With his pants still around his ankles and a lump in his throat from the excitement and disbelief, he gazed wide-eyed with incredulous fascination at the glistening brown back of the woman who was bent over in front of him, totally naked but for a pair of socks that only went as far as her ankles. Standing on her toes, she dipped her head, then flung her curly locks into the air, then looked back at him. Her exotic looks and sultry dark eyes entranced him. His rhythm was unchanged.

"*Kiss me,*" she commanded.

He leaned forward and obeyed, a willing student being led by a skilled teacher. Their lips engaged. She grabbed his right hand and placed it on her generous right breast. Near exploding, Billy Joe began to tense up. Sensing his release, she pulled away and fell to her knees. Placing her hands on his hips, he only pumped twice before a warm stream of essence shot forth in three short blasts, caressing her lips and mouth, bathing her neck and breasts. As he stood paralyzed with pleasure so sensitive it was almost painful, she pumped his warm flesh, then took it into her mouth.

All Lucy wanted was love. And this was the only love she knew.

It was a sad and sick connection to the only father she ever had.

* * * * *

Behind the closed front door in the living room, Lucy St. Claire gave Billy Joe Garner a slow kiss, making the adolescent youth want more. She gently pushed him away.

"No," she whispered. "Not now." She smiled, touching the chin of her young lover.

"Can I come by later?" he begged, sheepishly.

"You know you can come by anytime."

Billy Joe reached in for another kiss, but was gently pushed away.

"Later, baby," she said, and opened the door.

Billy whispered a "No..." as the door was opening, secretly wishing for a few more minutes of kisses from the object of his lustful desires. Defeated, but hopeful, Billy grabbed his pistol off the small table near the door and walked out with the shotgun shells he had come for in the first place.

Taking her shotgun off the rack near the door, she followed Billy Joe out.

"Bye, Ms. St. Claire," he chimed as innocently as possible, walking down the sidewalk back home.

"Bye, Billy," said Lucy neutrally. She saw his father Eric sitting on the porch of their house. She waved. He gave a subtle wave back as he puffed away on a cigarette.

After locking her door, she started walking to her car.

"Hi, Lucy," came a voice from across the street.

Lucy looked up. "Hi, Margie."

"Girl, I need to talk to you," Margie said with a knowing smile.

Lucy walked over.

Margie Montemayor was another divorcee who was doing just fine without a man. She was a stout woman, tall and bleached blonde. Her hair was still stuck in the eighties, minus the high bangs, instead curling downwards toward her forehead.

"Don't be hard on me now," Lucy said with a smile, extending her arms for a hug. They embraced.

"Looks like I wasn't the only one who was hard on you," Margie said, laughing. She was so Texas, even her laugh had an accent.

Knowing their conversation would be heard by the entire neighborhood, especially with Margie's booming voice, Lucy suggested, "Why don't we go inside? I'll tell you everything."

"Well, come on in, girl," said Margie, opening up the screen door. She led Lucy to her kitchen, where Lucy pulled up a chair at a small kitchen table while Margie went to the refrigerator to pull out some beer.

"Want one?" Margie offered, extending an unopened can of Miller Lite.

"Yeah," Lucy said, taking the can and popping it open. She took a long swig. She wiped her mouth and placed the can on the table. She then noticed the television still displaying the 'Technical Difficulty' signal. The television was muted, with the word "MUTE" standing still on the right hand corner of the screen.

"Why's your TV still on?" she asked.

Margie was pouring a bag of Chex-mix into a bowl. "You never know," she replied, leaving it unspoken that the television was like a comfort, a reminder of how things were. Television was sometimes the only friend to many—but to most everyone, it always provided some kind of comfort or support.

For a moment, they recalled the problem that was facing their nation and their own hometown.

"Lucy, what the hell are you doing with that boy?"

Lucy blushed. "Aw, c'mon, Margie. It's the *end of the world*, for God's sake."

"You're twice his age, girl," Margie pointed out, taking a handful of Chex mix and tossing it into her mouth.

"Margie, you know you'd let some strapping young boy fuck you if you had the chance."

Margie pursed her lips, suggesting she probably would, but still held fast to the moral high ground. "Maybe, but..."

An awkward moment passed. Then they both broke out into a hearty laugh.

"See?" Lucy said, still giggling. She took another swig of beer.

Not wanting to bring up Lucy's past, Margie instead asked, "How many times have you two been together?"

"Daily for the past two months," came the reply, accompanied by a smile.

"Girl!" exclaimed Margie, surprised but knowing. She was suspicious, but didn't think it had been going on for so long. "Is he any good?"

"At first, no. But I trained him well."

"Damn, girl," Margie said, laughing with a touch of jealousy. She turned to her living room. She was embarrassed that she did not notice her own sixteen year-old daughter silently reading a book. It was obvious to Margie that she wanted to hear the conversation. "Gina, go to your room," giggled Margie. Gina silently obeyed, walking back to her room, but making sure to keep the door opened a crack to listen in.

"Anyway, so how are things?" Lucy asked, trying to change the subject.

"Oh, I'm all right. That son-of-a-bitch Brent called." (*Son-of-a bitch Brent* was Margie's ex-husband.)

"What did he say?" Lucy asked, interested in the update on Margie's ex.

"Well," she said as her thick pink lips left the edge of the beer can with a kiss, "He's holed up in some office building in Houston. They've secured the place pretty well, but there's no food and no way out."

"Sucks for him," Lucy said.

"Yeah. Tough shit," Margie replied with a grin. "So, tell me more about you and Billy Joe."

* * * * *

"How's it look, mommy?"

"Why, that's great, Timmy."

Mary Moore and her five year old son Timmy were passing the

time coloring pictures of various children's television stars: Spongebob, Elmo, Dora.

The plague had visited its curse on the Moore family, taking the life of husband and father Bobby Moore. He had joined the men of the town in the initial effort to destroy all the ghouls and secure the city.

Though Sheriff McMurtry had broken the sad news, Bobby was considered a hero and was honored in a small ceremony two days after the city was secured. It did nothing to allay her grief. With Timmy being so young, Mary could only tell the boy that his dad had an important job to do to help the town, and would not be back for a long time. He sensed his mother's sadness, and they spent the days walking the stages of grief and loss together.

Since the fateful day, Mary and Timmy followed a simple schedule of reading, writing, coloring, napping, and watching movies.

Mary Moore was a meek person. Quiet and unassuming, she had a very uneventful high school career, keeping her grades up and spending most of her time absorbed in books. She had met Bobby at a Michael Bolton concert. He had been a sweet guy, though he was twenty-five and still quite the comic book fanatic. To secure his place in dorkdom, he was a big Star Trek fan. He was old school, preferring the classic, violent era of Kirk and Spock over the mostly tame era of Picard and Riker.

Mary and Bobby married two years later and had Timmy a year after that. Their life was the picture of happiness—*until last week*, of course.

"Mommy, can we watch a movie now?" Timmy asked. He sat in the middle of a mound of crayons. He had done a pretty good job of staying in the lines, and Elmo looked pretty good.

It was about that time of day that they watched a movie anyway, so Mary replied, "Why not?"

"Yay!" Timmy shouted.

"You clean up these crayons and I'll find today's movie, okay?"

"Okay, mommy," Timmy said, quickly picking up the crayons and tidying up the carpet.

Mary picked herself up off the floor. Her aching back reminded her that her body had seen healthier days. She walked to the living room and went to a shelf housing a few short stacks of movies. Several Disney films were featured in the stacks and plenty of other movies to boot. She chose *Finding Nemo*.

Before she knew it, Timmy ran in.

"I'm done, mommy," he said.

"Good. Look what mommy picked." She held up the popular Disney title.

"*Neeeeeemo!*" he sang, stretching the word like the sound of a bomb dropping from the sky.

"Now go prepare our snacks while I get the movie ready."

"Yay," he cried again, running to the kitchen.

She flicked on the television and was startled at what she saw. She had not seen it in weeks.

—Cable news.

Mary stood stunned for a moment as she took in the words from the anchor.

"*...officials are saying the plague is still dangerous and has affected every continent on the globe. The CDC has not yet been able to identify the strain. NASA and the space administration are also still trying to determine if the destruction of the Venus probe Sojourner Four—then on its return trip—was part of the problem.*"

Incidental news music began playing as a reporter was imparting the teasers for the news.

"*The President has signed a special Executive Order to allow U.N. forces into America. The cast of 'Grey's Anatomy' have a special message for America. The Center for Disease Control have a plan for preventing the disease. Stars and crew of the reality television show 'Island Challenge' reported stuck on their island. And millions are dead with millions more expected to die in the coming days as the Global Plague continues.*"

A large animated banner appeared on the screen, backed by dramatic music. The banner read, "Global Plague Update."

"*Hello again, everyone. I'm Julia Hall, CNC Headline News. Our top story today: the President of the United States has signed a special Executive Order allowing U.N. forces to join with Homeland Security and the Federal Emergency Management Agency to assist in rescue efforts and securing America. U.N. Secretary General Jefferson Williams has lifted sanctions to all*" *nations in an effort to expedite relief efforts. More to report in fifteen minutes.*

"But first, officials from the CDC have joined with the U.N. Peacekeeping forces and members of Homeland Security to vaccinate refugees secured at FEMA centers on the outskirts of major cities throughout the nation. Currently, all forty-eight states in the continental United States have secured at least one center in each..."

Margie Montemayor and Lucy St. Claire came walking through the front door. Their abrupt entrance made Mary jump and scream, which did the same thing for little Timmy, who was just entering the living room as the neighbors barged in.

"Oh, shit! Sorry," Margie giggled.

Mary started laughing. "Dammit, Margie. If it wasn't the end of the world..."

Timmy walked to his mother and held fast to her leg with one arm and securing an old teddy bear in the other.

"Sorry, Mary," Lucy said. "We just wanted to tell you about the TV coming on again."

"Yeah, I just found out, too. What did you hear?"

"The President is going to speak."

Mary gasped. "Are you kidding?"

"No."

"I'm going over to tell Audrey," Lucy said, running out the door.

"So what did *you* hear?" Mary asked, taking a seat on her living room couch.

"Well," Margie began, positioning herself on a nearby recliner, "When the TV came on, the CNC banner was on for like five minutes, then they went into their top-of-the-hour teasers. Something was going on in Isreal because of the plague—Like an invasion or something."

Lucy could be heard yelling across the front lawn at Audrey down the street.

Since Mary wasn't abreast of Middle East politics, she just nodded her head in approval.

"Then, something about U.N. forces coming to America to help secure major cities. Then the President was set to speak in fifteen minutes."

"About what?"

"Well, a state of the union, I guess."

"Is daddy going to be there, mommy?" asked little Timmy.

"Maybe, Timmy. Maybe," came the reply from his mother.

Lucy walked back in, clapping her hands and smiling. "This is so exciting. Check to see if the movie channels are back on."

Thinking Lucy's comment was a joke at first, Mary took a moment before switching to a movie channel. Box Office Hits, (or BOH as it was known,) had a banner that stated programming would resume at midnight.

"Yes!" Lucy exclaimed, "I wonder what's going to show?"

"Put it back on CNC," Margie said, a bit annoyed.

Mary switched back.

"...*encourage to find the nearest FEMA center for maximum protection and safety.*"

"What do you think the President will say?" Mary asked, holding Timmy in her lap.

"He's going to bring us together, that's what," Margie replied. She placed her shotgun on the floor and pulled a can of Miller Lite from her pocket.

"He did a good job when the terrorists flew a plane into the World Trade Center," Mary commented.

"He's a good man," Margie agreed.

"Let's not talk about that now," Mary said. "It still brings me to tears. All those poor people."

"So you think they'll show any of the movies that were supposed to come out last week?" Lucy chimed in. "Like the new *Harry Potter*?"

"I guess we'll see tonight," Mary said, incredulous.

"*Shhhhhhh,*" Margie hissed. "Here it comes."

On the television screen was the President at his desk. A camera slowly panned from wide to a tight shot on President Herbert M. Walker.

"*My fellow citizens,*" he began, somberly. "*It is with a heavy heart and sad soul that I join you here today. Yet with a duty to perform in respect to you to fulfill my responsibility to our nation.*

"*Our country has been attacked. We have been assaulted in a hideous and vile way. Something even more horrific than September*

Eleventh. One that has engulfed the world.

"The world has been attacked in a way that has never been seen in the history of man. A bizarre and unnatural plague has cursed our land. It is a cruel curse, one that does not show mercy. It is a deadly infection that has forced many of our fellow citizens—"

"Why doesn't he call us Americans?" asked Lucy.

"Shhhhhh," hissed Mary and Timmy.

"—to engage in horrifying acts of self and familial defense. Not since the Bubonic Plague of the Middle Ages has an infectious biological affected so many.

"But I come to you today to offer hope. To provide solace, and share crucial information that will set the course for a radical shift in our nation's future. Earlier this week, United Nations forces have joined with Homeland Security and our military. As we all know, our military has been stretched thin defending America, liberating nations and securing their future abroad—"

"How do you defend a nation abroad?"

"Lucy, be quiet!" Mary shouted.

Both ladies were somewhat divergent when it came to the Republicans and Democrats. Lucy was so liberal she was almost red. Mary was a compassionate conservative who supported President Walker's every choice with enthusiasm and trust. Though the war on terror was harvesting a bitter crop of American dead, Mary trusted him and his choices regardless of all the false and unsubstantiated data that put the war into question.

"The United Nations has joined our effort to rescue our nation from the literal mouth of these ghoulish enemy combatants. As we speak, U.N. peacekeeping soldiers have launched an effort in conjunction with our reserve forces to liberate cities and begin an unprecedented military strategy to sweep our cities clean of this blight.

"I urge every citizen who can hear my voice and has made it this far along to find the nearest FEMA center and join them. I urge you not to stay in your homes. They are unsafe, and no matter how secure you think you are, there is great danger around you.

"I recall a story I heard in a briefing three days ago. Sergeant John Homesley was a dedicated soldier and a great American. But his life was altered horrifically when he was patrolling a

neighborhood in Omaha, Nebraska, for survivors. It was at the height of the outbreak, and Sergeant Homesley saw a house boarded up. When he approached the door with his comrades, only one person answered his call. It was a little girl named Natalie. Natalie was seven years old, and had the wisdom enough to lock herself in her room. Hearing screaming coming from her room, Sergeant Homesley dashed to her window. Large boards had been screwed into the windowsill. Her cries were accompanied by a banging at her door. Sergeant Homesley could hear the growls, and knew it was only moments before the beasts—perhaps her own family—would break down the door.

"Trying desperately to tear down the boards, Sergeant Homesley was only strong enough to remove one board before her now infected family entered the room and devoured her.

"My fellow citizens, no place is safer in this time of despair than our own FEMA centers. I can assure you all necessary security measures are in place to ensure your safety. Every FEMA center is safe, secure, and well-stocked. At this point, it is important that you go there. We do not know how many lives across our great nation have been lost. As insidious as this plague is, it is not too bold to say that the numbers are in the millions. That is why you must find a FEMA center as soon as possible.

"To those of you who are safe and can hear my voice: you are the foundation and future of this great nation.

"Thank you, and may God Bless America."

After a slow dissolve, the "Global Plague Banner" came up on screen again.

"Well, it sounds like they think they can get this under control after all," suggested Margie.

"It's one thing to secure a town like we did. But a *nation*?" Lucy said.

"We should probably find a FEMA center," said Mary, holding Timmy close. "It would be safe there."

"Why? We're safe *here*," Margie pointed out. "I don't see any sense in leaving town. Hell, maybe we've done the U.N. a favor." She took another long swig from her can of beer.

"We sure have," Lucy agreed.

A knock came at the door before Audrey Garner entered into the living room. "Hey, ya'll," she said. The girls responded with a general response. "Did ya'll see it?"

"What? The state of the union?" Lucy asked.

"Yeah. What a douchebag, huh?"

"You don't need to talk like that now," Mary said.

"What do you mean?" Audrey asked. "They're saying a govern-ment-sponsored internment camp will protect us. That's bullshit. We can take care of ourselves."

"We have," Lucy said.

"Well, *yeah*," Audrey agreed.

"But we'd be secure for sure, Audrey," Mary said. "Why would he lie?"

"Because *his* self-righteous ass doesn't have to sit in one of those camps. He's probably in some underground bunker eating a five-course meal. *FEMA camp*," sneered Audrey, "My *ass*."

There was then a knock at the back door, but only Timmy heard it. The girls continued in a cordial yet fiery debate.

Timmy left his mother's arms and walked to the back door.

"Well, we *would* be guarded," Margie said. "Here we have to be policing the area twenty-four seven."

Timmy reached the kitchen. The sun cut a shadow of a human through the curtain on the door window.

"But we'd be disarmed," Audrey chimed in. "What happens if the shit hits the fan inside this protective camp?"

Timmy peeked behind the curtain. He saw Mr. and Mrs. Larson on the other side. He was excited to see them, thinking maybe their children, Betsy, Synda, and Orrin were with them, too.

"But the soldiers are trained to deal with the problem. It'd be safe," Mary said, trying to defend the plan.

Timmy clicked open the lock on the back door.

"Mary, they train soldiers for foreign occupation, not to protect Americans."

Timmy threw open the door with youthful excitement.

Mr. Larson had a huge gaping hole in his stomach. His innards were dangling out and his slacks were soaked in blood. Mrs. Larson was right behind him. Pieces of her arm were torn off. Behind her were the children. Their clothes were torn and bloody. Pieces of their flesh was missing from various appendages. The wounds of the family hadn't been noticeable at all to young Timmy through the window, and now they were about to consume him.

Mr. Larson raised his hands and advanced toward Timmy. Timmy screamed, dropping his teddy bear.

All the women turned to the kitchen. As Margie yelled out an expletive in surprise, Audrey and Lucy dashed to the kitchen, armed and ready.

Lucy was immediately tackled by surprise by Mrs. Larson, who was trying to bite the lascivious Ms. St. Claire. Her pistol fell to the floor nearby. Audrey was quickly surrounded by the Larson kids.

"*Timmy*!" Mary cried, dashing through the chaos toward Mr. Larson, who was chasing her son into an adjacent hallway.

Margie entered the kitchen and picked off one of the undead children, blasting a large portion of Orrin's head off with her shotgun. Audrey booted Synda in the face, then blasted Betsy's face off. Synda hit the kitchen table.

Lucy was on the floor with Mrs. Larson, who was close to biting her face. A string of dark drool dangled from Mrs. Larson's mouth. Using a primitive amateur wrestling-style elevator, Lucy rolled Mrs. Larson on her back, reached for her pistol and pierced Mrs. Larson's skull with a well aimed bullet.

She wiped the drool off her cheek where it fell.

As Synda rose, Margie and Audrey let the girl have it, all but beheading the child. Its bloody body fell to the floor.

"Mary!" Margie yelled, running to the hallway. Lucy and Audrey followed close behind.

When they walked into Timmy's room, Mary was punching at the back of the creature, both struggling on the floor. The creature was pulling at Timmy's jeans, attempting to bite into the boy's leg.

Audrey yelled, "Mary! Back off! We got him!"

Mary continued to pound on the beast. Timmy's leg inched closer to its mouth. The boy was wiggling with all his childhood might to try to get away.

The monster snapped at his leg. It missed.

"Mary!" Audrey yelled again. But it was no use. Mary was a woman possessed.

Quickly, Margie tackled Mary and knocked her off the beast, crashing into the dresser. A teddy bear fell off the dresser on the two as Mary screamed, struggling to free herself.

"Get off me!" Mary growled, her voice so deep it sounded like a demon had acquired the body of the sweet housewife.

The moment was all Audrey needed. The beast grabbed a hold of Timmy and would have taken a chunk out of the boy had Audrey not removed the ghoul's head with a gruesome blast. A spray of blood splattered across Timmy's toybox and across his face.

"Don't open your mouth," Lucy said. Grabbing a shirt, she wiped the blood off the boy's face. Mary was screaming and crying. Timmy was trembling. Lucy pulled Timmy away from the corpse of Mr. Larson. Mary reached for her child and they embraced.

Margie, Lucy, and Audrey stood in silence as Mary rocked her hysterical child in her arms. After a moment, Audrey nudged Margie, signaling her to the kitchen.

Margie hesitated. "Mary, are you going to be all right?"

"I'm fine," Mary moaned, rocking her child to and fro in her arms. Timmy cried and whimpered like a scalded dog longing for solace and wondering why such pain had entered its existence.

"C'mere," said Margie, lifting Mary to her feet. "Let's get out of this room, huh?" They walked out together.

In the kitchen, Lucy and Audrey looked at the mess. The funk was beginning to float in the air. The back door was still open, providing a bit of fresh air in the temporary tomb. A fly buzzed around the bodies of the now immobilized Larson family. Blood was caking on the floor. A large puddle of crimson formed an oval, looking like a macabre carpet. The teddy bear dropped by Timmy when the attack began was absorbing the blood, soaking up the genetic material like an unwilling sponge.

Audrey and Lucy knew Mary would need help cleaning up the mess. Neither really wanted to, but both knew Mary would need all the help she could get.

"Go check around for any more," Lucy suggested. "I'll start in here."

Another moment passed before Audrey moved out the back door. The sound of the television filled the kitchen.

"...*is dangerous. Keep all doors locked at all times and never let anyone into your house unless you are absolutely sure they are not infected...*"

75

Frank Garza
Goes Shopping

Frank and Dolores Garza drove their green minivan into town. H.E.B. was still accepting debit and credit cards, but still charging full price for their products. Frank knew a mom-and-pop grocery store near City Hall that would take cash and barter if necessary.

Dolores was still greatly upset at the death of Blanca. They had buried her and her friend together in the backyard in a shallow grave. Dolores spent the afternoon and early evening sitting by the grave.

Today, the Garzas needed supplies. They had a water purifier at the house, (as the purity of the town water supply had been put into question,) and they were hoping to find some dry goods and eggs.

Frank drove by the large police barricade set up around City Hall and the main plaza area, a basic fortification. He waved at the police officer on duty by the barricade.

"Hi Frank."

"Hi Fred."

Fred waved him through. Small town trust.

The city plaza and surrounding businesses were guaranteed secure by the local police and militiamen. Though secured, it seemed vacant, apart from the militiamen drinking beer in and around the plaza, the heroes of Beeville.

Finding a parking space, Dolores and Frank got out of their

vehicle. A friend waved at them.

"Hey Frank!"

"Hey, Benny. *Que paso, buey?*" Frank said with a smile, yet carrying with it a sad edge.

"*Pues, nada, buey,*" Benny replied, casually describing his uneventful day.

Benito Juarez Reyes was Frank's old high school friend. He was wearing a blue patterned shirt and Wrangler jeans with cowboy boots. A straw Stetson imposter sat on his head with Wrangler stickers on either side.

Benny noticed Frank and Dolores' sullen disposition. "*Ey,* what's wrong?"

"*Mi hija, buey,*" Frank said, tears welling up in his eyes as his body was fighting against his efforts to suppress the sadness.

Frank didn't need to say more. Benny gave him a hug, then held Dolores.

Benny backed away. "If you need anything, you call me. Or call Lupe at the house, okay?"

Frank pulled himself together and nodded in agreement, wiping tears from his eyes. He gripped his wife's hand tight.

"I'll come by later. We'll have some beers."

"Cool," Frank said. "Hey, did you hear about the TV's coming back on?"

"Yeah. We were watching it at Abuelita's Corner Store."

"Hey, that's where we're going."

"There's still plenty of stuff. She's got lots of fideo and tortillas."

"*Entonces, pues,* I'll see you later, okay?"

"Take it easy," Benny said, as the couple walked away hand in hand toward Abuelita's, which was close to City Hall.

* * * * *

Pulling up in the camouflaged truck was Gary Chapman and Wayne Crocker. They shared a friendly Texas nod with Frank Garza as they exited the vehicle and walked to City Hall.

"So, we say the college campus is still infested, right?" Wayne asked.

"Yeah," said Gary.

"And we couldn't do it alone, right?"

"Yeah. Would you relax?"

"All right, all right."

Benny approached the two guys.

"Hey guys. How'd it go?" They shook hands.

"Don't ask," Wayne said.

"Hey, you missed it. The television's back on."

"*What*?" said Gary.

"Yeah. The President spoke and everything."

"What did he say?"

"Is there pay-per-view?" Wayne asked, thinking about purchasing some of the latest porn titles.

Benny laughed. "I don't know about pay-per-view, but he said the U.N. has teamed up with Homeland Security to retake the U.S. or some shit like that. They think this thing will blow over."

"That's good news," Gary said.

"Is Cinemax on?" Wayne asked.

"We think so," Benny said, answering Gary and ignoring Wayne's query.

"Awesome," said Wayne, oblivious.

"No—*not about Cinemax*—about the military helping us," Gary told him. He turned back to Benny and asked, "Is the mayor in?"

"I guess," Benny said. "His car's here." He pointed at the blue BMW parked in an official spot near the courthouse.

"Cool."

"Hey, Frank Garza's coming over for some beers later. Wanna come by?"

"Who's Frank Garza?"

"Oh, you don't know him?"

"No."

"Well, anyways, we might be drinking later. Wanna come by?"

"I might," Gary said.

Wayne frowned at not being invited. "What about me?"

"You too," Benny said with a friendly smile.

"Cool," Wayne said, ready to get down to business with the mayor. "Call me later."

"Okay," came the casual reply from Benny as he turned and walked back to the other militiamen.

Gary and Wayne hit the front steps of City Hall and trotted up the stone stairs.

"So what do we say again?" Wayne asked.

"Just follow my lead," Gary told him.

"What if he's busy?"

"Would you relax? He ain't busy. It's the end of the world, remember? What would *you* be doing?"

* * * * *

"Oh, yeah! Fuck my titties, Lance! Fuck them!" screamed Stephanie Zapata as she looked up into the eyes of Mayor Lance Hickland. Her body was ready for the real action, but she allowed Lance to indulge his fetish with her breasts for a while after her perfect performance of fellatio.

Lance had been working throughout the day coordinating the city in its continued vigilant protective setup. Each command by Mayor Hickland made Stephanie shiver with desire. His power, decisiveness, and confidence turned her on.

It reminded her of her first fuck in High School. She had been a sophomore and a bit of a nerd, but she was in lust for the Beeville star receiver, senior Abel Benavidez. It only took several coquettish glances before Abel asked her out, prompting her to share her body for the first time ever with him in a car behind the *Texas Grand Dance Hall* outside of Beeville. She was surprised at how good he was and had no problem letting go in the back seat of his black '95 Camero. Despite the lack of space in the back of the vehicle, she proved herself flexible and willing for each awkward position.

The two high school students dated for about a month before Abel dumped her for two other girls. But her stock had risen and she was no longer looked upon as a nerd.

Stephanie held her breasts together, embracing Hickland's well-proportioned manhood. Well lubricated by her saliva, he thrust himself rhythmically between her generous bosoms. She teased him with her words, just like Abel Benavidez, her first fuck, asked her to do many years before.

After a few moments, Lance pulled away and tapped her nipples with the head of his piece. She wiggled with delight before scooting back on the desk and spreading her legs wide in aroused anticipation. Her black patent-leather high heels gleamed in the light of the room.

Before she knew it, Lance had thrust himself into her with lubricated ease. His steady rhythm coupled with the generous amount of foreplay was soon to help her reach new heights again.

"*Take it, baby. Take it all*," Lance whispered. Sweat dropped from his nose onto her belly as he gripped her behind the knees of her spread legs. Her legs dangled over his arms. Had her shoes been off, her toes would have been curled and pointing.

Lance didn't bother to take off his shirt or tie, but his pants were kicked off by his desk where the action started orally. The desk was just high enough for Lance to stand on the floor and bend at the knees a bit and lean in. Stephanie was wearing black thigh-highs and garters that attached to a lacy belt around her waist. Her black heels continued to swing in the air erratically. Her bra was only pushed up and not completely off, but her breasts were fully exposed. Her red blouse was only buttoned at the bottom. She hadn't removed her skirt either.

"Fuck me, Lance! Oh, fuck me!"

"*Oh, yeah.*"

* * * * *

"It would be nice if the regular season started again in August," Wayne thought aloud, contemplating the cancellation of the regular season for American-style football. He and Gary were walking through the front door of City Hall. The hallway was dimly lit, illuminated only by the light from outside shining through the windows of the front doors. The light on the secretary's desk outside of the mayor's office was still lit.

"Are you *kidding*?" Gary said. "Who would go to a football game after all this?"

"What do you mean? Lots of people would go."

"Wayne, there's no way those games would go on. They couldn't make any money."

"*Yes*, they could."

"Wayne, think about—" Then Gary paused for a second, picking up on something he heard. They stopped. "Wait. You hear that?"

Both men stood quiet for a moment and picked up on Stephanie's moans and the slapping sound of flesh colliding with flesh.

"*Oh, shit,*" Gary whispered.

"You thinking what *I'm* thinking?" Wayne asked with a perverted smile.

In front of them stood the door to the mayor's office, slightly agape. The two men crept slowly to the door. The translucent glass revealed nondescript movement within the room, but nothing that could be positively perceived.

They peeked in.

Mayor Hickland had his secretary bent over on the arm rest of the couch near the desk, pounding her from behind.

The men moved away from the door against the wall.

"The mayor's fucking his secretary," said Gary.

"No shit, Sherlock," said Wayne, giddy as all get out. They moved back to look in again for a few moments.

Lance was still giving it to her from behind, *hard*. The steady rhythm of the slapping of flesh resonated around the room. Both participants were moaning in ecstasy.

Gary and Wayne moved to the wall again.

"What kind of shit is this?" Gary asked with incredulity. "The world's falling apart. There's a national crisis, and he's fucking his secretary during business hours?"

"I'm getting my video camera," Wayne said, shaking and hopping, hardly containing his glee of watching two people fucking in real life—something that was pretty much foreign to him.

"Are you crazy?"

"It's in the Suburban. I can get it."

Before either of the men could do anything, they heard the main door open. The bright light of day beamed into the hallway, making a silhouette around the approaching person like a dark specter entering from the netherworld.

Gary mumbled, "Oh, shit…"

"What? Who is it?" asked Wayne. The figure approaching them revealed the distinct form of a pregnant woman. The person walking toward them and the office was unmistakable.

"It's *Evelyn*."

"Who's Evelyn?"

"The mayor's *wife*," Gary groaned. "Listen, follow my lead."

"As always," Wayne said.

Gary nudged Wayne to follow him and they both approached

her.

Evelyn Hickland was of average height and had a charming freckled face, even without makeup. Short brown hair caressed her neck and a very loose pregnancy shirt, adorned with flowers, gave her a sense of maternal beauty.

Gary was not necessarily on a first name basis with the mayor and his wife, but they were casual acquaintances. And though he really did not care either way, he did not want to be a part of what was probably going to happen.

"Hi, *Missus Hickland*," said Gary, loud enough to seem casual, yet low enough that the mayor and his secretary could not hear.

Evelyn abrubtly spun around to reply, "Hi, Gary. What's going on?"

"We just came by to see your husband, but he's not here."

"Though I think he'll be coming soon," chimed in Wayne with a mischievous smirk. Gary scowled at the pun, but held his composure even though he wanted to smack him.

"Well, his car was outside," said Evelyn, feeling a bit uncomfortable at being led back toward the doors.

"He probably went to lunch," Wayne said.

"It's *two-thirty in the afternoon*," Evelyn replied, immediately becoming suspicious.

"Well, a *late* lunch," Gary said.

"He's eating *linner*. Like lunch and dinner combined, you know?" offered Wayne. Gary was now finding it extremely difficult to refrain from striking his friend.

As they were about the reach the door, Stephanie Zapata cried out in intense pleasure.

"What was that?" Evelyn asked, turning back toward her husband's office.

"It's one of those monsters!" Wayne yelled. "Quick! Run!" Wayne took off out the door as if he had seen a ghost.

Gary stood, helpless, and shrugged. The jig was up. Lance's groaning, melding with Stephanie's, really did not help much either.

Evelyn started to whimper. She put one hand on her round eight-month belly and one on her mouth.

"Did you know about this?" she asked, glaring at Gary.

"We just walked in on it, too," said Gary with regret. "I swear."

Wayne came back to the door. "Quick! The monster! Run!" and disappeared back out the door, foolishly continuing his futile tactic.

Evelyn's sadness turned to anger and she began to stride to the door. She had to see it for herself.

Wayne popped back in the doorway.

"C'mon, ya'll! Let's—"

"—Forget it, man. Let's get out of here," Gary said, exiting the building.

Evelyn pushed the door open quietly.

On the couch was her husband, pumping what was left of his essence on the neck and breasts of his secretary like in a porno movie.

"Lance!" she yelled with an unearthly growl.

Both lovers jumped at the cry and their moment was lost. They turned in horrified surprise at the pregnant wife. She had never been by the office, at least before the zombie holocaust. A huge lump formed in Lance's throat and butterflies fluttered in his stomach. His body became charged with a frightened energy that made him shake with adrenaline.

Stephanie stood up, adjusting her skirt so it covered her legs again, then snatched her panties up off the floor. She turned her back and started wiping the evidence off her chest and neck.

Lance ran to his trousers and put them on without his underwear, in such a hurry he almost zipped them up while the zipper's path was still obstructed.

He grumbled, "*Evelyn. Goddammit.*"

"Don't you goddamn *me*, you son of a bitch!" she screamed. "How could you, Lance?! How *could* you?!" She started to cry.

"Evelyn, listen," he began, moving towards her.

"Get away from me!" she yelled, moving away. "I loved you, Lance! I gave you everything you ever wanted! Why?! Why?!"

"Evelyn, please," said Lance. Stephanie had buttoned up her blouse, put her hair in a *chongo*, and stood silently.

"You have no home now. Don't set foot back on our property ever again," Evelyn said, breaking down into tears again.

She turned around and ran out the door. As she slammed the door, the frosted window shattered. Pieces of glass crashed to the floor, resounding through the abandoned City Hall, and revealing the hallway. Lance watched Evelyn running down the corridor and out the door. He bowed his head in shame.

Stephanie approached her lover and whispered, *"You're welcome at my place."* She touched his arm and returned to her desk.

Lance stood alone in his office, a leader of his city, but a failure as a husband.

* * * * *

Frank and Dolores had found plenty of supplies at Abuelita's store. The proprietors gave them a special discount as well, providing many goods for free, including bottled water.

Dolores' head was bowed in grief. Frank held her hand, driving with the other.

"I love you, Frank," said Dolores.

Pleasantly surprised at the comment, Frank responded with, "I love you, too."

She sat silent again.

Frank took in the world around him as he drove through the most secure area of town back to his house near McCann Street.

Two large truck trailers were standing alone in the parking lot of the "Hobby House." Large chains secured the locks on the back. An ambulance sat still next to the trailers. Nearby, a group of men with rifles sat on the tailgates of their trucks, drinking beer. A police car was nearby, and the policeman was enjoying a beer with the men.

Further up the road, men were stacking up bodies in a pile in one lane of the road. Large cans of gas stood ready. Two dark, late model Ford F-150s were having their contents emptied on the pile by several men. Two others were standing guard with rifles. Red handkerchiefs covered their mouths and noses. Gloves protected their hands. The men were dragging the bodies of the dead off the trucks with meat hooks and tossing them on the piles. As the bodies flew from the hooks, large chunks of flesh tore off of them. The pieces fell on the tailgates and on the ground by the pile of bodies, forming a pile of torn soft tissue below the tailgates.

Frank grunted.

In a playground, three dead bodies were strung up by their necks on an old metal swingset. Seven young boys of different cultural backgrounds ranging from ages six to fourteen were taking turns with a bat and taking shots at the bodies. Among them, protective goggles, gloves, and a bandana was passed around. A joyous laughter erupted with each blow to the dead body, especially when they smacked the one that was female, who looked like she had been young when she died. Across the way, two young girls took turns on a slide while two more young girls played with dolls in a sandbox. There was an adult female sitting on a park bench nearby, a rifle at her feet, a tall can of Busch beer in one hand, and a cell phone up to her ear as she casually watched the children at play.

Frank and Dolores turned onto McCann Street. He politely waved at the strangers along the street. Audrey and Eric Garner waved back at the couple.

Up the road further was another body dangling from a tree. This one seemed to be a young boy of African-American descent. There was something strange about it, though. Frank looked closer. The face seemed bruised and swollen. The legs and hands were bound. Beer cans were spread along the yard and a Confederate flag hung in the window, curiously mocking the black child. Two large men sat in a lawn chair near their front porch, hunting rifles at their side. Frank did not associate with the family, as they were never too friendly—and though Frank drew his own conclusion, he still drove home in silence.

Frank and Dolores pulled into their driveway. After checking the area, Frank signaled for Dolores to exit the vehicle. They swiftly advanced to the front door, unlocked it, and entered the house.

Dolores placed the groceries on the table in the kitchen.

"Well, we're home," Frank said, consoling himself more than Dolores.

It took him by surprise when Dolores screamed and started to cry. Frank looked toward the kitchen to see Dolores peering out the window into the backyard. He came toward her for a closer look.

Outside, three ghouls had dug up the bodies of his daughter and her friend and were eating them.

Frank pulled out his pistol and opened the back door.

As he stepped out, a zombie in a suit and tie attacked him, seemingly waiting at the back door for some fresh meat to happen by. It tackled him to the ground and snarled at his arm. Frank moved away fast enough that the beast was only able to bite his sleeve, pinching his flesh but not piercing the material enough to penetrate his skin. It gave Frank enough time to shove the ghoul off of him.

He stood. The beast was trying to get to his feet but was met with a boot to the nose. The nose was literally kicked off, revealing dark flesh and two holes as the ghoul stumbled back. Frank sent a bullet through its forehead.

Thinking it might have attracted the attention of the other monsters, he aimed the gun at them, only to find them concentrating solely on their meal. He kept the gun trained as he stepped closer. Large chunks of flesh were being shoved into their mouths. Dirt mixed with flesh and blood oozed from their lips.

Slowly, Frank picked off all three. They collapsed, unmoving. Putting down his gun, Frank peered into the crudely exhumed grave.

Below, he saw the partially consumed body of his daughter. Her legs were still buried in the dirt. Her stomach was torn open. The beasts had pulled her ribcage apart in an effort to get at the heart. Her face was ripped away. One glazed eye peppered with dirt gazed into the sky. Alyssa's body suffered the same fate.

Dolores' cries echoed in Frank's ears as he realized that there was only one other way to protect the bodies of Blanca and Alyssa.

Sadly, he walked to the shed to get the shovel and a can of gasoline.

* * * * *

Night once again threw its black pall over Beeville, displaying a grand orange and yellow twilight before tossing out the twinkling stars of the sky.

Sheriff Sam McMurtry was checking on the east barricade outside of town. Things had been quiet and nothing like the morning massacre he had witnessed. Every car that stopped at the barricade was redirected to Corpus Christi or elsewhere. Since the televised address of the President, traffic had picked up a bit, but with no trouble. Due to the new amount of traffic, McMurtry advised each of the barricades to create a sign reading, 'NO FEMA CENTERS HERE' in an effort to divert traffic. It seemed to make a difference.

After finishing the last sign, McMurtry got back into his car and started his drive to the next barricade.

It was hard for him not to think about his son, Edgar. Surely he was safe, perhaps in a military bunker underground somewhere. But he wanted to know for sure. Since the outbreaks, the last letter he got said Kuwait was great. Great beer. Great food.

Since the outbreak, McMurtry never felt so alone.

The cloudy sky created a canopy of darkness. The headlights of his cruiser cut through the night like lasers. In a short distance, the high beams began to pick up the form of a creature. As the car accelerated closer, it was more easy to see: a man in a white shirt and slacks, probably a resident of the nearby subdivision, stumbling along the road.

Angry, McMurtry accelerated and rammed the zombie. It flipped forward onto the hood for a brief moment, then sucked under the vehicle. The hood ornament got planted in its chest, penetrating just below the area where the ribcage separates. It ripped open a portion of the chest as the ornament tore off, embedded in the chest of the monster, as McMurtry continued to drive forward. The beast was ground into the pavement, bouncing the vehicle up and down before being spit out in its wake. McMurtry hit the brakes a few yards away from the body.

Instinctually, he reached for the CB radio.

"This is McMurtry to dispatch. I'm stepping out of the vehicle to examine..." He stammered. "To help a civilian at country road thirty-four, three miles away from barricade..." He could not recall which barricade.

"Dispatch to McMurtry. Please repeat your twenty."

Leaving the engine running, McMurtry opened the door and exited his vehicle, ignoring the query from dispatch. He pulled out his flashlight. Taking his gun from his holster, he approached the body behind his vehicle. The beam of illumination from the flashlight pierced the night. The red taillights were glowing in the darkness, like the scarlet eyes of a large sinister demon watching McMurtry approach the body. A ring of white radiance was created by the flashlight and danced on the road, wiggling around the body as the sheriff advanced closer.

He looked at the cadaver. To his dismay, he recognized the monster—or, at least, who the monster *used* to be. It was his son's sophomore math teacher, Mr. Jacoby.

Mr. Jacoby was in bad shape. Apart from his being a ghoul, his arms had been ground to mincemeat by the car. His face was scarred with road rash. The right leg was twisted awkwardly at the knee. A dull groan was emanating from his mouth. He seemed to be shaking, as if quivering from the pain.

The ghoul began to move in an apparent attempt to rise, but was quickly halted by a bullet to the head.

Dispatch, having waited for nearly a minute for a response, repeated its query. *"Dispatch to McMurtry. Please repeat your twenty."*

The funk from the fallen zombie was hitting McMurtry's nostrils, so he returned to his vehicle. He opened the door and the interior light came on. He sat down in the driver's seat.

With the world turned so upside down and the stress of wondering where his son was, he reached under his seat. Pulling out a small wooden box, he then reached into his shirt pocket and pulled out a packet of Zig-Zags.

After a minute or two, Sheriff McMurtry had rolled himself a nice joint—or a *"doobie,"* as he liked to call it. With the world tipped on its ear and the stress he was under, he felt justified. Normally this kind of criminal paraphernalia would never be in his car, but he took advantage of the global crisis and started bringing some along.

Taking a lighter from his cup holder by the steering wheel, he lit the marijuana cigarette and took a deep breath. He held in the gentle smoke for a moment, then exhaled what was left. The smoke hung in the stagnant air as he contemplated his future, recalled his past, and feared for the present.

What the hell is going to happen? he wondered. *With the U.N. coming in to help, things might be better. But what then?*

He knew, in essence, the "liberation" of the U.S. would basically be an occupation. When would they leave? How would they treat his fellow Americans? Foreign troops on U.S. soil was a predicament not seen since the Revolutionary War. Would there be any Americans left to save? And what about other nations?

He took another long hit off the doobie and closed his eyes, reclining in the seat before exhaling. A gentle mist of second-hand pot smoke wafted around the driver-side door.

Looking around the dark countryside, he thought about his family: Larry and Jane McMurtry, his loving parents, and Arthur and Jade McMurtry, his older brother and younger sister.

Then he thought about Lydia Jane, his wife. He remembered the first time he ever saw her during a college spring break. It was a nice spring day, and the river had been moving swiftly. Sam had joined two of his buddies, Vance and Johnny, for tubing down the Frio river in Concan, Texas. Though the river was flowing, there had been several areas that were still too shallow to ride. So he had walked them.

At one point, a small gaggle of girls had gathered in a deep area of the river. It was almost like an oasis of women to him. After his friend Vance had taken the initiative to ask the girls if they needed help, they ended up hanging out and chatting for about thirty minutes before they all journeyed down the river again. Sam had chivalrously offered to carry Lydia's tube during the shallow parts.

Sam took another long hit from his joint. The cherry turned bright orange for a moment, then subsided. He exhaled.

Their relationship at first had been a hard sell. Lydia had been a bit of a snob, and Sam's background had not helped matters much. But his affection had been simple and charming, and Sam eventually won her over several months later. Within a span of three years, they were married.

McMurtry was suddenly shaken from his reverie. He sensed some movement across the road. The night was still, and the groan was unmistakable.

Taking out his pistol again and standing, McMurtry took a final hit, then put the roach on the dashboard. He began to walk toward the shadowy creature. In standard police fashion, he advanced with his flashlight in one hand and his pistol in the other. The marijuana had worked its magic, though. He stumbled over several embedded rocks on the side of the road, awkwardly regaining his footing each time.

As he moved closer he spotlighted the creature square in the face. Its eyes squinted and its hand came up. It stumbled around, blinded by the light. McMurtry started to chuckle as he watched the beast try to regain its footing. It turned into a full blown laugh as the beast fell. The "happy grass" was alive and well in McMurtry's body. The beast rose, struggling to see through the bright radiance.

After chuckling some more, McMurtry squeezed the trigger and punched a hole in the creature's neck. It staggered a bit as a large amount of black muck fell from its neck onto its white shirt. The name badge dangling from the shirt of the abomination was indecipherable, covered in black slime. The head hung awkwardly toward the side of the neck that was removed by the gunfire. It extended its hands once again and approached the wire fence that separated it from the sheriff.

Taking aim again, McMurtry let another bullet punch a hole in the creature's chest. Its head flung forward as it was pushed back over a bush.

Before the beast could get up, literally losing its head, a set of groans sounded to McMurtry's right side. He shined the flashlight into the brush in that direction. A movement from a bush informally invited another bullet toward an unknown and invisible target. Fear sent yet another in the same direction. Naturally-induced confusion made him stumble backward and fall on his ass. His flashlight fell to the ground as well as his pistol.

A certain rustling made him turn to his left. A once-young zombie girl stumbled over the wire fence. Barbs tore at her shirt, piercing her arms and stomach and exposing her dead breasts.

Her blonde hair became a red mess in the back as a bullet sent the living dead girl to the ground by a sheriff struggling to regain control.

He was dazed. The shot was dead on, but lucky. Had he fumbled for the flashlight and gun just a few moments longer, he might have been in grave danger. His head was spinning. Had he smoked some bad shit? He looked at the dark clouds overhead, still sitting on his behind. A northeasterly wind was moving the clouds across the sky. As the beast that was trying to hold its neck together was rising, McMurtry was still entranced by the clouds. The moonlight was coloring the darkness with some light. A ray of hope.

Then, somewhere in McMurtry's ears, a familiar tune sounded. It took an extra second for his drugged mind to register the reverberation. It was his phone humming the *Sanford and Son* theme.

—It was his son calling.

He rose to his feet, fearful that hands would grab him in the darkness. He fumbled and dropped his flashlight, somehow anticipating being grabbed and bit. But there was no creature to attack him, just a confused and jumbled phantasm of his own creation.

Turning to his patrol car, the cell phone ringer playing its programmed melody caused his heart to skip a beat. A moment passed in stillness as a large ghoul shambled toward the light of his open car door.

The ringtone continued into the familiar tune. Instinctively, McMurtry raised his gun only to notice the slide had locked back, indicating an empty weapon.

The large creature turned to him as the tune played on.

"*Fuck*," McMurtry breathed, his reflexes a moment slower. He pulled out his steel baton and flicked it to its full length as the cowbell portion of the song sounded. He chuckled then, and whispered, "*More cowbell.*"

He somehow regained his senses. Positioning the baton in his hand, he jabbed it into the face of the monster, bursting its left eye. As goo fell forth from the punctured eye socket, he quickly pulled the black weapon back and swung it against the cheek of the monster. He completely followed through, then brought his arm back around, catching the creature on the other side of the face. Concussive physics apparently still in effect, the beast stumbled and fell away from the open door.

Diving into the driver's seat, McMurtry reached for the phone.

The phone fell silent.

Looking at the face of the phone, a digital message manifested on the screen: *1 Missed Call.*

Urgently fumbling with the buttons, he checked the missed call menu to find the number. A connection of letters popped up instead of numbers: *PRIVATE CALLER—NUMBER UNAVAILABLE.*

McMurtry took a moment to sulk in the driver's seat. The door was still wide open. His head fell into his hands.

A groan from just outside the vehicle made him step out of the car once more, first grabbing the shotgun off the rack on his side of the prisoner cage. The creature he had clocked was rising from the pavement again, blood dripping from its punctured eye socket.

McMurtry emptied his shotgun on the lone beast, leveling it to ground chuck in mere seconds.

The car's interior light illuminated the ground around him.

Looking down at the mess he had made of the creature, he noticed a large glob of blood and flesh. Somehow, the shape it took on the pavement reminded him of Mickey Mouse.

Sheriff Sam McMurtry snorted, then laughed big and loud.

Saturday Afternoon

Bless me, Father, for I have sinned. It's been a while since my last confession."

Father O'Leary gently asked Frank Garza what he wanted to confess from behind the finely latticed partition in the solitude of his confessional.

"Father, I shot my daughter in the head."

The Father was silent, and a bit shocked. However, considering the circumstances, he measured the possibilities.

"She became one of them. One of her friends grabbed her arm and..." Frank trailed off and started to whimper.

"Whenever you are ready to continue, my son."

Pulling himself together, Frank started again. "She was bit by one of her friends and..." He just could not do it.

After listening to Frank whimper, O'Leary tried to ease his obvious pain.

"My son, in her time of need, did you express your love to her?"

"Yes, Father."

"And as her soul left her body, did you show all the compassion that you had in your heart?"

Frank felt guilty, remembering how he strapped her to the chair. "Father, I put her in bonds..." He began to cry again. The guilt was scourging his soul.

"My son, you were expressing your love to her, which was sharing God's love with her."

"Yes, Father."

"And God—our Father—protects his flock, as you were only protecting yours when you placed her in bonds."

"But Father, was she gone? Was she dead when I shot her?"

O'Leary had been contemplating that very question. And with the Vatican keeping silent since their last communication to the world at the start of the crisis, it was up to him to choose the words he was about to say.

"My son, our souls are within our bodies. Our physical bodies are merely a shell for our souls—our spiritual being. When she passed, did her soul return?" He paused. "Did you look into her eyes and see your daughter?"

Frank took another spiritual scourging, knowing that he did not allow a moment to pass as his daughter rose again only to collapse from a crude metal projectile passing through her head.

"I don't know," Frank said, weeping.

"Reach into your heart, Frank," said O'Leary, "Did you see?"

Frank thought for a moment, wiping tears from his eyes. He said, "I don't know."

"You *do* know," O'Leary insisted. "What did you see? Did you see her smiling face? Did you hear her voice calling to you?"

Frank knew neither had happened and he faced the truth. His daughter had lunged at him, restrained but dangerous, only seconds before being silenced. And he remembered—remembered her *eyes*.

Dark. Empty.

"No," he admitted.

"Then you must make peace with the fact that she had already gone to join Jesus in Heaven with our heavenly Father. Your daughter was in Heaven. You experienced the cruel fate of her shell." O'Leary hid the horror of the thought of shooting the risen daughter.

Frank broke down again.

After several silent moments of gloom and sorrow, O'Leary gave his judgment: "My son, you have committed no sin. Do not despair. You are doing God's bidding. You have done no wrong."

The whimpers slowly faded after a few moments, and Frank felt a warm embrace. He took several deep breaths, regaining his

96

composure.

"Go forth, my son, and continue to do God's bidding. Your penance is only to pray for your family, your town, and the world."

"God bless you, Father," Frank said.

He exited the confessional.

O'Leary couldn't help but feel sad for him. The confession was a symptom of the national and global crisis. He bowed his head in prayer. After making the sign of the cross, he took a swig from a decanter bottle of whiskey.

Within moments, Lucy St. Claire entered the confessional.

She said, "Father, I sin."

*   *   *   *   *

"Pass me a mustard packet."

"They're right beside you."

"Oh."

Red reached for the red-flagged mustard packet, opened it with his teeth, spit out the corner, and spread the mustard onto his slice of Mrs. Baird's bread.

Red and Alex had missed the exit to Poth and decided it might be best to work their way to Karnes City. But in the meantime they found a shady spot near the side of the road to have lunch out of their supplies gathered while at the San Antonio Mercado. The spring sun began to warm the grassy field. A crisp breeze blew through the trees. For a world falling apart, the Texas countryside was a serene departure from the global epidemic.

Red and Alex were eating sandwiches.

"You know...," Alex began, and then paused. "I forgot."

"Huh?"

"I forgot what I was going to say."

"Oh, c'mon. You know what you were going to say," Red said, taking a swig from his can of Coke. In the distance, a cow shambled into the field they were sitting in.

"You were a real asshole to stick your gun in my face. You know that?"

Red didn't expect the remark. Since that moment, Alex did not feel as safe around Red as he used to.

"Man, I'm sorry," Red said. "I overreacted."

"Fuck yeah, you overreacted."

"I'm sorry, all right?"

Alex paused. "I forgive you, my friend." Though he really did not, he opted to keep things amicable. There was still a lot of road to cover. It was best to ease the tension than to fight it out. After all, he liked Red.

Red changed the subject. "You know," he said, " I can't help but feel, like, *free*, you know?"

"It's weird, though," Alex replied, "I just can't help to feel totally unsafe. *Anywhere.*" The subtext was clear.

Red chose to ignore it. "Well, I don't blame you," he said, chomping on his sandwich. The cow mooed in the background. "Not every day the dead rise and attack the living, right?"

Another groaning moo emanated from the distant cow.

"That's another thing," Alex said. "What's with them wanting to eat flesh? Why don't they attack animals?"

"They *do*," Red said. "I saw one eating a dog that was chained up in a yard back in San Antonio."

"No way?"

"Yeah. It was when it was all first starting. I remember running down the street. It was the best thing to do since the traffic was all jammed getting out of town. The sidewalks weren't crowded even though people were running. I remember hearing a loud squeal. I looked into the backyard of this white trash family."

Alex reached for a handful of chips as a cowbell sounded nearby.

"Well, this pit bull was tearing at this guy's arm. But the guy had grabbed it and bit into the nape of the dog's neck. The dog wouldn't let go, though, even as blood was dripping all over the guy's pizza delivery shirt."

"Domino's?"

"No. Papa Johns."

"Oh."

"Anyway, so the dog snapped at the guy's face, taking off the dude's nose."

"Aw, man," Alex breathed.

"I'm serious," Red said. "But it gave that guy a chance to bite back, right into the throat."

The ketchup on Alex's sandwich suddenly did not look so

appetizing anymore. He put it down and burped.

"You okay?" Red asked.

"Yeah," Alex said, swallowing back a bit of upchucked food.

The cow mooed again, ambling closer to the picnicking pair.

"Dude, I didn't mean to make you puke."

"I didn't puke," Alex said, wiping his mouth.

"In your mouth, I mean."

"Puke was in my mouth, but I didn't puke."

"Puke as a noun. Puke was in your mouth, therefore you puked."

"Red, it's not a noun. You used it as a verb. I *puked*."

The cow was much closer.

"You *did* puke, though."

"No, I didn't. I didn't spit it out. *That's* puking."

"You don't have to spit it out to puke in your mouth."

"So puke is regurgitation whether you spit it out or—"

Alex was interrupted by a loud and painful moo from the cow. Both men jumped in surprise, shouting frightened colorful metaphors as they scrambled to their feet. They looked at the cow, who was dripping a thick black fluid from its mouth. Red goo was dangling from its nose. Its eyes were bloodshot and glazed. Its muzzle was caked in dried blood. It stumbled about the picnic area, dripping filth from its brown behind.

"It's infected," Alex said, pulling out his gun.

"Holy shit!" Red exclaimed. "No way!"

The cow bucked, wiggled its head, then eyeballed Alex. It then raised its tail, which was facing Red. Diving, Red dodged the warm stream of urine flying out the cow's rear end. It was accompanied by a load of warm cow excrement, which fell all over their food.

A warm stream of vomit flew from Red's stomach out his mouth in a stream.

"*Now* you puked," Alex said with a chuckle. "That's puke."

The cow bucked again and lunged at Alex. A wild shot from Alex's gun pierced its shoulder.

Wiping his mouth, Red yelled, "You're making the cow with Mad Cow mad!" Then, catching a whiff of the cow's mess, threw up again.

"You puked again," Alex said, getting some distance from the animal.

Red picked himself up off the ground and ran towards Alex, who was aiming at the cow with his .38. He popped off another shot, putting a round in the cow's head. Its legs buckled. Alex squeezed off another and the beast fell, squashing what was left of their picnic.

They paused.

"Infection burgers, anyone?" Red joked.

"You're nasty, man," Alex said.

They both continued to look in disbelief and despair at the mess that was once their picnic.

"So much for the sandwich meat," Red said. Their food was either crushed by the cow carcass or soaked in waste. Red gagged, thinking of the food.

"Don't puke again, man," Alex said.

"I didn't," said Red.

"I know. *Don't*," said Alex, struggling to make amends with his constitution.

"Hey, what the hell is that?" Red asked, looking back at the highway.

White Hummers were cruising down the road.

"*Get down*," said Alex.

The both hit the ground, hiding in the weeds. Peering over the stalks of grass, they examined the vehicles.

"Holy shit! The U.N.!"

"It's the U.N. all right," Alex agreed. As a pair of conspiracy kooks, this did not bode well in their minds.

"I knew it. These bastards were behind all this. Just like with AIDS in Africa."

"Be quiet," Alex said. "Check it out." He pointed to a Hummer that stopped by their vehicle. They had made no effort to camouflage the blue and black F-150, simply parking it on the side of the road. Alex suddenly regretted it.

"Aw, damn. They're going to loot our vehicle. Shit. My *Credence* tapes..."

"They're not going to loot our vehicle, dumbass. They're checking for us." Alex tried to keep himself calm at the now dangerous circumstance. A bolt of fear charged through both of their bodies. They watched quietly.

Soldiers speaking in a foreign language scattered about. Several came into the field. Both Red and Alex remained still and quiet. Two men began walking into the tall grass.

"*Dude, they're going to see us. We've flattened this patch of grass,*" whispered Red.

Alex replied by putting his finger to his lips.

The soldiers edged closer.

Red put his hands over his head. Alex remained still, yet frightened.

The soldiers edged even closer.

Alex checked to make sure his .38 was still off safety.

The soldiers were in a position to see the flattened grass, but a radio message stopped them. They paused, spoke in a foreign tongue, then turned back. Within a minute they were back in their vehicles and driving away, returning to their convoy.

Alex and Red took a deep breath.

"You were right," said Red.

"About what?"

"There is a difference between 'puke' and 'puke'."

The two shared a laugh and walked back to their vehicle.

Before Red climbed in, he noticed a small canister on the ground by the front wheel.

"Shit! Alex, don't move!"

"What?"

"C'mere and look. *Slowly.*"

Alex walked around the back of the vehicle to the driver's side door. At the foot of the front wheel stood a small metal container. In large black stenciled letters was written 'U.N.' Below that was stenciled, 'TXZ-68788805'.

"What is it?" Red asked.

"It's a trap," Alex replied. "Don't touch it."

"It's in front of the wheel," Red said.

"Behind it."

"Behind it, in front of it—who gives a shit when it blows up our ass? We have to move it."

"What do you mean *we*? You got a mouse in your pocket?"

"Well, it's not ticking."

"That doesn't mean it's not going to level the place."

"You don't even know it's a bomb."

"Then what *is* it?" said Red, irritated.

"Aw, hell," Alex grumbled, just as irritated. He got to his knees and approached the device.

It appeared to be made out of aluminum, though it seemed heavy. He noticed a clip with a pin stuck through it.

"It's a grenade. Or flash-bang. Or something," Alex hypothesized.

"How do you know?"

"It's got a pin."

"Well, don't pull it."

"I'm not gonna pull it," Alex said. He quickly picked it up. Red flinched and yelped in fear. It was a bit heavy and was definitely larger than a flash-bang or hand grenade.

After a collective sigh, they examined it closer.

"I think it's a gas canister," Red said.

"You might be right. But what kind of gas?"

"I don't know, but I know it must stink."

"That was a dumb joke."

"No, your mom's bad gas is a dumb joke."

"Hey, my mom's farts smell like roses," Alex retorted, putting the canister in the back of the truck.

"What are you doing?" Red asked, watching in disbelief.

"I'm keeping it," said Alex, smiling.

"What?!"

"Maybe we could use it. We don't want to be wasteful with weapons, right?"

Red still thought it was dumb, but Alex was his friend. "All right. But if my truck blows up, I'm kicking your ass."

"Aw, shut up and drive," Alex told him, getting into the passenger seat. "This day's been long enough already."

The two drove off, unconcerned that the canister was rolling around, unsecured, in the back of the vehicle.

* * * * *

Frank and Dolores Garza sat in front of their television set, mesmerized by the news Cable News Channel was regurgitating.

In regard to television broadcasts, the large cities that provided programming for the rural communities were wrecked. A week after the plague hit, TV stations went off the air. It had been a week since local programming was on, eventually being replaced by twice-a-day CNC coverage. At around the same time, Colombia Broadcasting Company played reruns of regularly scheduled shows, with the news shows replaced by the CNC shows from earlier in the day. And the movie channels started running as well, though no set schedule had been confirmed since the outage.

CNC was in full information mode, provided with the latest news by the five-cornered Pentagon, and Frank and Dolores were trying to take it all in at the top of the hour.

"Pentagon officials meet with high-ranking leaders from the U.N. The President signs an Executive Order allowing U.S. military and U.N. Peacekeeping forces unlimited power in the U.S. Britney and Kevin are reunited, and a simple tech gadget that can save your family's life next on CNC."

The Global Plague Update banner glided onto the screen. A colorful backdrop accompanied an ominous soundtrack then faded into the newsroom where sexy news anchor Natasha Valerio was ready to spout the news. The random news ticker was in top form, dancing across the screen under the modest bosom of the Latin anchor. A box with the U.N. insignia appeared in the upper left-hand portion of the screen.

"Good evening everyone. I'm Natasha Valerio. Our top story tonight: Pentagon officials are meeting with high-ranking leaders from the U.N. today in a secret location in New York City. They are working on a plan to re-secure the United States. Nicole Elmore has more."

A caption appeared below stock footage of U.N. soldiers marching on a foreign land. The caption read, '*U.S. joins with U.N.*' Nicole Elmore invisibly spoke her report.

"The United Nations has been activated in the U.S., and U.S. leaders are happy at the prospect of more security for the American people."

A shot of Massachusetts senator Ted Kinney appeared on the screen. His name appeared below. Television did nothing for his looks. His eastern U.S. accent was in great form.

"I was happy to encourage the President to accept our non-partisan committee recommendation to allow U.N. forces to patrol the streets of America in an effort to eliminate the threat within our country."

"New York senator Carl Shumer also voiced his support."

Another shot, this one of Carl Shumer standing in front of a blue curtain, appeared on the screen. He was casually dressed with no tie.

"I think all Americans will benefit from this U.N. peacekeeping force."

Stock footage of the U.N. keeping peace in foreign nations appeared on the screen as Nicole Elmore continued with her report.

"The United Nations has sent several thousand troops and a surplus of military vehicles to help the U.S. man and equip the various rescue stations and FEMA centers set up around the nation. But they've also been allowed to secure entire cities in an effort to retake them. But some are not happy with the two massive militaries joining forces."

An interview from an unknown FEMA camp revealed a short man of Hispanic descent, (and very young,) voicing his opinion. Below his face read his name: Fabian Murphy.

"I think the U.S. should take care of this problem themselves. Inviting the international community into our nation to walk our streets with guns puts all of us in danger."

Another opinion was shared, by one Thomas Martinez.

"The U.N. peacekeeping forces will do no such thing. They have a nasty reputation of not keeping the peace when invited into nations. They will only cause conflict."

Another stock footage package of FEMA camp members was flashed across the screen as Nicole went on, *"But some are happy with the United States getting assistance from the United Nations."*

Pablo Roca was the next to share his voice.

"I love being here in the FEMA camp. I've never felt so safe and secure. The soldiers running it have been great. With all the guns the FEMA soldiers have protecting us, there's no way any of those things will get in here."

The screen fell back into images of despondent, yet happy images of FEMA camp members waiting out the madness as Nicole concluded her report.

"The U.S. is hopeful that all Americans will embrace the U.N. support of the U.S. military, which will provide many Americans with a chance at surviving the plague."

An image of a small child with his mother was revealed on the screen as Nicole wrapped up her report. The child smiled at the camera and gave a thumbs-up sign before hugging his mother.

"Nicole Elmore, CNC news."

Natasha's alluring, well-kept face and strategically placed bosoms appeared on the screen.

"The United Nations joins with the United States in encouraging all citizens to find and join the nearest FEMA camp, or allow U.N. and U.S. forces to secure your city, no matter how secure you might think it is.

"The United Nations has also asked all U.S. citizens to turn in their guns and firearms at the FEMA center. Citizens found to possess private firearms will be subject to prosecution and incarceration."

Frank Garza looked down at his pistol laying by the votive hands on the coffee table.

He knew there was absolutely no way he was turning that in.

Trains

R
ed and Alex pulled into Karnes City, windows rolled down. The pleasant breeze caressed their faces. But around them, zombies, bodies, and blood greeted them on the main roads in.

"So who would win," Red began, "Batman or the Punisher?"

"I go with Batman," said Alex, intentionally steering his vehicle off to the left just enough to knock over a zombie.

"Why? Punisher's got all the weapons."

"Wait a second. Do you notice something?"

"What?" Red asked. It took him a moment to figure out what Alex was talking about.

Though the duo was driving through a global apocalypse, with the dead wreaking havoc on the living, there was something different with this city.

—Then it came to him.

Craters lined the roads. Cars seemed blasted in two—not from car accidents, but from artillery shells. Holes were not burned, but punched into the sides of buildings. The city, though still infected, looked more like a war zone than a city contaminated.

Then something else caught their eyes, making the situation glaringly obvious.

A large mass of creatures were massed around what seemed to

107

be a line of bodies lying symmetrically on their backs and stomachs. Holes filled the brick wall behind the bodies. The creatures were all digging into the cadavers, like hungry men, women, and children at the CiCi's Pizza buffet. To the conspiratorial eyes of Alex and Red, it was obvious the beasts were eating the remains of people who were brutally executed.

Red chose not to stop, and instead drove on, seemingly trying to ignore the obvious possibility of the military-style executions. But then something else caught their eyes.

"Oh, shit! Pull over! Pull over!" Alex exclaimed.

Red put the vehicle in park, and the two exited.

They peeked into a side street near the central plaza of the city. Within the plaza, U.N. troops were securing the city hall. A perimeter had been set around the square and soldiers were sporadically shooting zombies as they placed sandbags.

"They're setting up shop," Red commented, gazing at their work. "But why?"

"Who knows. And why would they care about this town?"

"Hell, I don't—"

Before Red could finish his sentence, something grabbed his shoulders. Flinching, he turned to see the rotting face of a creature. The bloody white garb suggested he might have been a formal barber at one time. A small moustache under slicked-back hair illustrated his face. A bite in the neck confirmed his infection. Red screamed.

The beast snapped at Red's neck to no avail as Red quickly wiggled away in dread.

As the beast lunged at him again, a large portion of its head was blown off by Alex.

"Shit!" Red yelled. The bullet was close enough to spook him, but far enough to not be a danger, though the blast made his ears ring.

"You all right?" Alex asked.

"No," Red answered, looking back at the truck. It was surrounded by several creatures.

"Aw, hell," Alex grumbled, knowing that the ruckus could attract the U.N. troops.

Raising his weapon, Alex put down the two creatures near the closest door. Red knew what Alex was doing and went for that door.

Alex was close behind, fearing more for the possibility of the U.N. coming after them. They re-entered the vehicle, with Alex in the driver's seat this time around.

With quickness, Alex took the vehicle out of park and into drive. Pedal hit metal and rubber met a corpse before hitting the road. They drove off.

"Where are you going?"

"I don't know," Alex said, trying to figure out a way around the occupied city.

An open field stood ahead at the end of the street. A set of tracks lined the edge of the green field. As the big blue vehicle made it to the intersection, yet another sight put the men on guard and sent another bolt of fear through their bodies.

It was a train station. The U.N. troops were herding the residents of the town into the boxcars. A voice from a loudspeaker could be heard unpoetically reciting a stern diatribe.

"*Attention. Attention. U.N. forces are here to help. Remain calm. We will not tolerate civil disobedience.*"

Red and Alex stared in awe.

"*Eat your heart out, Benito Mussilini,*" Red mumbled.

"I told you, man! I told you!" Alex exclaimed. "Create the crisis, then pose the solution!"

"Where are they going?"

"A FEMA camp somewhere down the line, I guess," Alex said. "I'll be goddamned..."

For years, Alex had done research on FEMA. He discovered that much of the money given to the agency actually went to black ops and other clandestine projects within the U.S. and beyond. There were also claims that camps would be set up for Americans during a time of crisis. He was now witnessing his worst nightmare come true.

"Hey!" a voice called out. Red and Alex turned toward the street corner on the driver's side. Standing, flabbergasted, was a U.N. soldier in blue camouflage, who immediately raised his weapon.

"*Get down,*" Alex said, gunning the engine again and advancing forward. Hot smoke blew from the tail pipe. Black tires peeled out on the pavement.

The soldier opened fire, peppering the side of the big blue truck with holes and barely missing the tires. The back window shattered and glass sprinkled into the cab.

Red turned in his seat and returned fire with an M-16 he acquired in San Antonio. The soldier dove for cover, giving the two just enough time to get away.

Sitting back in his seat, he noticed Alex grimacing in pain. One hand was on the wheel. The other was gripping his left leg.

"Alex..."

"Don't worry about me, man. Just keep your eyes peeled for more men in blue."

Scared for his friend, Red took a deep breath and pointed his machine gun out of the passenger side window as they sped out of town.

* * * * *

Billy Joe strolled up the street, pistol in hand. There was no real danger on McCann Street aside from the alleys behind the main road.

It had been another pleasant afternoon of sex for him and Lucy St. Claire. He wanted to stay longer again, but was prompted to leave with the promise of more sex later tonight or tomorrow, depending on if his parents would let him leave the house again.

Billy Joe was so busy reminiscing that he neglected to see his father Eric sitting on the steps of the front porch.

"Billy Joe," he said, gruffly. A shotgun stood at his side.

"Hi, Dad."

"Where have you been?" He knew where he had been, watching him come out of Lucy's house, but wanted to hear it directly from his son's own mouth.

Knowing that he was probably caught coming out of Lucy's house, he admitted, "I was helping Ms. St. Claire with some things she needed moved around the house." Gulping after completing the sentence did not help much.

His father remained suspicious. "She pay you?"

"It wasn't much to move, just a little heavy."

His father nodded, then took a drag off his cigarette. "Your mom's inside. Go tell her where you've been."

"Okay," Billy Joe said, walking up the steps into the house.

His mother Audrey was sitting in front of the television with a small box of Bon-Bons.

"Hey, where've you been?"

"I was helping Ms. St. Claire move some stuff," he said. "I'm going to my room."

"You should put it on CNC when you get there. There's some fucked up shit going on in the world."

"Okay," he said, and dashed to his room.

Audrey watched the television intently.

"...Thank you, Natasha. Today's special report, Storing the Dead. Across the nation, hospitals are overrun with humans dying and returning to life. Hospitals are now using a government-sponsored disposal method that has raised controversy, but is currently being used by FEMA centers across the nation. Julio Jones has more."

Footage of hospitals in chaos were projected on the screen as Julio Jones reported.

"The dead rising. Families torn apart. Hospitals in disorder... It was a sign of the times. Across the nation, as the infection spread, hospital officials were using a controversial technique in storing the massive amounts of dead that began to pile into buildings...

"Truck trailers."

Stock footage of training videos and actual footage filled the screen as a member of FEMA talked about the procedure.

"The procedure was originally intended for a smallpox outbreak. But when that didn't happen, we encouraged hospitals to use the procedure for the current plague.

"Hospital officials were ordered to place people who were moments from dying in body bags. When they expired, nurses were told to record the time, then zip up the bag, securing the zipper with a small lock. After that, they were wheeled to a truck trailer that was waiting outside."

A doctor who was in a FEMA camp described the procedure as people walked around behind him.

"It worked fine for the first few days, until the streets became littered with the walking dead, making the procedure difficult and ultimately impossible."

"Amazing. Fuckin' amazing," said Audrey as she popped another bon-bon into her mouth.

* * * * *

Several miles outside of Karnes City, Red and Alex pulled over. The afternoon sun was washing the gentle Texas countryside with warmth. Alex sat on the tailgate.

Alex loosened his buttoned denim shirt, gritting his teeth in pain as Red gingerly examined the bullet hole in his leg.

"You think you can pull it out?" Alex asked.

"It's not in deep," Red told him, "But you're going to have to take off your pants if I'm going to wrap it." He then subtly gulped.

A zombie meandered in a field in the distance.

"That's fine. Just don't pull any of your homoerotic shit, all right?" Alex retorted, getting off of the tailgate and unbuckling his belt.

"Hey, you're the one that wanted to give me the back rub, you fag," Red said, laughing off the comment.

Alex was relieved some of the tension had worn off. "Man, shut up and go get the pliers. They're on the right side of the toolbox." He pointed at the large toolbox near the passenger side and under the broken window.

Alex got to his boxers and painfully brought his leg up on the tailgate and sat down again. Red found two pairs of pliers. He chose the needle-nose and walked back to Alex.

Alex noticed the creature in the distance.

"Hey, how much you want to bet I could pick off that thing over there?"

Red looked in the direction Alex was indicating with his finger. "Well, what if he's not a monster?"

"Of course he is," Alex said. "Look."

"I'll put money on you killing a real human," Red said, getting ready to work on the leg.

Alex stopped Red before he dug in with the pliers. He exclaimed, "Whoa! Wait! You didn't sanitize those!"

"What?"

"You didn't sanitize those. They need to be sanitized before you go digging around in my leg."

"Well, what do I use?"

"Rinse it with water, then dip it in some whiskey."

"Are you kidding?"

"I'm serious. I saw it in a movie once."

"Oh, yeah. Now I'm *sure* it will work," Red said sarcastically, chuckling and moving to the cab to get the suggested supplies.

Alex picked up the M-16 and set it to single shot. Shouldering the machine gun, he squeezed off a round. His wound ached as the shot rang out, but was not extremely painful.

In the distance, the creature stumbled backwards. A large portion of its right shoulder was removed. It continued to walk.

Red returned with a cup of whiskey. He prepped the pliers in the cup, soaking it in the fine alcoholic beverage. Both he and Alex ignored the fact that the cup was not washed.

"Oh, yeah," Alex said, shouldering the weapon.

"*L'Amour?*" Red asked, referring to the large jug of fermented beverage he had poured from. "What kind of cheap whiskey is this?"

"Don't matter what it costs. If it's whiskey, it gets the job done," Alex replied, popping off two more shots that missed. The zombie could be heard groaning, as if fearful of the shots. "Man, I missed."

Red returned his butt to the tailgate where Alex was aiming for one last shot. He squeezed off another while Red watched.

In the distance, the zombie twisted and fell to the ground.

"All right! I win! One to zero!"

The two chuckled and shared a high five. But the slap shifted Alex's torso momentarily, sending pain rocketing through his body.

He yelled, "Ow!"

"Oh, damn. Sorry."

"Just get the damn thing out, all right?" Alex groaned.

Red went to work. Alex winced and looked again towards the creature in the field in an effort to take his mind off the primitive surgery. The zombie apparently wasn't neutralized, as it was trying to stand once more.

"So what would you rather have, an M-16 or an AK-47?" Red asked, digging in.

"M-16 all the way," Alex replied, wincing.

"Even though the AK doesn't jam, even in the desert?"

"Maybe, but the accuracy is crappola. Ow!"

In the distance, Alex watched the creature making an effort to stand, but it fell several times before finally making it to its feet.

"*Ow*," Alex groaned again as Red twisted the pliers in his leg, reaching for the bullet that wasn't too deep.

The creature walked with a stumbling gait. It groaned with a sorrowful misery. As Red found the bullet in Alex's leg and began to pull it out, Alex couldn't help but compare himself to the creature.

"I got it," Red said triumphantly, dunking the round in the whiskey along with the pliers. He began to wrap the wound.

The creature in the distance groaned again. Alex couldn't help but know exactly how it felt.

"Hey, Red," said Alex.

"What?"

"Promise me you won't let me turn into one of them." He indicated the stumbling monster in the distance.

Red looked out at the zombie. It shambled along in torment and distress. Red then reached for the M-16, shouldered it, and squeezed off a shot. A large portion of the creature's skull disintegrated, and the beast fell.

"You'd do the same for me," Red said. He gazed down at the weapon in his hands. "Shit, you're right about the M-16." They both let out a hearty laugh. "Now, c'mon. Let's get out of here."

"Where we going?"

"Beeville, I guess. It's the next big town along the way."

Just another day in Beeville, Texas

There was an old expression that went something to the effect of: *Wise people talk about ideas, Intelligent people talk about events, Slow people talk about people.*

Small towns in Texas had something of a reputation for having people who chose to stay in town after graduating from High School. Usually, their choices were either eat, drink, or fuck. Or any combination of the three. Holding down a job at a local fast food joint or perhaps even a better job working for the school or the city was ancillary. Mostly, the ones that stayed behind just drank and gossiped. Holding a position in the city or at a school was the prime place for tittle-tattle.

For the most part, the men just hung out and drank together. Just another day in Beeville.

Today, trends remained the same, with a bit of a job to do. Today, Benny Reyes, Frank Garza, Gary Chapman, and Wayne Crocker were patrolling the neighborhood several blocks from McCann Street. Frank's wife, Dolores, was hanging out with Lupe, Benny's wife. And, in typical small town fashion, the men were enjoying a few beverages while out. *Milwaukee's Best Light*, to be precise. When trouble began to peak around town, it was the priority of many to secure as many twelve packs as they could from local stores. Benny was no exception.

The day was particularly brisk. A cool breeze eased the intensity of the spring sun.

"And then Jesse fell down," said Benny, laughing. Frank and Wayne joined in with a hearty laugh as Benny finished the joke. So far, they had seen no zombies.

"Man, Jesse is so dumb," Wayne commented.

"Well, but Jesse's cool, though," Frank said. "I saw him once help a *viejita* buy her groceries. She was short, like, twenty dollars. And he gave her the money to buy it."

Gary took a long swig from his can of the *Beast Light*, then said, "He's a jackass, Frank."

"He might be a jackass. But he's a cool jackass," Benny said.

"Once I..."

But before Wayne could finish, Gary stopped in his tracks and muttered, "*Motherfuckers*," as he gazed at a tree down the street.

Wayne and the others stopped as well and followed Gary's gaze. Frank knew exactly what they were staring at. The body of a young black child was dangling by his neck from a rope. It was the same child Frank saw the day before.

The four men stood silent for a moment. Then Gary ended the moment and walked closer to the dangling body. The men followed.

Gary looked up at the corpse.

"It's *LeRoi*."

"LeRoi?" Wayne asked.

"LeRoi Henderson. His parents turned and were put down during the first wave here in town. I heard he's been in hidin' around town. Various houses. People taking him in." Anger began to build in Gary's body. "I know for a fact LeRoi was not infected. He was with me just two days ago."

"Anything could have happened since then," Benny said.

"I tell you he wasn't infected," stated Gary, firmly.

Something else drew their attention. Someone was screaming at the house across the street.

"What the heck is that?" Wayne asked.

"Probably one of those ghouls," Frank told him.

They almost drew their weapons and advanced, thinking it might be a creature. But the cause of the screaming was soon revealed to be an adolescent boy walking out of the house across the street, pulling up his zipper. His white, freckled face was complemented by a dirty mullet and a faded *Lynyrd Skynyrd* concert shirt.

A younger girl, perhaps thirteen, followed close behind, barefoot, yelling angry obscenities at the boy that would make a sailor blush. She was wielding a knife. Her face and arms were bruised and scratched. Her nose was bloody, and a small portion of her brown hair seemed to be torn out. Two little boys, perhaps her little brothers, were close behind her. They were crying, too.

"*You fucking asshole! Goddamn you, you motherfuckin' sonovabitch!*"

"Aw, you liked it, you fuckin' whore!" he screamed back.

"I'll kill you," she said, impotently brandishing the knife as she stood just outside the door.

The boy turned around and pulled a gun. The men flinched. "Do it. Come do it, bitch."

The girl, only moments from having been violated and defeated, fell to her knees and wept. Her little brothers stood by her and joined their sister in bawling.

The boy approached the men, walking toward the house where LeRoi was hanging. All four men stared at the defiant youth. Gary caught his eye.

"What the fuck are ya'll looking at?" the boy growled, his hand still on his gun.

"What did you just do?" Benny asked, though he already knew the answer.

"None of your fuckin' business, wetback."

Benny fumed. Frank suddenly became frightened, knowing the moment was escalating quick.

"What are you looking at, nigger?" the boy growled, meeting Gary's gaze with an equal amount of anger.

"You better watch that *nigger* shit, cracker. I don't have any problem putting you down, child."

"Who you calling *child*, bitch?" the boy said in total defiance and disregard, continuing to walk backward to his house. He watched Gary flinch, making a move to raise his weapon, but holding back. "C'mon, do it! Do it!" the boy challenged, still walking back as if the whole conversation was a waste of his time. In his mind, he was just calling Gary's bluff.

The boy turned around and walked straight toward his house.

"Gary, walk away," Frank said.

But Gary was already in a trance. He was staring at the boy, recalling a moment years ago in Vietnam.

* * * * *

He had been walking down a stretch of sweltering road with his unit, marching to their command post in a nearby town. They had been slogging for over two hours and Gary had run out of water early.

As they had entered the town, Gary saw a well. He took a moment, telling his commanding officer that he was going to get some water. The officer had no problem, and two others joined him.

The command hut was in Gary's line of sight as he filled his canteen and shot the breeze with his battle buddies. As he was taking a swig, a young adolescent boy appeared wearing black. A paddy hat dangled down around his back and shoulders. His brown sandals floated above the muddy ground. Somehow, Gary connected with the boy as he looked into his eyes. Immediately, Gary felt a sadness emanating from the boy. As the boy came closer, he stared at Gary. And it was then Gary knew there was a problem.

As the boy passed the well, it was obvious he was heading toward the command hut. Gary observed the boy and noticed a small wire coming out from under his black shirt into his hands. Gary dropped his canteen, instinctively lifted the butt of his machine gun to his shoulder, and let a bullet fly. The bullet hit the kid in the shoulder, flying out the front and clipping one of his teammates in the leg.

The shot scared his unit, but not as much as the kid, who then set off the suicide bomb strapped around his waist. The bullet made him scream, but the scream was cut off by a massive explosion that knocked down Gary and his comrades.

The command hut was safe and a majority of his comrades were uninjured. Only two soldiers were hurt.

When Gary picked himself up off the ground, he looked at where the boy was standing. What was left of his legs had been flung in two different directions. His upper body was tossed in the opposite direction. Massive amounts of blood and tissue were scattered around the blast site and dripping from the body parts.

As the villagers and soldiers scrambled to secure the area, Gary slowly walked to the severed torso on the ground. The kid's face was frozen in fear. Blood was dripping from his mouth, nose, and ears. His ribcage was totally exposed and there was no way to identify the organs and flesh under the chest that oozed around on the ground.

It was bad enough that he was killing his fellow human beings. It was worse that he had to kill a kid. He had to make a hard choice, and there was no real winning pick.

*　*　*　*　*

But today, the choice was much easier to make. His old programming kicked in. As the kid was reaching his front porch, Gary shouldered his weapon, put the kid in his sights, and squeezed off a shot.

The kid screamed as he fell forward, the bullet penetrating his shoulder and bringing him to the ground.

"Oh, shit!" Wayne yelled. Fear and guilt filled Frank's soul. Wayne gasped in surprise, as well as Benny. They watched the kid quiver in pain.

Gary lowered his weapon. "Go cut LeRoi down," he commanded Wayne.

Snapping back to reality and choosing to side with his friend, Wayne did as he was told and approached the rope. "C'mon, Benny," he said, bringing Benny into the conspiracy. Benny stood for a moment, then chose to follow Wayne.

Frank knew he would be asked in next. Shaking, Frank uttered, "*I can't do this. I can't do this*," and turned to walk back to Benny's house.

"You'd better not say shit, Frank!" Gary barked, walking to the quivering and crying boy.

"I'm not!" Frank yelled back. He dashed back to the house.

The girls and her little brothers were crying even more, the brutal images before their eyes adding to the dreadfulness of their day, scarring their young minds forever.

But it wasn't over.

Wayne and Benny cut down LeRoi. They both noticed a hole in the young boy's head.

Gary stood over the wounded mullet boy, who was whimpering and cussing at Gary, holding his shoulder in agony.

"You fuckin' nigger! My family is gonna lynch your ass, you coon-ass sonov—"

Before the boy could finish, Gary buried the butt of his rifle into the boy's face, breaking his nose. The boy screamed as Gary continued to stand quietly over him.

"Fuck you, nigger!"

Gary punched the boy in the face, directly on his broken nose. The boy screamed in pain and terror. Gary's fist was stained red as blood dripped from the boy's nose all over his mouth and chin.

"Hit me again!" he yelled, stubbornly holding on to the remnants of his pride.

Gary obliged. His hands were thick and heavy.

"Again!" the boy yelled, defiant.

Gary obliged.

Wayne and Benny stood in shock, watching the beating. They had released LeRoi from the noose.

"*Fuck you*," mumbled the boy, losing interest in continuing the beating.

Gary gave him two more for good measure, cracking the boy's cheek bone. He then kicked him in the wounded shoulder.

Gary pulled out some spare fishing line from his coat pocket. He rolled the boy over and put his hands behind his back, tying him with the fishing line at the wrists. The boy screamed in pain, as the angle his arm was taking was particularly painful to his shoulder.

Gary stood the boy up and walked him to Wayne and Benny. The kid tried to kick Gary. Gary reeled back and punched the kid in the wounded shoulder again. He picked up the boy and walked him to the noose. He put wrapped it around the boy's neck.

Benny now knew what was going to happen, and that he was about to be a real part of it, and got cold feet. "I can't do this, guys."

"Just don't say shit, man, you hear?"

"Yes, sir," he replied respectfully before running back to his house.

Gary turned to the boy, who was trying to break free. Gary stopped all that with another punch to the face. The boy fell on his ass, the fall shooting another surge of pain from his shoulder to his mind, making him scream.

Gary lowered himself down to the boy and stared at him straight in the eyes. He whispered, "Don't you worry about being alone in hell, because when your dumbass white trash piece of shit family comes for me, I'm sending them to see you." He then spit in the boy's face.

The boy screamed, "*Nooooo!*"

Gary approached Wayne and said, "Let's pull him up just a little bit. There's one more thing we're doing."

Wayne finally figured out what they were going to do. He had thought they were going to need a horse or a car or something to yank the boy up, but realized they were going to pull him up themselves.

The two pulled the boy off the ground. He gagged before Gary lowered the rope just enough to put the child on his toes.

"Hold on to this," Gary said to Wayne, who had to lean back a bit to maintain leverage and keep the boy elevated off the ground.

Gary walked to the boy's house. The door was locked, so Gary kicked it in.

Wayne stood alone, looking at the boy. The kid was struggling to catch his breath, literally dancing on his tiptoes. The boy tried to fall down, but Wayne leaned back even more, countering the fall of weight. It choked the boy even more, and he got back on his feet, then his toes.

The boy swung around and faced Wayne. In a last ditch effort, he pleaded for his life. "*Please don't kill me,*" he gasped. "*Please.*"

Wayne gulped in guilt, but knew the kid was a rapist and a murderer. It was hard for him to continue the torture, but he did not want to let his friend down. He was always taught that it was wrong to kill another person. But he continued in the interest of justice that—at this point—would probably never be served by the laws of the old world.

Gary reemerged from the house with a piece of paper. He duct-taped the paper around the chest and waist of the adolescent, securing it on his body.

Gary joined Wayne at the end of the rope. Looking at the boy, Gary said, "Burn in hell, motherfucker," before yanking the rope, bringing the boy off the ground several feet. He coordinated with Wayne and yelled, "Pull!" as they hoisted the boy into the air in the exact location LeRoi was hanging. The boy writhed in pain, desperately searching for a way to breathe.

Then the wiggling stopped. For a few moments the body swung to and fro, still.

"Let's get out of here," Wayne uttered.

"One more thing," Gary said.

They stood for a few moments.

Then suddenly the boy started to wiggle again. Slobber dangled from his lips and fell to the ground below.

He was a zombie.

Gary pulled out a small caliber pistol and let a shot go, piercing the kid's skull.

"Now we can go," Gary said, turning around and heading back to Benny's house.

The beaten body swung forward, revealing to the world what was written on the chest:

RAPIST

* * * * *

Monsignor O'Leary sat alone in the office of the rectory. He took yet another long swig of Mr. Walker. He had been drinking for the entire day, confused at the situation his Lord had placed the world in.

Taking the bottle in his hand, he poured another glass over the melting ice. Some of it got away, spilling onto the desk.

"*Aw...*" He almost voiced an expletive, but refrained. Taking a napkin, he sopped up the liquor, then wrung it out into his glass. He then took the worn paper napkin into his mouth and sucked out the remaining malt.

He gazed up at a crucifix prominently displayed on the wall in front of the desk. The paper in his mouth was forming a ball in the palate of his mouth and his tongue caressed it with alcoholic glee. But his mind was angry. He wondered why God would unleash this plague on humanity.

Standing up, he tripped over his own feet, knocking papers and books off the desk. He fell to the floor. As he hit, he gagged on the towel in his mouth. He promptly spit it out. It smacked against the floor. Slobber splattered around the soaked white napkin.

Picking himself up, he began to collect the items that had fallen off the desk. The room was spinning. He gathered the papers and put them back in a manila folder with all the organization of an inept secretary. He reached for two Confirmation study guides and placed them back on the table. Then he reached for a Douay Bible that had fallen to the floor.

As his hand came closer, a sharp sensation jolted his hand away for a moment. He thought he had been bit by something. He grasped his hand. Inspecting it, he noticed nothing unusual. He looked down at the book, expecting to see a bug or other insect.

Instead, he saw the book open to *Saint John's Revelation.* Something drew his eyes to chapter nine. Picking up the book, he read closer:

Chapter 9

The Fifth Trumpet: [1]Then the fifth angel blew his trumpet, and I saw a star that had fallen from the sky to the earth. It was given the key for the passage to the abyss. [2]It opened the passage to the abyss, and smoke came up out of the passage like smoke from a huge furnace. The sun and air were darkened by the smoke from the passage. [3]Locusts came out of the smoke onto the land, and they were given the same powers as scorpions of the earth. [4]They were told not to harm the grass of the earth or any plant or tree, but only those people who did not have the seal of God on their foreheads. [5]They were not allowed to kill them but only to torment them for five months; the torment they inflicted was like that of a scorpion when it stings a person. [6]During that time these people will seek death but will not find it, and they will long to die but death will escape them.

"People will seek death but will not find it," whispered O'Leary. "And they will long to die but death will escape them."

He looked up at the crucifix again. The eyes seemed to be staring back, condemning him.

O'Leary put his face in his hands and cried.

* * * * *

Red LaRue and Alex Rich arrived in Beeville later that afternoon. The roads had been relatively clear and they didn't have any run-ins with Homeland Security or the U.N., though they did see several Homeland Security posts abandoned.

Up ahead, the blockade to Beeville was coming into view.

"Check it out," said Red, pulling up near the barricade.

"What is it? Homeland Security?"

"Looks like cops."

"No way..."

Both Red and Alex had seen for themselves how police had rapidly and effectively transformed into tools for Homeland Security. As the national state of emergency effectively made the rule of *posse comitatus* null and void, local police were working openly with the military.

As they pulled closer to the orange and white barricade, a voice sounded from a loudspeaker.

"*Attention people in the vehicle. Stay away from the barricade. No one will be allowed in.*"

"Oh, yeah," said Alex, pointing to the large sign in front of the barricade that read, '*NO FEMA CENTERS HERE.*'

"Well, *shit*," Red mumbled. He then yelled a reply out the window. "No one's infected! We can help you!"

"*No one is allowed in. You need to find another place to stay,*" came the reply.

"What do we do?" asked Alex.

"Well, I guess we drive, huh?"

Putting the truck in gear, Red started to drive.

"We should really find a way in there," Alex said.

"What? Why?"

"Well, if they've secured the city, then this would be the perfect place to hole up."

Red considered the possibility. "What about the U.N.?"

"What do you mean?"

"Well, if they come down the road and find Beeville, they'll wipe it out."

"Red, they're not going to waste their time with a secured city. They're on a time-table, you know. They have goals."

"What if the cops decide to let them in anyway?"

"I think once they see the city is secured, they're not going to fuck with it. Soldiers aren't as expendable as they used to be, you know, with how things are."

"That's true," Red said, conceding.

They were close to a mile away from the checkpoint when Alex had an idea.

"Slow down, man," he said.

"What?" asked Red nervously.

"I've got an idea."

"What?"

"Did you see that gate back there?"

"Yeah."

"Pull into it."

Red had an idea where Alex was going. "Okay."

He pulled the vehicle into a U-turn on the road, far from the blockade. He drove back up and turned into the dirt driveway. The metal gate was closed and locked. A 'No Trespassing' sign hung on the front of the gate.

"Now what?" asked Red before Alex stepped out with a pistol. Limping to the gate, Alex shot the lock, knocking it off. He flinched and looked around. They both looked back up and down the road. Alex then pushed the gate open and signaled for Red to enter.

Red pulled the vehicle through the gate and stopped. Alex closed the gate and threw what was left of the lock and chain around it. He limped back to the truck. Dust floated around on the ground, finding a home on Alex's boots, the truck tires, and undercarriage.

"So?" Red asked.

Alex shut the truck door. "Look, let's drive down this road. Maybe we'll find a trail that will take us to the road they were blocking."

"What about the people in town? They won't recognize us as members of the community."

"Beeville is not that small, man. We can just say we're from the other side of town."

Red was a little scared, but knew the potential and protection of the town could be a good place to spend time while the plague wound down.

"Let's do it," said Red, putting the truck in gear.

The big blue Ford F-150 glided across the dirt road. A large line of grass stood up in the middle of the road where tires rarely treaded. The field was filled with brush and mostly barren apart from the south Texas bushes. Though it was spring, the brush, trees, and weeds were a dusty brown. A long puff of dust created a veritable smokescreen behind the truck. The gentle breeze pushed the dust cloud in a diagonal direction behind the truck, like a long tail drifting in the wind. Thorny bushes scratched the side of the vehicle and the occasional deep hole made Red and Alex bounce in their seats.

The trail curved into a section that was a bit more dense with bushes, brush, and the occasional tree.

"What do you think?" Red asked.

"Just keep driving," Alex replied. They hit a large rock in the road that jostled Alex, causing his wounded leg to throb intensely in pain.

"You all right?" Red asked.

"I'm fine," Alex groaned.

They entered a clearing where a ranch house stood. Red stopped. The dust from behind the truck was still in motion and enveloped the truck momentarily, then blew away. Red drew back from the dust.

"What do you think?" Red asked again.

Before Alex could answer, a shot rang out, punching a hole in the back of the vehicle. Alex and Red jumped.

"Oh, shit!" Red exclaimed, stomping on the gas pedal and blazing his own trail through the brush. As the truck rocked back and forth leveling weeds, Alex held fast to the door and gritted his teeth in pain. Another shot rang out, putting a hole through the tailgate, then lodging itself in the rear of the cab, confirming to Alex that Red's choice was necessary.

Leveling another bush, Red found a clearing and another trail for vehicles. Instinctively, he turned right onto the trail. After crushing two more bushes, he leveled the vehicle on the grassy road.

Alex relaxed, but glowered in pain.

"Are you sure you're okay?" Red asked.

"I'm *fine*. Just get us out of here."

Red drove for several minutes across the land. The ranch was large and spacious, a picture of south Texas beauty. Large and spiny round cactus shared the land with ancient Mesquite trees. In the distance, an old decrepit barn stood silent near rusty old farm equipment and machines.

"Pull over for a minute," Alex told him.

Red slowed down and pulled over. He asked, "What's wrong?"

"I just need to readjust my leg," Alex said, shifting painfully in his seat.

A door on the old barn slowly crept open as the vehicle came to a stop. The tail of dust began to envelop the barn. Red's eye caught the movement in the rearview mirror.

"Hold on," Red said, pulling out his gun and turning back to look at the barn door through the broken rear window. Alex turned to look as well. The dust glided into the cab and clouded their vision for a moment. A dark, ragged figure emerged from the barn, clouded by the dust.

Red pointed his weapon. Alex signaled quickly for him to wait.

The dust tail drifted away and the dark, ragged figure stood still. For a moment, no one moved.

Then the figure spoke. "*Senor?*"

"*Hola, senor,*" said Red in broken Spanish.

Another figure came around the barn door, followed by a small child about four years old.

"Wetbacks," said Red. "They must work for the ranch owner."

"Don't call them *wetbacks*," said Alex.

"Why not? They probably are."

"Just don't do it. It's rude."

"*Donde esta senor* Bannon?" said the first man.

"*No se, pero—*"

Before Red could finish, the man interrupted, "*Mi hermano esta enfermo. Uno de los monstruos lo mordio.*"

"*Hijole,*" said Red.

"What did he say?" Alex asked.

"His brother was bit." He turned back toward the immigrants. "*El va a morir. La mordida de los monstrous es peligroso. Mata lo,*" suggested Red, informing them that his brother was infected and he needed to kill him.

"*Chingate, buey! No voy a matar mi hermano!*" the man angrily replied, obviously refusing the advice.

"*Esta bien*," said Red, shrugging, "*Sabes como podemos llegar a* Beeville?"

"*Si. Aya atras de esse porton vas a encontrar la calle que te llevara directamente a* Beeville."

Another figure appeared behind the man, then stepped in front of him. He said, "*Puedo ir con ustedes?*"

"This one wants to go with us," said Red to Alex.

Alex shrugged.

"*Si. Esta bien*," said Red, "*Pero no tenemos espacio en el frente. Te puedes ir atras*," indicating the space available in the truck bed.

"*Gracias*," the man replied and, after running into the barn for a brief moment, reemerged with a large backpack.

Red gave one last warning to the first man: "*Amigo, se que tu quires a tu hermano. Pero ya esta muerto. Cuando el muera, su cuerpo va rececitar, y ustedes van estar en peligro.*"

"*Si el muere, se muere. Pero no lo voy a matar quando todavia tiene su alma.*"

The comment stunned Red. He had never considered what happens to the soul of a person. Before he could contemplate the spiritual quandary, Alex spoke.

"What did he say?"

"Something pretty deep. Let's talk about it later."

The man who had retrieved his backpack from the barn threw his gear in the back of the vehicle and climbed in. He then noticed the glass scattered on the truck bed.

"*Que paso?*"

"*Soldados*," said Red.

The man stood for a moment, possibly reconsidering his choice, before sliding glass away from a spot to sit.

"*Como te llamas?*" asked Red.

"Miguel," he said, offering his hand. Red accepted the callused, dry hands of the ranch helper. Alex waved, and Miguel waved back.

Miguel sat back against the truck bed and was poked by a protrusion from the side of the truck. As the truck drove off, Miguel noticed it was a bullet hole. He was no stranger to such things, as rival cartels had been carving pieces out of his mother's hometown of Nuevo Laredo for the past decade. They had only become more and more flagrant in their aggressions, openly walking into hospitals and newspaper presses and murdering rivals in broad daylight. They went so far as to have the chief of police executed just hours after being assigned the duty. Nuevo Laredo was rough. But now, Miguel became nervous once again as the trio drove to the back entrance and found the road to Beeville.

Miguel looked at the metal container rolling around in the back.

"Que es eso?"

"No sabemos."

Bowie V. Ibarra

A
SECURITY BREACH
on McCann Street

Y ou see?! That was the only play Kevin Greene was even
remotely a factor on!"

"You're right, though," agreed Gary, crumpling up
another Milwaukee's Best Light, trying to get his mind off of the
lynching.

After hanging the kid, Wayne suggested they take their minds
off the moment and watch some of his Cowboy tapes he had recorded
off the television over the past few years. Today, Wayne had picked
the Cowboys/Los Angeles Rams game from 1993, the Cowboys' first
Super Bowl season since the seventies.

"Novacek was wide open in the flats," groaned Wayne.

Wayne's house was unkept. The wooden screen door hung
crooked from its hinges. Old beer cans littered the floor. Posters—
not framed pictures—lined the living room wall. Emmitt Smith and
Troy Aikman in action poses greeted anyone who entered. Stacks of
marked and unmarked videotapes lined the floors around the small
entertainment center. Wayne did not make much of an effort to hide
the porno. Large video boxes and DVD cases were lying on the coffee
tables.

The phone rang and Wayne paused the video to answer it. It was
an old rotary phone shaped like a yellow oval. "Hello?" He paused to
listen. "Hey, Benny. What's up?" A pause. "Cool."

"Who is it?"

Wayne signaled for Gary to wait as he talked into the phone.

"Benny, thanks, but we'll pass." He paused again. "Cool. We'll talk later. All right. Bye."

"Who was it?" Gary asked, standing up with his rifle.

"Benny. Asked if we wanted to go to church. Said no."

"Cool," Gary said, stretching. "I think I'm going to head home."

"No, wait. The game's almost over."

"Okay then. I'll hang out," said Gary kindly. He knew Wayne was super lonely and with things outside being a little crazy, he decided to stay and watch the rest of the game.

"Who is *that*?" Gary asked, frozen halfway sitting and halfway standing.

A large blue truck passed on the road in front of Wayne's house, cutting through the haze of a colorful twilight.

Wayne looked out. "I don't recognize it."

"How'd they get through the blockade?" Gary asked, already assuming they were outsiders.

"Who knows?"

The truck made a left and drove away.

"Looks like they're headed to McCann Street. Give Audrey a heads-up. They might be looters."

"Cool," said Wayne as he picked up the phone. He then picked up the contact list organized in the early days of the plague, found her number, and dialed.

* * * * *

Up the road on McCann Street, the old phone rattled as the bell within the device rang out loud in the Garner house. Audrey and Eric could hear it from outside on the porch through the screen door. Eric got up and went inside to answer it.

"Hello," he grunted, taking a quick drag off his cigarette. "Uh-huh... All right. Bye." He hung up the phone and went outside.

With his perpetual scowl he said, "There's some looters coming. Blue pickup. We should stop them."

"*Fuckin' douchebags*," Audrey mumbled, upset that she could not complete her fingernail painting. She quickly placed cotton balls between her fingers and stood up. Her red lips gripped the dual-colored cigarette butt as she took a long drag while carefully pulling the bolt on the M-16. She started making her way to the middle of the street. Eric followed close behind with his Spas-12.

The blue truck turned the corner, and as Audrey stepped into the street it gunned the engine, trying to make a break for it.

She whispered, *"You ain't gettin' away."*

Audrey and Eric opened fire, unloading a spray of bullets into the vehicle. The front windshield cracked and the front tires blew out. The truck shimmied then started into a barrel roll, tossing three people from the flying vehicle like circus acrobats, along with several cardboard boxes full of stolen electronics. Audrey and Eric moved out of the way as the vehicle came to rest upside down on the curb opposite their house. Then silence.

The phone in the house began to ring again as Audrey and Eric puffed on their cigarettes.

"You okay, babe?" Eric asked.

"Yeah," she replied, rattled, but coherent. She studied her hands. "Nail polish is perfect."

Margie Montemayor exited her house with her pistol. Her daughter Gina followed close behind. Margie called to Audrey, "Hey! What happened?!"

"Looters!" Audrey shouted back. She started making her way to the three bodies.

Lucy St. Claire came out with her rifle as the phone at Audrey's continued to ring. "Everything all right?!"

"Yeah! We're fine!" Audrey yelled. She then began putting holes in the heads of the three bodies that lay in tangled messes on the asphalt.

The phone stopped ringing as Margie and Lucy ran to Audrey and Eric. Billy Joe had answered it.

He said, "Hello?"

Mary Moore exited her house with her son Timmy behind her. She saw Lucy and Margie running to the wreck. She hollered out, "What's going on?!"

Audrey gritted her teeth, sighed heavily, and shouted, "For the *umpteenth* time, everything's going to be fine! It was just some looters!"

Mary stood on the porch to watch.

Billy Joe ran out of his house onto the front porch. He yelled, "Mom!"

Audrey responded, "Give me a minute, Billy Joe!"

Billy groaned at being dismissed in front of the whole neighborhood. He crossed his arms and tapped his foot impatiently.

Margie asked, "Is that truck going to blow up?"

"No," Lucy responded. "That's just in the movies."

"Mom!" yelled Billy Joe again. This time, he was ignored completely. He raised his voice even louder: "There's a supposed to be a second truck! More looters! Will you *listen* to me?!"

He groaned again, then saw the second blue truck turn the corner—the same one he was just warned about over the phone. A shot of fear hit Billy as he pointed and yelled with more urgency. "Mom! Look!"

The second truck took the group by surprise. Audrey fumbled for a new clip. The cotton balls fell from between her fingers and her nail polish streaked across her skin. Eric frantically worked to reload his weapon. Lucy and Margie turned and pointed their weapons at the vehicle.

Inside the vehicle, Red LaRue and Alex Rich both flinched, in unison, as they looked at the wall of people pointing guns at them.

—And behind the people with guns was a totalled blue pickup truck and three dead bodies.

"You should slow down, man," said Alex. "I'd rather not test the neighborhood watch."

"Uh, *yeah*," Red replied. "Good idea."

Miguel looked toward the front. He was scared again, second guessing himself on why he joined the two wanderers.

"Man, that chick's hot," Red said. "Wow..."

"Which one?" asked Alex as the vehicle came to a stop.

"The one in the *Daisy Dukes* and denim top," Red replied, putting the vehicle in park. "There's just something about a woman holding a firearm that's hot."

"Yeah. Except when it's pointed at you," Alex stated, rolling his eyes.

Margie was a bit nervous. She turned to Lucy and asked, "They stopped. What do we do?"

Lucy yelled, "Who are ya'll and what are you doing here?!"

Audrey and Eric reloaded their weapons and moved to either side of the vehicle.

"*No dispares! No dispares!*" begged Miguel with his hands up, crouching submissively in the back of the truck.

"*Calmate*, Miguel," Red told him. "*No te van a matar*, Miguel."

"Who are you and what are you doing here?!" yelled Lucy again.

"Are they gonna shoot them, mommy?" asked Timmy.

"No, baby. Everything's going to be fine. Go inside now." Mary had no idea what they were going to do, yet judging by what happened to the first truck, she knew her neighbors weren't above settling things the easy way.

Red answered, "We don't mean you any harm! We're just looking for a place to stay!"

"Where are ya'll from?" asked Margie, her voice more calm than Lucy's.

"San Antonio," said Red. Alex nudged him, as they were abandoning their original plan of feigning to be town residents.

"How'd you get past the police barricade?"

Lucy came around to Red's side. Nervously, Red waved and smiled. She grinned and gave a coy wink. Red nodded his head in approval.

Alex chose to be more direct. He told them, "We took a side road. Listen, we're not here to loot or cause trouble. We just need a place to stay." He then used a different tactic. "And we, uh... We came to warn you. We have a sneaking suspicion those monsters aren't the only thing to be worried about."

"The U.N.?" asked Audrey.

"Precisely," said Red.

"We have something in the back, too," Alex stated. "Something we found that maybe someone here in town can identify."

"What? The wetback?" Margie asked. Red and Lucy snickered. Alex and Miguel grimaced.

"*No*. We found a canister of something. We think its some type of weapon. It didn't go off, so we kept it."

Lucy and Margie looked in the back.

"It's there, alright," said Margie to Audrey, suddenly anxious to distance herself a bit more from the truck.

"Well, the guy you need to talk to is Mayor Hickland," Audrey said. "He's usually at City Hall just up this road."

"He usually goes home at night, though," Eric said.

It was getting late. An orange haze was burning the blue that was the day, charring the sky into night.

Alex made a suggestion. "Listen. I've been shot by those troops. I can use some first aid and all three of us can use a place to sleep. What can we do for ya'll to get this?"

Margie peeked in the side to look at Alex's leg.

"He's been shot," said Margie with suspicion.

"He's probably another looter," Eric whispered to his wife. Both simultaneously took a drag from their cigarettes and blew out the smoke opposite each other.

Lucy peeked in on Red's side, pretending to look at Alex's leg, but actually checking out Red's package beneath his pants. She paused a moment, then said, "The least we can do is show them proper courtesy. I'll take one of them in." She then held a glance and smile with Red a second longer than etiquette would normally allow. She added, "This guy can stay at my place, if he wants."

"Hot damn," Red whispered, grinning. He slapped at Alex's leg. The wounded leg—right on the injury.

Alex moaned. Red said, *"Oops,"* and got a knuckle sandwich in the arm. He mumbled, *"Ow... Asshole."*

"I've got lots of medical supplies. I could help you out, sir," offered Margie. "Pull into my driveway. It's over there." She pointed.

"Thank you," said Alex.

"Say, is that truck going to blow up?" Red asked, pointing at the flipped vehicle.

A collective *"No"* came from the group of Beeville survivalists, with one dissenting voice saying, *"Well... maybe."*

Mary reentered her house, taking little Timmy with her.

The truck pulled into Margie's driveway. Margie and Audrey helped Alex from the vehicle, up the porch steps, and into the house. Red was led to the house of Lucy St. Claire just across the street. Margie grinned and shook her head, watching the two new friends walk to the house as the night swallowed what was left of the day.

On the porch several houses away, a young Billy Joe Garner watched the object of his lustful desires lead another man into her den of pleasure. He glared at the couple as his father walked up to the steps.

"Billy Joe, come inside."

So as not to arouse suspicion, Billy Joe obeyed his father as all good children do. But inside, he began to seethe with jealously.

Breaking Up
is hard to do

The dark night enveloped Beeville in a celestial death shroud filled with twinkling beacons of hope. The moon waxed near completion. The city, though secured in most places, was still dangerous. The infection was insidious. Though efforts were made to make sure all remaining citizens were healthy, many still flew under the radar hiding in their houses, bringing their sickness to fruition in secret.

Night, for one reason or another, seemed to be the prime time for sick humans to die and reanimate. It was also time for many creatures in hiding to make their move. Somehow the creatures seemed to comprehend the danger of walking around in the daytime and would hide themselves in shadows, dark corners, or behind large objects. Though many still wandered openly during the day, they eventually paid the price. If one were able to observe them for an extended period of time, one would assume a bit of a learning curve taking place. The beasts were picking up on the danger. Somehow, as the moon grew larger, the creatures seemed smarter.

Wiser.

Motivated.

Mayor Lance Hickland only noticed three unchecked creatures on his drive back to his house with Miss Zapata. He didn't bother to destroy them, contrary to his edict set down on the city to do as

139

such. His mind was occupied with how in the world he was going to make up with his wife, though he had already accepted the fact that things would never be the same again between them. Ever.

Yet, he knew he had to make an effort. Or in the very least, he had to begin to put new pieces into place to secure the future for their unborn child—his future and his legacy.

Stephanie Zapata sat silent in the passenger seat. A Glock was secure in her left hand. Without a manual safety, she would have to be cautious. Her arms were crossed. Though she was wanting the mayor again since the affair was brought to light, she was supportive of her lover and gave him plenty of space to work out his problems. Somehow, she remained seemingly oblivious to the nature of their affair.

They pulled up onto the driveway of the mayor's house on a hill in the affluent part of town. He kept the motor running and switched the headlights to low beam.

"Would you like me to come with you?" Stephanie asked.

Lance chuckled in disbelief. "No, but thanks."

Stephanie smiled deviously.

Lance took his shotgun in hand and exited the vehicle, leaving Stephanie to fend for herself. Walking deliberately toward the front door, he scanned the area for danger. He saw none; it appeared his citizens had done very well. The windows on the first floor of his three-story red bricked house were boarded up. While there seemed to be no danger, he thought he could hear groans in the distance. Pulling out his key, he took a deep breath and unlocked the door.

He entered the house.

A gun blast was heard and a piece of the wall next to Lance's head crumbled and flew off. He cringed and froze, expecting another blast to punch him in the face or forehead.

But nothing happened. Only a sinister voice demanded an answer.

"What are you doing here?!" growled Evelyn Hickland, holding the .45 pistol her husband had bought for her three years before. He had even taught her how to use it.

Lance opened his eyes and saw his wife. She was wearing a white shirt fit for pregnancy and pink pajama pants. She wore a belt that was filled with knives dangling below her pregnant belly.

Lance raised his hands. "Evelyn, please. Hear me out. Don't shoot me."

"You have one minute," came the quick response.

"Evelyn, be reasonable. Let's talk this out like adults."

"Fifty-nine seconds."

She was serious. Knowing his wife would not bend, he began his argument: "Evelyn, I admit I fucked up."

"You're goddamn right you fucked up."

"And I know there's not a whole lot I can say now to make it better. But I want you to know now that I love you. There is no one else I want to spend the rest of my life with."

Evelyn gave him his promised time, though she was burning to respond.

Lance went on, "The fact is we need each other now. We might have these issues to work out, but all we have is each other now. Your family's in San Antonio. Mine's in Austin."

"Ten seconds," she said, moving a little early on the time. His argument wasn't much. She cocked the hammer.

"Evelyn, you need someone to defend you," Lance desperately said.

"Do I?"

"Yeah."

"*Do I?!*" Her anger was at an all-time high. She placed her hand on her stomach as her baby kicked.

"*Yes, Evelyn. You need me,*" he stated firmly, stressing each individual word.

Evelyn turned her back and walked to the kitchen. Lance followed, calling to her and asking where she was going. She did not reply, but instead ripped away a few boards from the back door and opened it, much to his horror and surprise.

"*Evelyn, no!*"

She stepped outside. Bright backyard lights illuminated the lawn enough to see all around, but left scattered shadows near the fence line and the open field behind their house. Several shadows staggered in the distance. Several large shadows seemed camouflaged in the darkness cast by the fences.

Lance stood speechless in the doorway.

Evelyn stood in the middle of the backyard. Facing the shadows along the fence line, she slowly and methodically returned her .45 to its holster, then pulled a heavy knife from a sheathe below her belly. Turning her left hand up, she sliced a portion of the palm of her hand. It was deep enough for blood to immediately flow. She held her palm up and directed it toward the shadows. Blood began to form red rivulets down her arm, dripping onto the grass at odd intervals.

"Evelyn!" Lance called out.

In an instant, the silence was broken as three creatures revealed themselves from the shadows. All three groaned in a chorus of greedy desire. It was as if the sight—or perhaps the *smell*—of blood lured them from their apparent hiding places, exposing themselves.

The swiftest of the three walking cannibal corpses was a female, a large Hispanic woman with a tattered plain green shirt.

Flipping the knife in her right hand, Evelyn delivered a vicious overhand strike with the knife, catching the beast in the left eye socket. Black fluid flowed from the juicy busted eye as Evelyn removed the knife. Repositioning the weapon in her hand and keeping the now stumbling beast at bay with the other, she jabbed it again, attempting to scramble the brain or sever the spine.

It was working. The beast began to shake and convulse before Evelyn again attacked with an overhand strike, coming down hard and cracking the skull. The long knife blade remained lodged in the stabbed and mutilated head.

As the beast fell at Evelyn's feet, she pulled out her pistol and took aim at another beast, directly on her right side. This one, a zombiefied male store clerk, took a bullet to the genitals, causing it to stumble. Then Evelyn caught it with an aimed shot that entered just above its right eye, blasting enough brain to send it to the ground.

She turned with enough time to eyeball a shot that took out the right kneecap of the third and final zombie. It fell to the ground. Evelyn nonchalantly walked up to it and let fly the last two bullets from her .45.

Lance was flabbergasted.

"I don't *need* you, Lance," she said, slowly turning around to face him. She glared at her adulterous husband. She opened the chamber to her gun and reached into her pants pocket for more bullets. Bloody fingerprints blessed each bullet as she walked deliberately toward Lance.

"Evelyn?"

But she was not listening, just swiftly reloading her weapon. Her left arm was a red hand of death. Three bullets remained to be loaded.

Realizing the lost cause, Lance took several steps backwards, then turned completely and dashed through the kitchen.

Evelyn yelled, "Your minute's up, Lance!"

Lance sprinted through the house and threw open the front door. His heart pumped as he ran to the car. The front yard never seemed so big. He expected to be cut down at any second. Stephanie stared at him from the passenger seat with confusion and fear. She opened the driver's side door, doing for him the greatest favor of his life as Evelyn appeared inside the open front door.

Lance swiftly shifted to reverse and hit the gas, leaving burnt rubber in the driveway. Evelyn deliberately strode toward the vehicle and opened fire from her .45.

Stephanie screamed as the windshield cracked and splintered. The leather interior began popping as bullet holes suddenly appeared.

Lance shifted to drive and floored it, fleeing his once peaceful home.

Evelyn emptied her weapon into the trunk of her husband's car. Two clicks of a hammer caused her to stand still for a moment. She watched the taillights speed away.

For a moment, she stood still. Silent. Then a groan nearby brought her back to reality. Tears began to form in her eyes. She tried to wipe them away, only to smear the left side of her face with blood from her own slashed palm. Crying, she ran back through her front door, a red-masked woman bawling like a banshee in the middle of the desolate and dangerous night.

* * * * *

Night rarely makes anyone feel safer, regardless of what they are. Man or animal, the dark always seems to signify one of two things: danger, or romance.

Perhaps that is why the night has so much appeal to lovers. The night could be dangerous, so the company of the opposite sex could inspire a kind of confidence—of *safety*.

Margie Montemayor somehow felt safer, tending to the leg of Alex Rich in her kitchen. Alex was a nice man, in good health and in good shape—and judging by their conversation over the last hour, a man of strong convictions and true Christian faith. He was also good-looking in her opinion. Gina sat in the living room, reading *The Three Musketeers* by Alexandre Dumas, silently observing her mother.

Margie had only felt the comfort of a man sporadically since her divorce three years ago. No one had even come close to being someone she would spend the rest of her life with. Even fewer were enticed to even spend the night. Not that she did not try, but her values and looks prevented intimacy at any regular intervals. She was not ugly, but after the divorce, she had let herself go.

As she tended to the wound, she wanted to talk even more to Alex. But Alex was absorbed with the current CNC coverage.

The Global Plague Update banner spun onto the screen again as the quarter hour worked its way to the top of the hour. Margie and Alex stared intently at the message. A lovely but slightly disheveled blonde whose name neither of them caught began her report as a ticker flashed news headlines at the bottom of the screen.

"The global plague is showing signs of stopping, say officials from the Center for Disease Control."

A caption with the CDC logo stood to the right of the news woman's head.

"The infection rate is reported to have peaked, with over eighty percent of the world's population estimated to be afflicted. But opponents say otherwise, believing the disease will eventually envelop the world. Sarah Novetti has more."

The screen displayed footage of scientists working in a lab.

"The Center for Disease Control has estimated that the rate of infection has peaked, and that infections are on the decline. But that doesn't mean the people who have protected themselves from the plague are safe from danger."

A still photo of Dr. Leonard Slawowitz appeared on the screen. His comments seemed pre-recorded.

"People in large cities are in the gravest danger with the high population rates per square feet. It would be surprising if anyone made it out of there alive. However, in rural communities, especially in the south, reports have confirmed that FEMA and Homeland

Security have secured the citizens of many small towns."

A video of the early days of infection flashed prerecorded images of the terror, accompanied by a voiceover: *"The Association of Southern Law Enforcement says otherwise."*

A picture of Sgt. Ralph Wilson appeared on the screen. The news ticker continued to flash blurbs and updates.

"The claims of the infections peaking are unfounded and ridiculous. There's absolutely no way they can know any of that. No real numbers have been counted or confirmed around the world. The fact is, it's just getting worse, and I'm not just pulling facts out of my..." The final word was bleeped.

More footage of the chaos was played as another point was made.

"But FEMA could not confirm either claim. We cannot say that the infection is growing or lessening among the world population. Only that within America, our centers have been taking in less and less people."

Another scene of zombie chaos appeared on the screen under a final voiceover.

"With the numbers of dead unconfirmed, the numbers could reach the millions in America alone. Sarah Novetti, CNC news."

Margie tried to get Alex's attention again.

"How's it feel?" she asked, referring to the bandage.

"It's fine," he said, casually blowing her off.

Another report began.

"The U.S. military has confirmed a coordinated effort with U.N. forces to begin securing military bases, both operative and inoperative, in the United States."

Alex's eyes widened in shock as the U.N. insignia faded into view in a box to the right of the anchor's head.

"Though other U.N. efforts have been initiated in England, Germany, and Russia, the main emphasis has been in the U.S... Katy Elmore has more."

Stock footage of U.N. training drills were shown.

"The United Nations Peacekeeping Security forces are taking the global plague head on."

A still photo of U.N. Secretary General (and smarmy former U.S. President,) Jefferson Williams, was shown. His voice narrated, *"We are pleased with the member nations and especially the U.S.*

Congress for allowing us to coordinate security efforts in the wake of this global pandemic. We have begun efforts in Europe and the U.S. to re-secure major cities..."

(More stock footage of the U.N. under the correspondents' voice.)

"*Major efforts have begun to strengthen the members of FEMA and Homeland Security within the U.S.*"

A U.S. General's face appeared on the screen.

"*We're pleased to have the U.N. join us in our crusade to re-secure America.*"

(Back to the news anchor.)

"*A spokesman for Homeland Security had this to say about the rescue efforts within the U.S.: There has been little to no resistance in our efforts. Some looters have been captured and incarcerated, and any insurgency against our collective efforts have been minimal to nonexistent.*"

Alex finally broke out of his trance with a start. He breathed, "I can't believe its finally happened."

"What?" asked Margie, sensing an opening and positioning herself behind Alex. "What's happened?"

"The U.N. has begun an occupation of America."

Margie began to rub Alex's shoulders. To her surprise, he was extremely tense. Her daughter Gina winced.

Alex made an unpleasant curious face and went on, "They've been looking to cause something like this for decades now—and now they *have*."

"Well, I don't see what the big deal is about not staying in town, especially if our town is secure."

"It's not about *security*, it's about *control*. You've got to help me meet the mayor."

"You seem like a man who's in control," Margie said, complimenting Alex and moving close to his face from behind.

He could feel her breath on his neck, and lips touching his ear. He hesitated, then said, "Margie, please. I can't do this right now." He tried to be as polite as possible.

An awkward silence ensued.

Gina stood up from the couch and went to her room.

Margie slowly returned to her seat. Not another word was shared for the remainder of the evening.

* * * * *

In a back room of Margie's house, Miguel DeLaMontana was on his knees, clutching a rosary, praying in the dim candle light. The candle was held in a large glass container with a picture of the Virgin of Guadalupe on the front. Miguel kissed the crucifix on his rosary before he reclined on the blankets he had situated on the floor to go to sleep.

* * * * *

"What do you like to drink?" asked Lucy St. Claire, standing by the sink in her kitchen.

Red was sitting at the table, listening to Lucy's country mix tape.

"What do I *like* to drink or what do I *want* to drink?"

Though the television was turned on the news, neither were paying attention.

"What do you like? I'm sure I have what you want." She winked at Red behind one of the dark brown strands of hair that was falling across her face.

Accepting the open pass with a smile, Red continued, "Well, would there happen to be a *Lone Star Beer* in the fridge?"

"Well, let me have a look-see," she said, sauntering to the fridge. She opened the fridge door and bent over, her hands on her knees, her round and shapely rear facing Red. The woman was comfortable with her sexuality and aggressive in her pursuit.

Man, I'm going to score, thought Red.

But in the shadows of the backyard, a human figure from the back alley pushed open the back gate. It slowly crept across the darkness of the lawn.

Inside, Lucy pulled a bottle from the refrigerator.

"Will a *Coors Light* longneck be all right?"

"Why, *yes*, thank you."

She served the beer to Red as if she were a waiter at a fancy restaurant serving the most exquisite bottle of wine, placing the bottle on her forearm.

Playing a sophisticate, Red said, "The *born-on-date* says last month. A fine vintage ale, *garcon*."

"*Garcon?*" she giggled.

They both laughed.

Outside, the figure crept closer to the back porch, moments away from exposing itself to the light.

"You know, you're really cute," said Lucy, sitting side-saddle on Red.

Excited, Red replied, "Well, I must say I was thinking the same thing about you, too, my lady."

The figure reached the back porch and was suddenly emersed in artificial light. It peeped through the kitchen window and saw the happenings inside the house.

Billy Joe Garner scowled.

"Really now?" teased Lucy, taking a swig from Red's beer, then placing it on the table.

"Yes, ma'am," said Red, placing one hand on her powerful thigh and the other on her back. "You are quite a country lass."

"I have a country ass?" she said with a smile. They both laughed.

Billy Joe began to breathe a little faster as his bitter jealously built. His forearms were twitching. All ambient sound was tuned out. Only anger echoed in his ears.

From the shadows of the alley, a former living citizen of Beeville— now dead and ambulating—stumbled forth. It caught sight of Billy Joe near the distant window.

"That, too," said Red.

"Why, thank you," said Lucy, rising and shaking her thing for Red.

"*Yes,*" whispered Red as Lucy continued to wiggle for him, squatting down with her hands on her knees, spreading her legs then quickly bringing them back together again. She was moving in rhythm to the country song on the player, George Strait's *The Fireman* as she stood back up, arching her back to make her rear more pronounced.

She finished her brief dance and turned and giggled. Red laughed with her.

Billy Joe was steaming mad. He knew that very same ploy was used on *him* only months earlier.

The ghoul edged closer to Billy Joe.

Lucy straddled Red and made sure to sit very close to feel his excitement.

"You know, there's nothing like a good... *longneck,* don't you think?" said Lucy.

"A longneck can certainly provide joy to everyone," stated Red, playing along with the overt seduction.

"You can provide your own longneck if necessary, right?" she asked, become more aroused as she slowly rubbed and grinded her sensitive area against his fully aroused part beneath his pants.

"*Naturally. Can you feel it?*" Red whispered, beginning to breathe a little faster.

"I most certainly can," she said, grinding on his lap.

His hands helped themselves to both cheeks of her rear end as she began to add a bounce to her grind. Lucy quivered and ran a hand through her hair. She bit her bottom lip. For several moments, only the radio played, continuing George Strait's popular old song, as the two continued their movements. Red caressed her neck with his lips, tugging gently at her earlobe with his teeth. They then gazed into each other's eyes, the rhythm of Lucy's grind slowly moving faster. Lucy's full red lips moved towards Red's.

Billy Joe had seen enough. He pulled a knife from his back pocket and went to knock on the back door.

But before he could knock, the ghoul grabbed him by the hair and arms. With a solid grip and the element of surprise, the beast bit into Billy Joe's neck. The bite removed a large portion of the boy's neck. Billy Joe screamed in pain and alarm as his adolescent blood poured onto his *Ramones* shirt and stained the mouth of the ghoul.

Hearing the scream, Lucy bounced off of Red moments before their lips locked. Red grabbed a pistol from the table and looked out the back door. He adjusted his pants.

"*Shit.* One of those things is eating some kid."

"What?!" Lucy moved to the back door. They both looked through the boarded-up window.

"I think this kid was peepin'. The monster snuck up on him. I've gotta blast 'em."

"No, wait!" Lucy exclaimed, grabbing Red's arm.

"What?"

Billy Joe started to cry for help.

"*Get 'em,*" said Lucy, changing her mind.

Red removed three boards from the door and opened it. He

stepped onto the back porch. The beast was smothering Billy Joe before Red blasted a hole in the back of its head, then immediately opened a hole in Billy Joe's head.

"*Got 'em,*" Red said with confidence.

Lucy frowned.

A frantic knock came at the front door, followed by an erratic ringing of the doorbell.

"Crap!" Lucy shouted, yanking Red back into the kitchen. She slammed the back door. She growled, "Don't let anybody back there."

Red cringed in surprise. "*Uh...* okay."

Lucy dashed to the front door. Placing the small chain lock on the door, she opened it as far as the chain would permit.

It was Audrey and Eric Garner. Lucy gulped.

"Lucy, everything all right?" Audrey asked. She had her M-16. Eric had his Spas-12.

"Fine, fine," Lucy said nervously. "Everything's fine." She wondered if they were suspicious.

"What was that?" Eric asked.

"A monster tried to come in the back, but Red got him. Right, Red?"

Red, not expecting the question, replied, "Yeah. It's fine. I got 'em."

"*Them?*" Audrey asked. "I thought you said one monster?"

"No. He said *him*—right, Red?"

"Yes. Just one. There's just one dead back here."

"See?" said Lucy with a smile.

"Need help disposing with—"

"—No, no. We got it. Thanks, though," she said, realizing she was probably safe, but needed them to scram.

"Okay," Audrey said. "Listen, if you need anything, just holler, you hear?"

"Sure will," Lucy said, smiling. "Don't worry, we got things under control. Thanks."

Audrey and Eric cautiously walked back to their house. Lucy closed the door, and leaning against it took a deep breath. Then she went back to the kitchen.

Red, uncertain about what just happened, stared curiously at her as she entered.

"What's going on here?" he asked.

"What do you mean? We killed some monsters, that's all."

"What about the kid? Who was he?"

"No one. Just a *peepin' tom* that got his. Now I need your help to get rid of these—"

Red assertively grabbed her shoulders and stared into her eyes. *"Who was he?"*

Lucy paused for a second, then answered with a gulp, "He was their *son*." She almost revealed that the boy was also her lover, but chose not to. If she played her cards right, Red would be a useful substitute.

"Aw, Jesus Christ, Lucy. I killed their *son*?"

"He was already dead. You saw him."

"Jesus Christ. I'm out of here."

"No, you're not," Lucy stated, with authority. She grabbed his arm with surprising strength. "You're going to help me bury him. You're in this now as much as I am." She glared.

As intimidating as it was, and as much as Lucy was making him angry, he could not help but feel turned on. This woman was wild, but smart—very smart. Red got the feeling he could fulfill some of his wildest fantasies with this woman and she would appreciate it. Considering the possibility, he agreed to follow her lead.

"Okay. What do you want me to do?" he asked.

A devious grin came across Lucy's lips and she coquettishly gave Red a peck on the lips. She said, "Follow me and I'll tell you."

She was thinking: *Mommy's got a new toy.*

Alex meets the Sheriff and Monsignor takes a walk

Margie and Alex woke up the next morning, had some breakfast, and drove to find the sheriff. Gina stayed with Mary.

"We can start at City Hall," said Margie, driving her four-door Cutlass. "That's where the mayor is basing his operations."

"The mayor?"

"Yeah."

"Well, hell. Then take me to the mayor. I thought the sheriff would be easier to find."

"Most of the law is out by the barricades. Sheriff McMurtry is usually going between all three three times a day."

"Thrice."

"Huh?"

"Never mind."

Within five minutes, they were through the security barricades around City Hall and into the plaza. Margie pointed out the mayor's car. "He's here." She parked, and the two of them strolled into City Hall.

Miss Zapata was at her desk, made up like a doll, as per usual.

"Hi, Margie."

"Hi, Stephanie. Is the mayor in?"

"He's in his office. Would you like to speak with him?"

"That'd be great."

"Give me a moment." Miss Zapata pressed a button on the phone. "Margie Montemayor and..." she paused, waiting for Margie's guest to give his name.

"Alex Rich," he said.

"...Alex Rich are here to speak with you."

"What do they want?" came the gruff reply. The sounds of bottles and other glass items clanking could be heard. Margie shot a glance at Alex.

Alex volunteered, "We have some news that might be critical to this town's survival."

Judging that Mayor Hickland heard Alex, Miss Zapata waited for a response.

"Give me a minute," came the mayor's reply.

"The mayor will be right with you," said Miss Zapata with a smile.

"Thank you," said Alex.

There were several seconds of awkward silence.

"Girl, you look like you're holding up just fine," said Margie, for conversation's sake.

"If only you knew," Miss Zapata replied.

"Oh, girl. You gotta tell me now," Margie said, waiting to get the dirt.

Mayor Hickland opened the door.

"Wait just one minute," Miss Zapata whispered to Margie, gently.

"Hello, Margie," Mayor Hickland said.

"Hello, Mayor," said Margie, noticing how uncharacteristically bedraggled he was. Usually Lance Hickland came across as very metrosexual. But today he was unshaven, unkempt, and tired-looking—far from stylish. "This is Alex Rich. He says he has some news for you that you might want to hear."

"Hello, Alex," said the mayor, offering his hand.

"Mayor. Can I have a moment of your time, sir?" Alex said, mustering the formality of a diplomat.

"Please. Come into my office," said Hickland, leading Alex into the adjacent room.

"I'll stay here," said Margie.

Alex nodded, then closed the door. A large sheet of paper was taped over the broken window on the office door. Alex didn't ask, assuming it was part of the disaster that was currently America.

Inside the mayor's office, the formalities continued.

"Please, have a seat," said Mayor Hickland. Alex thanked him and painfully took a seat in a chair in front of the mayor's desk. His hand rested on something gooey. Assuming it was a booger, Alex wiped his hand on his pant leg. He almost gagged.

Alex noticed some spent bottles of beer in the trash can. Two bottle caps were near the notepad and pen the mayor prepared to write with.

"So, how did you get here?"

"From San Antonio. Margie is my cousin," said Alex with a great poker face. Without Red around to screw things up, he was confident his bluff would work.

"Oh, really?" said the mayor, suspicious but not too concerned. "What happened to your leg?"

"That's part of what I'm here for. At any rate, I have reason to believe that a small army of U.N. forces is headed this way to capture and occupy this town."

The mayor was hopeful of the possible help that could be provided by the peacekeepers, but surprised at the unveiled sinister accusation.

"What do you mean *capture and occupy*?"

"Well, sir, me and my compatriot witnessed in Karnes City what we thought were stacks of executed people and also citizens being rounded up and put on trains."

The mayor reasoned, "Well, the news reports have said that the people are being gathered to be sent to FEMA centers for protection."

"This may be, sir," Alex said, being assertive, yet diplomatic, "But I feel they are not providing choices for the communities they are 'liberating'." Alex made 'quote signals' with his fingers.

The mayor remained cordial. "I can understand your concern..." His words trailed off as he burped. He breathed out, and Alex caught a whiff of his beer breath. He politely faced away for a moment. The mayor continued, "Excuse me. I understand your concern, but the reality is there is nothing to fear. If these forces were to arrive here, they would most certainly see that we have secured our fine city and move on to the next town in need of assistance."

Sensing that the mayor did not understand the threat, Alex tried to plead his case one more time.

"Mayor, if you would please consider the possibility of these forces using their powers against us. In the very least, I think it would be wise to come up with a contingency plan to deal with them if they threaten to 'liberate,'" (he used the finger quotes again,) "and occupy this city."

The mayor chose to humor Alex. "Though I disagree with the U.N. potentially using such heavy-handed tactics, I will concede that a contingency plan should be in place. I will contact my sheriff who is in charge of securing our city and we will devise a plan in order to deal with any aggression by these forces, if they get here."

Feeling conned, Alex forced the mayor's hand.

"Can we call him *now*, sir? At this point, they could come at any minute. It would be important to inform your charges of the possible confrontation and establish a plan in advance."

The mayor was impressed with Alex's negotiating skills but in no mood to continue the discussion. He decided it would be wise to delegate.

"Mister... *Rich*, is that right?"

"Right."

"Right. Listen, please wait in the lobby. My secretary will call the sheriff, and you can inform him when he arrives."

"Thanks," Alex said, offering his hand.

"You're welcome," said the mayor, taking his hand and showing him the door.

Margie and the secretary abruptly stopped talking as the two men emerged from the office. The mayor informed his secretary of what to do. She did as she was told, and Alex was welcomed to sit in the lobby.

After informing Margie of what was to come, he said she could leave. After hugging Alex, she told him she would be back in about thirty minutes, then walked out the door.

Alex took a deep breath, the pain in his leg still strong, and sat down.

*   *   *   *   *

Monsignor O'Leary had spent the afternoon in an effort to reach out to the community within the church's neighborhood. Armed with a shotgun filled with slugs, he hadn't faced any danger until now.

Most of the houses he went to did not answer their doors, and some of the ones that did kindly refused his offers to attend mass.

He was halfway to McCann Street when a man wandered onto the sidewalk in front of him. It did not take O'Leary long to realize it was a zombie. The blood caked on the man's mouth and the dismembered arm were a literal dead giveaway.

O'Leary took aim and removed the head of the beast. It fell to the ground. Dark blood poured from the head and soaked the sidewalk.

O'Leary lowered his weapon. The body of the zombie quivered, then became still.

He took a deep breath and turned to a boarded-up house. A figure seemed to be looking outside, but ducked away as O'Leary turned to look at them.

He looked back at the body. He was still very conflicted as to what God's plan was. Were these ghouls still with souls? Or were they the shells? Had he committed murder? Even though the Vatican had said their piece, he was still confused.

These people will seek death but will not find it...

Putting his questions aside, he scanned the neighborhood in the warm April morning for any other threats. He then prepared to give the creature Last Rites. Bowing his head, he began the ritual.

As he quietly began reciting the prayers, his mind started to drift off and spin. Something was being pulled into his mind, his soul, and Monsignor drifted into a trance.

On the top of a desolate yet green hill stood a square stone building. Black clouds and lightning flashed behind the building. O'Leary found himself looking out from window. It took only a moment to figure out that he was in the stone building, looking at the approaching storm.

He turned and looked around the room. Dead bodies were scattered on the floor in front of him. He looked at his hands. Blood dripped from them. Sitting at his feet was a disemboweled body.

Looking back outside, the storm was striking the land with blades of water and a thick foggy mist was approaching, soon to envelop the building.

He turned back to the room. The thick mist penetrated the air, filling it with a thick gray cloud. It infiltrated his nose, mouth, ears, even eyes, pushing the optical organs back into his head.

He fell to the ground.

Before long, he rose again, standing alone in the thick gray fog. His eyes had returned to their rightful places. He shambled around in the mist slowly, then stopped, sensing movement.

Before him stood a lone figure, enveloped in fog, silhouetted in black. Large red eyes beamed through the mist. Suddenly another figure appeared by its side, dark and with the same red eyes. Then another. Before long, the room was filled with the figures.

The one in front gestured him to follow them as they all turned and marched into the fog.

A hand touched O'Leary's shoulder, shaking him from the dream. He shook in fear, thinking that a beast must have just caught him unawares.

But it was not a beast. It was Benito Reyes.

"I'm sorry, Father. I didn't mean to scare you. Are you all right?"

The holy man shivered and jumped away from Benny, looking into the sky, expecting to see the impending darkness and fog. But nothing but blue skies were smiling at him, floating over the infected world.

"Father?"

Confident that the illusion had disappeared, Monsignor Ralph O'Leary smiled and looked at Benny. "Yes, my son."

"Father, can you take a confession out here?"

Realizing one of his flock needed assistance, he confirmed that he could. The two moved under a large tree that offered a green canopy of leaves, a respite from the sun.

After formally beginning his confession, Benny revealed his painful sin.

"Father, I was a part of a murder."

Thinking that Benny was referring to the zombies, O'Leary said, "My son, these creatures are *shells*, merely—"

"Father, my sin is for someone who was still alive, yet seemed to have no soul."

Benny then retold the story from the previous day involving the cruel young boy and his friends. Astounded, O'Leary poker-faced the confession, realizing the lawlessness that was another symptom of the new world.

As Benny finished, O'Leary offered his judgement and penance.

"My son, Jesus appreciates your heart and confession. You know, many people ask the question *'What Would Jesus Do?'* Though Jesus believes in forgiveness, he also knows that man can be cruel and that his sins will—*ultimately*—be judged by God. You could have made other choices to prevent this lost soul from hurting other girls, but you chose to assist in his murder."

Benny closed his eyes and lowered his head.

O'Leary went on, "I can see both sides of your sinful predicament, and though only God will tell you if you chose right or wrong, you will still have to live with that. Meditate with prayer. Pray your rosary twice a day for the next three weeks to cleanse your sins. And while you pray, ask God and Jesus for forgiveness. I'm sorry this lost soul has put a scar on your heart. Rest easy, my son, knowing that our ever-loving God in His infinite love will ultimately grant you forgiveness if you ask for it from your heart."

Tears of guilt welled up in Benny's eyes. He nodded, made the sign of the cross, and said "Amen" with Father O'Leary.

* * * * *

Alex was reading announcements on the bulletin board as the clock logged forty minutes on his wait.

An announcement for a spring festival at the park.

A flyer for a trailer park.

A disclaimer about child abuse.

—Remnants of the old world.

Stephanie Zapata wasn't much for conversation, but made Alex nervous at her curious glances in his direction.

Margie returned after Alex had waited roughly thirty minutes, and was making conversation with him.

Just before the clock logged forty-five minutes, the sheriff entered through the double doors at the front of the building. He closed the doors behind him and greeted Alex with a smile and a hearty handshake. As the two men conversed, Margie said she'd wait in the truck.

"You're Alex, I guess."

"Yes, sir. Alex Rich."

"Well, good afternoon. I'm Sheriff McMurtry. What can I do you for?"

"Sheriff, a foreign invasion force is on their way here."

"What?"

"I mean to say a United Nations peacekeeping force is on its way here. We've watched them—"

The sheriff put a hand up to silence Alex. Though he himself had his reservations about the U.N forces, he had to stick to his guns. He said, "*Whoa, whoa, whoa.* Slow down, now. You understand our president has allowed these forces to enter our country to back up our military?"

Alex realized then that the sheriff was a war hawk neo-con, a new kind of conservative who he considered very narrow-minded, (not that the liberals were any consolation to his political ideology.)

"Yes, sir, but..."

"Are you saying they're coming to *fight* us?"

"Yes, sir. They've shot me," Alex said, indicating his leg, "And I've seen what they did in Poth, and—"

"I don't believe you," stated the sheriff, bluntly and without remorse.

Alex thought he was on the *O'Reilly Factor*, not getting a chance to complete a sentence before being steamrolled with words that did not necessarily contribute to the discussion, but were meant more to belittle without clearly stated points. He felt he had an 'ace' though, and played it. "Well, sir. I can show you some device they placed near our vehicle that has markings. Perhaps..."

"Sure. Let's see this so-called *device*."

Alex limped away and led the skeptical sheriff to Margie's truck. Margie was waiting for him.

"Hi, Sam," waved Margie.

"Hi, Margie," said McMurtry in response, still stone-faced and smug.

"I guess you met my cousin Alex?" she said with a grin.

160

"Yes, we've met."

Alex grinned. The levity was appreciated, as the sheriff was coming across to Alex as a bit of an asshole.

Alex reached into the back of the truck for the canister. He handed it to the sheriff.

"This is a military-style canister all right," confirmed the sheriff, closely examining the object and looking surprised.

"Gas?"

"Can't be anything too dangerous," assumed the sheriff, downplaying the revelation and trying to sound authoritative, even though he had no idea what the canister was. "Seems like it could be meant for a small distance or maybe a two or three story building. I can't let you keep it, though."

Alex was totally supportive of that idea. "That's fine by me."

"Well, it's a danger to our community, especially since we don't know how dangerous or powerful it is. We can also use it as evidence of wrongdoing in the future if this thing blows over." Though the message seemed to mean something against the U.N., it came across to Alex as a threat to his own well-being.

"I can live with that," Alex sincerely replied.

"We wouldn't want any insurgents or terrorists getting to this," McMurtry threw in, overtly indicating Alex.

Alex changed the subject: "What about contingency plans to counter an offensive from a peacekeeping force?"

Despite the curious canister, the sheriff concluded the whole idea of a U.N. offensive against the town was ridiculous. He said, "Well, I'm making my rounds, so I'll prepare them for what might come, including amicable agreements. How's that sound?"

"Fantastic. Thank you, sir," said Alex, leaving it on the sheriff.

"Yes, sir," said the sheriff. He shook Alex's hand, then went inside to show the canister to the mayor. When asked where he should leave it, the mayor said anyplace but his office.

After taking in Miss Zapata on the way out of the mayor's office, he made his way upstairs to the third floor, where he placed the unknown device in the cabinet of what once had been the city clerk's office.

And there it remained, hiding in the darkness of the closed cabinet, unassuming yet unforgotten.

*   *   *   *   *

Miguel Mercado DeLaMontana had made a sandwich and was eating it in Ms. Montemayor's kitchen. He had tuned the radio to a Spanish station that was delivering news in his native language.

Miguel had been born in Guadalajara, Jalisco. His birthplace could be suggested by the red and white striped soccer shirt he was wearing. Closer examination would reveal the emblem of his hometown team, *Chivas*. He was an orphan and had been raised by his aunt. She was a strict disciplinarian and made Miguel walk the line. He grew up to be a respectful and hard-working man.

In an effort to make a life for himself, he took a risk, hiring a "coyote" to lead him across the border illegally. It was an arduous journey on foot through the cold south Texas night, but he eventually found the camp he had been directed to in early January. He was lucky, as January was a time when the Border Patrol was particularly active during the holiday season.

The camp leader had been a nice man, but Miguel didn't understand a word he said. Eventually he was driven to Beeville where he began work as a ranch hand for Mr. Mark Bannon. Bannon was very good to Miguel and his family, not only providing generous pay, but giving them a living space in an old barn near his ranch house. Bannon was good friends with Sheriff McMurtry, who had always made sure to head off any random Border Patrol searches at Bannon's ranch.

Things had been going great until the plague broke out.

Miguel took a handful of chips into his mouth when he noticed a movement at the front porch. Then a knock sounded from the door. Miguel jumped, then picked up a pistol that had been left for him.

He approached the door.

He peered outside.

On the other side stood Monsignor O'Leary. Noticing the white collar, Miguel realized the man was a priest and opened the door.

"*Bueno,*" greeted Miguel.

Realizing he had to speak Spanish, O'Leary replied, "*Hola, senor. Yo soy* Padre O'Leary *de la iglesia* Our Lady of Perpetual Forgiveness."

"*Hola*, padre," Miguel replied with a smile. He was happy that the priest knew how to speak Spanish.

"Um…" O'Leary began, thinking of how to word his broken Spanish. *"Todo los dias, hay iglesia a las nueve en la manana. Quiero invitarle a iglesia para servir nuestro Padre Christo."*

"Seguro que si," said Miguel, confirming that he'd love to go to church. He then asked for directions to get to the church at nine every morning, as offered.

Father O'Leary was happy to find someone who wanted to attend. He was even happier to be asked to pray for Miguel's family and friends back on the Bannon Ranch.

As the door closed, O'Leary knew the trip had been worth it. But then again, his service to his Lord was always worth it to him.

He walked to the next house and knocked on the door.

Little Timmy
has an adventure

L ittle Timmy Moore was gazing at his turtle in its artificial amphibious world. Timmy and his mother had put the little simulated world together two months earlier.

It was while on a trip to Corpus Christi. Timmy visited a large aquarium with his mother. He saw octopi, rare fish, and what was to become his new favorite animal: the giant turtle.

Two weeks later, his mother, Mary, took him to a pet store and bought him a little red-eared turtle. He named it *Rock Climber*, because the moment he removed it from the bag, the little amphibian had climbed up his shirt to his neck.

That night the duo put the artificial environment together. The turtle had a new home.

Timmy loved his turtle. That is why today, when the simulated moon lamp went out, Timmy got concerned. He looked around the room and knew it was not a failure of the electric company.

He stood up. A bit scared, he went to his door, which was closed. A tremor of fear washed over his body for a moment. He stopped, somehow sensing danger. Perhaps it was *paranoia*, but he didn't know what that was.

"Mom?!" he called out. No answer.

Taking a moment to gather up his courage, he approached the door.

He turned the knob.

The door clicked open.

Silence.

He slowly peered outside his door.

He looked to his right. He looked to his left.

Nothing.

"Mom?!" he called out again, a little louder.

Still no answer.

He almost closed the door to his room again when a noise came from his bedroom window.

He turned and saw a shadowy figure stumbling on the other side of the curtains. The afternoon sun revealed the silhouette of a creature outside his window.

Timmy looked out his bedroom into the still hallway again. He felt trapped. Somehow he knew there was a beast waiting, hiding by the wall at the end of the hallway, ready to snatch him up and bite him. But there was certainly something outside his window. That was for sure.

Gulping, he decided switching on the hallway light would be a good start. The switch was directly in front of his doorway.

He wanted to do it in one movement, feeling any wasted movement would be detrimental. Recalling the adventures of *The Blue Panther*, his favorite cartoon character, he knew a jump was in order. In his mind, the hallway was now a bottomless chasm in a jungle temple. The light switch was the key to cover the pit.

Taking a few steps back from the doorway, Timmy ran. Then, near the edge of the doorway, he took flight with plenty of air, hit the switch and collided with the wall. The light switched on, illuminating the hallway as he hit the floor.

The switch had closed the chasm.

Now another trap lay ahead, where the monsters were certainly waiting by the exit of the hallway into the living room. The couch lay just ahead. He could jump it. He knew he could. *The Blue Panther* could always make the jump.

Getting his footing and taking a deep breath, he started his run. As he neared the edge of the hallway, he could almost see a pair of arms coming to grab him from the border of the corridor.

He took to the air with the energy of the cartoon Blue Panther.

The hands could not catch him. His stomach hit the cushioned armrest, and he clawed his way to the couch.

First, he noticed the hallway entrance. There was nothing there. No monsters. No beastly arms. Then he looked around the room.

No monsters.

—But also no mother, either.

He called out again, "Mom?!"

Still no answer.

He dashed to the front door, dodging the poisoned darts that were flying from the walls. He made it to the door. Opening it, he looked out the screen door. No mom in sight.

"Mom?!"

Still no answer.

The screen door was open. Timmy deduced that his mother must have gone to visit one of her friends without telling him. But who?

Taking on the mind of *The Blue Panther*, Timmy looked for clues.

Looking ahead, the Blue Panther noticed all the doors of the houses in his sight line closed except for Ms. St. Claire's. Her screen door revealed an open wooden door, and a fuzzy sight line into her living room. All the other houses had their doors closed—leaving his mom vulnerable if she had to go and knock, he reasoned. Exposing yourself to danger without guaranteed admission into a house would be foolish. Certainly his mom would know that.

Timmy the Blue Panther also noted the creature at his bedroom window could be coming through it right now—or even worse, coming around the corner to the front door.

His heart racing, he put his money on his mother being at Ms. St. Clair's.

Throwing the screen door of his house open, Timmy the Blue Panther raced from the doorway across the porch and into the yard. Hands were rising from the ground around him as he cleared the front yard and ran into the street.

The street was a river of lava, with small patches of land spread among the red flow. Blue Panther Timmy Moore bounded from land mass to land mass until he got to the other side. The flipped truck in the street was a silent sentinel of an ancient temple. Clearing the front yard of Ms. St. Clair's house that was filled with ancient buried monsters, he leaped up the steps, hit the porch, and yanked at the screen door.

It was locked.

Danger was near. Timmy could feel it.

A hole in the screen just above the lock gave Timmy enough room to flick the lock from the latch and enter. He wisely kept the screen door from slamming.

The Blue Panther was successful.

"Mom?" Timmy said, confident of a reply.

No answer.

But he could hear people talking in a back room. Timmy casually followed the voices.

As he entered the hallway, a door was slightly ajar. The voices, or sounds, were certainly coming from the room. But what were they saying?

Before Timmy gave himself a chance to think about the choice he was about to make, he pushed open the door.

"*Mom*?" he whispered.

Before his eyes stood a frightening sight—a vision that struck fear in that he could not understand what was happening.

The curly-haired red-headed stranger was naked and seemed to be violently forcing himself into a just-as-naked Ms. St. Clair, at least to Timmy's virgin eyes. The image was so violent by his perception that he immediately moved back into the hallway.

Lucy, bent over the dresser, stopped moaning for a second and noticed the door in the mirror. "*Oh, did the door open? Oh, oh...*"

Red continued to drive into her from behind, watching Lucy's scrunched-up face in the dresser mirror.

"It's just the wind, baby," he said, not stopping for an instant.

Lucy closed her eyes again and started to moan louder. Their bodies collided harder and harder. The slapping of flesh resonated around the room.

Timmy started to cry.

Before his sad groans could be heard, he quietly dashed to the front door, sad, scared, and ashamed.

Bounding across the street, his focus on his front door so intense that he ignored the figure on the sidewalk. The tunnel vision denied the sight of the hands reaching for him. And when they did, in the bright afternoon sky, he screamed in fearful surprise.

"What are you doing out of the house, young man?!" the accompanying voice demanded to know.

* * * * *

At the Garner residence, Audrey and Eric were clueless as to the whereabouts of their son, Billy Joe.

"When was the last time you saw him?" Audrey asked.

"We ate dinner and he went to his room at around ten. I thought he went to bed."

"Well, so did I."

There was no sign of blood in the room, and though a window was unlocked, the screen was still on.

"Why would he leave?" Audrey asked.

"He wasn't seeing a girl, was he?"

"Maybe, but she lives across town."

"Well, he certainly wouldn't do *that*," said Eric with assurance.

"Goddamn, I can't believe this shit," Audrey said, breaking down and crying. Her tears turned to black lines running down her face. Eric held her, then offered her a cigarette. She wiped her face, and took several grateful puffs off the nicotine stick.

"He's all right, babe, he's all right. He'll be back."

Yet somehow, they both suspected otherwise.

Two Days Later...

S o, are you going to church?" asked Wayne over the phone.
"I don't know," said Gary from home. "I've seen too much shit and done too much shit to believe there's a God."
Wayne agreed, though he could not even begin to comprehend what Gary had seen during the war. However, Wayne was slowly starting to understand why it was so easy for Gary to do what he did to the redneck boy several days ago. Wayne was a bit of a dummy, but he could comprehend how war and the killing of other human beings could desensitize a soul.

"You'd think I'd know by now. But *no*...," Gary said.

"Yeah. I'm thinking I might go," Wayne said.

"Oh, yeah?"

"Would you come with me if I did?"

"I'd have to think about it."

Wayne was a little impatient, as he had had to pause his porno selection, *Older Guys, Younger Ladies 5*, featuring his favorite star, Amber Lynn.

"Well, give me a holler when you've decided, cool?"

"Cool."

"All right. Bye." He hung up the phone before Gary had a chance to say his goodbye.

Wayne immediately took the movie off of pause and started his ritual. It was right in the middle of a sex scene. Amber Lynn was playing a librarian who was enticed into sexual intercourse by some tables near the card catalog—a top-notch plotline.

So Wayne, in boxer briefs, laid down with the couch cushion near his crotch, and began coital movements. Mostly, he kept his movements in sync with the male performer on screen. While he drove himself into the porn star, Wayne drove into his imaginary woman. When he was close to releasing, he would lay off for a minute until he calmed down.

He closed his eyes and imagined women from his past—women he had never had—but women he *could have* in this self-indulgent intimate moment.

There was that blonde girl that worked the box office at the movie theater. And his Ninth-grade English teacher, Mrs. Burress. And Lucy St. Claire. And the busty and leggy fifteen year-old named Denise at the video store.

The actress on screen moaned in staged delight as Wayne slowed down, close to blowing his load for the third time.

As the sexed-up Miss Lynn bounced on top of the well-endowed male actor near a card catalog, Wayne lost his concentration. He remembered the boy hanging from the tree.

—The boy he helped murder.

He remembered the close call at the college dorms. Students who would never see their parents again.

Then he thought about himself. His own future.

An only child, and both of his parents deceased before the plague, Wayne only dreamed of sharing his love of the Cowboys and a little bit of his lonely soul with a beautiful woman. Someone who would appreciate his quirky humor. Someone that would help him get porno out of his life. Someone to go through life with.

As the world established future difficulty for the entire global population, he realized as Amber Lynn bent over the checkout counter that he would never find a girlfriend—not with the world falling apart.

He recalled the only girl that might have ever given him attention. Her name was Lois Bevelaqua. Wayne would see her every Sunday at the local sports bar, *The Nineteenth Hole*, during football season cheering for the Cowboys. She was around his age and presentable, though nowhere near being a knockout. Both of them would talk and have a jolly old time. But Wayne had never had the courage to advance their relationship. He resigned himself to keeping it just at the bar.

Then one Sunday he planned to ask her out. But just his luck, on that Sunday, she never arrived. It was to be another victory for the Cowboys, but another mark in the loss column for Wayne. He later found out that she had moved to Dallas and got a job with a computer conglomerate.

And he never saw her again.

In his mind, he wondered where she was and prayed for her well being.

As the male porn star shot his load onto Amber Lynn's mouth and face, Wayne began to cry in shame. He was a true loser, a man more focused on sports than women.

—A man so selfish he was destined to be forlorn, forever living and loving alone in his mind.

The Arrival

The day finally arrived, much to the dismay of Sheriff McMurtry. The United Nations peacekeeping mission led by Captain Phillip Carson had sent a scouting team to do reconnaissance, and that team was now facing off against the police blockade.

Alex Rich had been right.

Up ahead, Sheriff McMurtry could see the white Hummer with the unmistakable U.N. letters on the side.

He had come up with two plans. The first was to negotiate away the troops, convincing them that the city was contained. The second was to fire if fired upon and hold the line. With the small numbers of policemen at the barriers, the second plan was the least appealing.

Morale was already at an all-time low. The massacre over a week ago was still fresh on the minds of the police officers.

Deputy Anderson walked over to the sheriff's vehicle as he pulled up. Three U.N. soldiers in blue camouflage stood behind the orange and white barriers yards away from the line.

Anderson greeted McMurtry, then briefed him on the situation.

"Four men have pulled up in a Hummer. The three up ahead are calling for the city's surrender. The head of the team is Corporal Heinrich Helkegaard. He wants to talk to you."

McMurtry could not believe what was going on. Without replying to Anderson, he strode halfway between the line and the roadblocks. He stopped and called out, "May I speak to Corporal Helkegaard, please?"

"*Ja*," came a reply in a heavy German accent. A short man came to the sheriff, throwing his machine gun over his shoulder and offering his hand.

"*Gutten tag*. Hello," said Helkegaard with a smile of yellow and crooked teeth. McMurtry had never met a man so blonde and with such blue eyes.

In his strong German accent, Helkegaard explained, "Mein leader has informed meich to communicate to you that your town is now under U.N. control as mandated by your president. You are to send your people to FEMA camps in Corpus, or arrange to create one in your town."

The sheriff did understand that creating a FEMA center in town was humanitarian, but sensed underlying danger. Though the infected within city limits was minimal by comparison, bringing in people from surrounding towns could expose the people of Beeville to more infection, and more chances for it to spread. So he made an executive decision.

"I appreciate your offer, Corporal. But we choose to keep our city as it is without U.N. control and sanctions. Our city is secure, *armed*, and safe." He made sure to stress '*armed*.'

Corporal Helkegaard politely nodded his head and smiled. A courteous messenger.

"I honor your decision, Sheriff. I will communicate your decision to mein leader. Thank you. *Auf wiedershen*."

Politely, the corporal walked to his two blue collegues without a parting handshake.

Deputy Anderson approached McMurtry and asked, "What happened?"

"I told them we were fine."

"What'd he say?"

"He was going to tell his boss."

They both paused and watched the baby blue trio walk to the Hummer.

"What do you think they're going to do?"

"I don't know."

"If they decide to try to take us, I don't think we can match their firepower."

"I *know*," McMurtry said. His voice trembled.

"A pre-emptive strike?"

"Then it's a guaranteed war."

Two blue soldiers entered the Hummer and drove back up the road, while two soldiers stayed behind and started to dig a ditch near a stack of charred bodies—the charred bodies of the people of Three Rivers. After the massacre, the police had stacked and burned the bodies.

McMurtry figured explaining it to the U.N. soldiers at this point would be useless.

He said to Anderson, "We gotta wait."

"They're coming back, you know," Anderson replied.

"I know it."

"We gotta warn the city. Things are about to get crazy."

McMurtry groaned, "*Jesus, Mary, and Joseph.*"

Back in his cruiser, a digital message blinked repeatedly on his phone:

1 Missed Call.

Blue Skies

It had been two days since the initial contact with the United Nations Peacekeeping force.

Spring had already arrived in Beeville, Texas, but as Father Time flipped the calender to May, Mother Earth turned up the Texas heat another notch. April showers certainly brought May flowers. Bluebonnets and other native flora colored the countryside.

Yet a special blue was falling from the sky a distance away from town—a sinister blue contrasting with the gorgeous blue Texas sky.

Frank Garza was the first to notice the air drop. He squinted and held his hand above his eyes.

Audrey Garner picked up on it out of the corner of her eye as she was sorting through some of the looted goods in the flipped truck outside her home.

"Be careful, babe," Eric told her. "That truck might blow."

"This shit ain't blowing, or it woulda' done it by now."

He noticed her looking into the sky. He turned to look as well.

At the blockade, Sheriff McMurtry had a much closer view.

And meanwhile, Monsignor O'Leary was using the city's automated telephone call system to invite all citizens to mass at *Our Lady of Perpetual Forgiveness* that night, regardless of their religious denomination.

* * * * *

Captain Phillip Carson was standing in a blue tent about a mile from the Beeville blockade. This was to be his temporary base of operations. The soldiers and equipment were dropping in a nearby field.

A soldier came up to Carson.

"Sir. All personnel are accounted for and most of the equipment is here as well."

"Good. When the equipment is accounted for, organize it for efficient move-out at *o'five-hundred* hours. We begin operations in the morning."

"Yes, sir. Also, sir, we have captured a local. She says she has information you might be able to use."

"Bring her in," said Carson.

"Yes, sir."

"And go get us some coffee."

"Yes, sir."

The soldier exited the tent, then returned with the local.

It was Katy Russell. Despite living on the run in the brush around Beeville, she was well-kept.

"Hello, sir," she said formally.

"Greetings, my lady," Carson replied, openly checking her out. He lifted his gaze from her breasts and said, "Please, have a seat."

He motioned to a chair nearby. She sat down.

"Tell me if this counts as a war crime," she began, a scheming smile piercing her lips.

* * * * *

Red stood outside watching the military personnel and equipment float to the ground in the distance. He knew what was to come. He turned around and walked back into Lucy's house.

Lucy was looking out her kitchen window. Though the lights were off in the house, the sun provided adequate lighting for interaction. Lucy stood by the sink. A beam of sunlight streaming through the window gently illuminated her body, massaging her skin with warmth.

Red gazed at her figure. A tight sleeveless white shirt was worn over a pair of cutoff shorts. She wore white tube socks pulled down to the ankles. Her head was hanging low, facing the sink in a kind of melancholy. Her brown hair dangled down along the side of her face. Her lips were naturally pursed.

Red broke the silence. "I think the U.N. is arriving."

Uninterested, she replied, "Oh, yeah?"

"Yeah. I guess things are going to get interesting, huh?" He was trying to figure out her mood, as he was anticipating some more sex.

"Yeah," she replied, lifting her head and gazing out the window again.

Framed in the sunlight streaming through the window like a heavenly blessing, she looked majestic. Still, there seemed to be something *off* about her.

Red asked, "So, what's wrong?"

"I got a phone call," she said. "A recorded message from Monsignor O'Leary at *Our Lady of Perpetual Forgiveness*. He's invited everybody to church."

"Oh yeah?"

"I think I want to go."

"Oh... okay."

Her heart was hurting. She did not anticipate the emotional toll of watching the adolescent she manipulated dying on her back porch, and the subsequent conspiracy to hide his body.

Red seemed to pick up on the subtext, though was not feeling half as bad. He embraced her from behind, holding her close and kissing her neck with a comforting affection.

They both stood and looked out the window as the afternoon bathed them in a heavenly warmth.

* * * * *

The remainder of the afternoon was filled with anxiety and anticipation for the people of Beeville. They had an idea what would happen next, but they did not know when. There was no formal plan established on what the citizens would do if the U.N. penetrated the city, only uneasy speculation. Most everyone stayed inside, preparing themselves for the worst.

As the afternoon gave way to night, Monsignor O'Leary wondered how many people would show up for mass. As he prepared and dressed in his sacred raiments, he somehow felt the end closing in, an inevitable darkness encroaching on the city.

Something came over him as he looked into the mirror and adjusted his robe. He stood still and gazed at his reflection.

Somehow, the background within the mirror faded to black, and all that was left reflecting was his shadowy visage. O'Leary's eyes and mouth darkened. The darkness behind him turned to fierce flames and frenzied fingers of fire. A large, nondescript concrete building was ablaze. The flames died down and all that was left was the black shell of that large edifice. A bright light illuminated the structure. A column of ethereal magnificence rose from the building and into the sky, then dissipated. The land was silent. Then, ghouls began to walk from the remains of the building, charred and roasted black beasts. Then, slowly they melded back into the earth.

A tap on the shoulder brought the priest back from his moment.

It was Miguel. O'Leary almost blasted him had it not been for the Mexican's benevolent smile.

"*Padre, ya acave de barrer la iglesia. Hay algo mas que necesita que yo limpie?*"

O'Leary was sweating. He wasn't sure how long he was out. He responded by asking Miguel to repeat the question, then answered by telling him there was nothing more to clean and that he should prepare for mass.

O'Leary had been surprised to see Miguel come to the church the same afternoon they met. He came for confession and for prayers for his family. For an hour, the two contemplated theologically the plague and what God's plan was for the world and for them. O'Leary had wanted official word, but the Vatican remained quiet on the subject since the first communiqué.

It was then that Miguel told O'Leary he had been an altar server in Guadalajara, and said he was eager to help out O'Leary's church. He further explained that it was the only place he felt safe.

O'Leary allowed Miguel to stay there. He did not have much gear, so it was a perfect arrangement.

But it was about five minutes until mass was to start. O'Leary was afraid that not too many people would show up. He told Miguel to join him to light the candles.

Taking up the aluminum candle lighters, they walked out toward the altar. What O'Leary saw next shocked him.

—The entire church was filled with people.

After taking a brief moment to take it all in, O'Leary started lighting the candles.

* * * * *

Gary Chapman and Wayne Crocker stood outside the church, armed and ready. They were like benevolent angels prepared to protect the house of God with force, but they greeted those who came in with a smile.

"Hi, Kroeger family," Wayne said, waving at one of his acquaintances. They waved back. He whispered to Gary, "They're not Catholic. They're Baptists."

"I don't think it makes a damn today," Gary replied. "And that's a beautiful thing."

Alex Rich approached, limping, also armed and ready. He politely nodded at the men.

"Who's he?" Wayne asked.

"Dunno."

Evelyn Hickland, the mayor's wife, approached wearing a long-sleeved shirt.

"Hot, Evelyn?" Wayne asked.

"No," she replied, stone-faced.

Sam McMurtry walked up. He said with a smile, "Gentlemen, firearms are not allowed in church."

"I'll ask for Jesus to forgive me this once," Gary replied, shaking the sheriff's hand.

Benny Reyes and his wife Lupe walked up, followed by Frank and Dolores Garza. All four had rosaries in their hands. Benny and Frank just nodded at Gary and Wayne, who cordially returned the nods.

Eric and Audrey Garner showed up, puffing on cigarettes. Eric asked, "Can we take these in there?"

"Why not?" Wayne told him.

The pair puffed away and entered.

Margie and Gina Montemayor, accompanied by Mary and Timmy Moore, walked up.

"Gary!" said Margie loudly, giving him a big hug. "We're still drinkin' tomorrow, right?"

"I can't say that in front of God right now. He might get mad."

Margie let out a hearty laugh. "Wayne, how you doing, love?" she asked, giving him a warm embrace. He returned it, grateful.

"I'm fine, Margie."

"Oh, you give such good hugs," she said gently.

"Thanks," said Wayne, happy at the compliment.

"Go on in, girls," Gary said. "Seating is starting to get limited."

* * * * *

Alex took a seat. He was traditionally a Methodist and a devout Christian, but he decided to put religious dogma aside and hear the word, regardless of its denomination. He was pleasantly surprised at the turnout. The pews were packed with people.

Then Red LaRue and Lucy St. Claire walked in. Alex offered Red a seat near him, but he and Lucy chose to sit elsewhere. Alex didn't know why that upset him so much.

The mass started with little fanfare. Monsignor O'Leary used recorded hymns for the entrance, and the usual prayers, recitations, and readings proceeded.

As O'Leary began into the second reading from the book of Revelation, Mayor Lance Hickland walked in and sat down. A minute later, Stephanie Zapata walked in late and sat herself away from him.

As O'Leary ended the second reading, he began to walk back to the altar. The darkness came back to him again, and the altar area turned into a thick cloud of fog. Shadowy figures with red eyes stood all around him.

Red turned his head to Lucy and whispered, "What's wrong with the priest?"

Lucy shrugged.

O'Leary fell on the carpeted steps to the altar. The congregation gasped as Miguel ran to assist him.

"*Padre*," said Miguel.

"I'm all right," O'Leary said as Miguel lifted him to his feet. Taking a moment to regain his senses, he lifted his Bible and went into the Gospel, then the sermon.

"The eyes are the window to the soul," he said, pausing for emphasis. Then he repeated, "*The eyes are the window to the soul.*"

He continued, "It's a very clichéd saying, but I get the feeling we've all come to intimately understand what that means.

"Two days ago, I saw it for myself. Several times. The first instance, I came face-to-face with the problem terrorizing this nation. Those abominations we all know good and well. I looked into its eyes, and I saw sadness. I saw hopelessness. I saw the shell of what that person used to be. I looked into the window and I saw no soul. It was the illusion of life. The illusion of hope. An abomination.

"I then saw it again, in the eyes of a young child. This child had seen something so atrocious—so scary—he couldn't even tell me. But I looked into those eyes and knew his soul was there, and his soul was struck hard."

Lucy whispered to Red, "Wonder what happened?"

Red shrugged.

O'Leary went on, "I understood what it meant about fifteen years ago when I watched my father pass on. I say *watched* like I was there. I really wasn't. I was in college at the time. I had spent the previous two days there with him in the hospital. My mother was there, too. But I ended up leaving, only to get a call moments after getting home that he had died.

"So I packed up my stuff and a friend was kind enough to drive me back to the hospital. I reunited with my mother and she shared with me my father's final moments.

"She said that he had been convulsing every few minutes, gasping for air, wide-eyed, then returning to his pillow. My mother was reading to him about the miraculous appearance of the Virgin Mary at Lourdes, praying for her own personal miracle. God knows I was, too. Every day, I prayed. I prayed that when I went to sleep and woke up, it would all be different. Like a dream.

"Well, that day never came. We lost him that night, just several days before my own birthday.

"But back to that moment. Mom said he had been convulsing throughout the evening, but somehow she knew the final one was approaching.

"She said he convulsed, his eyes wide, looking at the ceiling.

"Then he smiled. He *smiled.*

"As his head returned to the pillow, mom closed my father's eyes. I imagined that my father was seeing not only his father, but *our*

Father. Somehow, I was assured that I would see my father again.

"But the eyes. His eyes remained open. *Why*, I asked. The windows to the soul. Perhaps that is how our soul leaves us, projected by some spiritual energy or plucked out and sent home by a guardian angel, its job done.

"But the eyes. *The eyes*. I knew my father's soul was gone.

"That's why I know when I look into the eyes of these poor cursed shells—these satanic abominations—I know they've no soul. It's like looking into the eyes of a baby killer or child molester. Behind those eyes is a dead or dying soul. An empty heart. A sad life.

"And that's why every moment from now to our end is important. Why we must choose to do good. Why we must fight against the remnants of a society that debases and diminishes our souls. The light in our eyes, it's a sacred flame, a spiritual energy that drives us to create, to laugh, to love.

"To *love*. That's our difference. We love. We love our family. Our children. Our selves. That is our gift to our fellow man. Love.

"That is why it is our duty to not only destroy the walking shells to put their souls truly at rest, but to fight for *ours*."

His sermon took a different tone.

"Outside this city lies an army that feels obliged to liberate our fair and secure city. To save us from a threat we've already contained. I haven't looked into their eyes, but they must be as cold as the blue they wear to assert themselves on this fine city.

"My brothers and sisters, I beseech you: Make right with the Lord. There is no better time than now. Make right with the Lord.

"In closing, I tell you this..."

He paused.

"When they look into my eyes, they will know my soul. They will see it, feel it, as I defend myself and my flock with all my might. And if they cause my light to fade, I pray someone will secure my shell.

"God help me, I'm going to defend this town. Our town.

"Our eyes.

"Our souls."

Monsignor Ralph O'Leary returned to the altar and sat down, letting his comments sink in.

The rest of the mass moved along normally, though there was an underlying sense of impending doom in the air. Yet the love everyone was feeling was resonating from their hearts, embracing the congregation and somehow warming their souls.

* * * * *

Outside the church, Gary and Wayne chatted. No creatures had shown their faces.

"What do you think about that sermon?" Wayne asked.

Gary didn't respond. He knew the priest was right. He had seen it for himself in the eyes of his dying friends in Vietnam.

Then something familiar resounded in Gary's ears. It caught Wayne's attention, too, but was not so connected as it was with Gary. It was the sound of rotors, a series of them suggesting several helicopters flying in formation across the city. To Gary, it reminded him of the Huey's back in 'Nam. He traveled back to a particularly nasty dust-off in which he was only one of three that ended up making it out of the shit alive.

He was brought out of his dream by visions of white floating down out of the twilight sky. He was right about helicopters flying in formation over the city, and was finally able to identify the stream of white. It was pieces of paper being scattered over the entire town.

Some gently fell to the ground around the church.

Gary and Wayne picked one up, standing in a gentle wash of falling sheets.

It read: *Citizens of Beeville must leave the city and join the United Nations convoy to a FEMA camp. Anyone remaining in the city after sun-up will be considered terrorists and part of an insurgency. All terrorists and insurgents will be eliminated.*

Gary frowned. Wayne stood in frightened awe. The two friends looked at each other as the communion hymn played in the background. Though the recording was old and sung by a choir not quite ready for the Metropolitan Opera, the voices were soothing to the congregation, but ominous to Gary and Wayne. The moon was beginning to reveal itself, two days from waxing to full as the voices sang the lyrics:

"And I will raise you up...

"And I will raise you up...

"And I will raise you up on the last day."

Bowie V. Ibarra

From Night,
to Dawn,
to Day

As the congregation made their way from mass, it became very clear that Monsignor's sermon was very relevant indeed. Everyone got their own paper off the ground, and by the time most people left the church, cars were already beginning to work their way to the highway where the U.N. had set up shop.

Most everyone had made up their mind what they were going to do. Since McCann Street was one of the major inlets into town, a generous band of resistance established themselves along that road. There was no real contingency plan, apart from holding out in what most figured would be a futile attempt to defend their town. The mayor was stationed at City Hall with Sheriff McMurtry. Leaders among the resistance were given communication devices to receive orders from City Hall.

The mayor said that the first wave of defense would be the police barricades. Once forces could not hold the line, they would draw back to McCann Street and the two other streets that the other barricades fed into, Largent Lane and Janacek Street. Militia positioned on those streets would hold out for as long as they could before falling back into the already barricaded plaza of City Hall.

The city of Beeville was in chaos. Car and truck-loads of people were fleeing the city, anticipating the worst.

Alex cautiously crossed McCann Street to look for Red. He

knocked on the front door of Lucy St. Claire's house.

No answer.

"Red!" he called out, scanning the front yard for monsters.

He heard two people giggling, then the door opened. On the other side was Red, wearing a straw Stetson hat over his red curls and leather cowboy boots—and nothing else.

"Can I help you, partner?" Red said, trying to do his best John Wayne impression. He and Lucy broke out in hysterical laughter.

Alex cringed, then turned away, stating, "Red, dammit. I need to talk to you—in *private*."

"You need to talk to my privates?" asked Red. More laughter from the two sang in the chaotic midnight hours.

Upset, Alex stated, "Red, we're getting out of here."

"What?"

"Get your clothes on. We gotta get outta here."

A zombie shambled into the street among the chaos. Alex aimed his gun at it and shot it in the head.

"Man, you gotta give me at least an hour."

"Red, they could attack at any minute."

Lucy St. Claire came to the door in a schoolgirl outfit. White knee-highs and high heeled 'Mary Janes' complemented her short red plaid skirt and white top. She taunted, "Let me serve my lunch detention, then you can have him back."

She shut the door on Alex. Giggling could again be heard from behind the door, along with a rebel yell.

Alex could not help but feel frustrated at his friend. He began to seethe with anger, but then calmed down. If his buddy was not going to go, then Alex would find his way on his own.

Cars, people, and some zombies criss-crossed McCann Street as the city fled. Though the town had been secured to some extent, there were still enough creatures about and locked in houses to cause a problem in the rush to evacuate. People were getting bit, zombies were being set free from houses accidentally, and the confusion caused by the number of people running in the streets began to spread the infection once again.

Gunfire sounded at odd intervals. People fought over property. A fistfight was occurring between young thugs on the sidewalk. Militia men were setting up their defenses.

Alex moved through the chaos to Red's truck, took the keys from under the seat, and started the vehicle. He took a last look back at Lucy's house. A twinge of sadness tapped his heart and a tear formed in his eye. He wiped his eye and shifted the truck into gear.

* * * * *

"Mommy, can you bring my books?!" shouted Timmy from the attic.

"Yes, baby! Just stay up there!" Mary replied from the kitchen.

"It's real hot up here, mommy!"

"I know, Timmy. That's why we've got a lot of water up there!" She was preparing an ice chest of sandwich stuff to hold them over the assumed invasion. Somehow, she thought she might be able to hide out through the upcoming skirmishes.

"Can I come down, mommy?!"

Mary stopped for a minute and took a deep breath. She thought maybe she was just overreacting to her fear. No conflict was occurring yet. So she figured there was no harm now in letting him come down.

She called to her son, "You can come down, Timmy, and go take a bath!"

"Yay!" he cried, climbing down the stairs from the attic.

Mary smiled as he ran to the bathroom.

* * * * *

"I don't give two shits who they are. We're stayin'," said Audrey to Margie over a couple of beers at the Garner residence. "I've fought too hard to secure this city to have it all taken away." She was also upset that Billy Joe was still missing, but did not voice her sadness.

"We need to head over there and let them take care of us," Margie said.

"Oh yeah, they'll take care of us, all right," mocked Eric.

* * * * *

"You ready for this, man?" Gary asked.

"No," Wayne replied. "But I'm ready to stand by you." Holding up his can of 'The Beast', Wayne proposed a toast. "Here's to you, Gary. You've been my only friend. And as shitty as this situation is, I'm fighting with you to the very end."

191

With regret, Gary said, "Cheers."
They tapped cans.

* * * * *

With the city secured and the plan for resistance in place, Mayor Lance Hickland made one last ditch effort to patch things up with his wife. He gave himself an hour to try to get Evelyn to come to City Hall with him. Despite regretting the affair, he allowed Stephanie to come with him, since she had no one else. It was a bumpy situation indeed, as they drove through the now dissipating madness to his house.

They pulled into the driveway.

"Stay here," Lance told Stephanie, handing her a pistol.

He took a shotgun and walked to the house. Several zombies were close by, and Lance leveled them. Taking out his keys, he opened the door.

The house was almost pitch black. At first, the only illumination seemed to be the moonlight sifting through the boarded-up windows, creating criss-crossing beams of light at odd angles against the wall. Then Lance noticed a thin artificial light was illuminating an area at the top of the staircase. Taking a deep breath, he slowly crept up the stairs. He knew exactly what room the light was coming from, and the prospect did not appeal to him for an instinctual reason.

As he reached the top, his suspicions were confirmed. The light had been escaping the narrow space where the bathroom door was slightly ajar. He paused for several seconds, not wanting to push it open further. Girding up his loins, he approached the door, put his index finger against it, then slowly applied pressure.

The door swung open.

His worst fear was justified.

In the tub was his wife. Naked. Dead. Her arms were gruesomely cut. A kitchen knife was lying on the floor next to the tub. Blood soaked the tub and the white tile around it.

He started to whimper.

As he looked at the diced and split arms of his dead wife, a sad joke entered his mind. It was a picture posted in a prank e-mail he had received that went something to the effect of, '*Remember kids, it's down the road, not across the street. Do something right for*

192

once,' (referencing the recommended way to slice your arm if you were attempting suicide.)

Moving closer to the body, Lance noticed several large masses of flesh floating in the tub of red water. It drifted between his dead wife's legs. Suddenly, the identity of the fleshy masses connected in his mind, and Lance was horrified.

It was his child, floating in the water, still connected by the umbilical cord. The placenta was floating nearby.

Lance remembered his Science lessons—especially the lessons about the human body, because they made him realize just how amazing that organism is. He knew the brain would shut down everything to survive when the body is near death. It would even expel an infant child from its mother in an effort to conserve energy.

Not knowing how long the baby was in the water, Lance made a choice.

In a desperate attempt to save his child, he dropped his weapon and reached into the pool of blood and water and pulled the baby out. It lay limp in his arms, the umbilical cord stretching from the placenta to the baby's future navel.

Desperate, Lance lifted the cord to his mouth and bit into the organ. It never occurred to him that he might get infected. He just knew it had to be done. Gnawing at the fleshy cord, he tore it in two with his teeth. He then gagged and vomited, turning his face away to avoid spewing it on his baby.

He then looked down at the lifeless body. Helpless, tears welled up in his eyes and he held the newborn boy close. He began to cry hysterically.

Then, as if granted a miraculous wish, the baby began to choke and kick. Fluid flew from the baby's mouth and nose. Instinctually, Lance sat down on the toilet and held the baby by the stomach, patting it on the back. The fluid flew from the baby's mouth, and the baby's first attempt at bringing air to its lungs resounded with a loud cry.

Lance's eyes grew large and a smile of loving disbelief crossed his face. He immediately reached for a towel, wrapping his baby completely in the soft blue fabric. He giggled at the color and couldn't help but think how appropriate it was.

As the baby cried its first crying gasp for air, Evelyn suddenly shook from her suicidal rest, shaking in the water and grabbing at Lance.

Lance cried out in utter terror, matching the baby's cry. He jumped back against the sink as the ghoul slipped around in the slick tub.

The tub was right by the door. He knew he only had one chance.

As the creature found its footing, Lance soccer-kicked the beast in the jaw, knocking it back, giving him enough room to hit the door.

With the quickness of a father longing to secure his child, he dashed down the stairs, out the door, and back to the car.

As the baby continued to cry, Stephanie gazed at Lance and the baby, astounded.

"Well, what are you waiting for? We need milk," he said, sternly. "I know Abuelita's might still have some. Take us toward City Hall."

Stephanie climbed over into the driver's seat, put the vehicle in gear, and took off.

Lance held his baby son close, crying with the sadness of a father knowing his child will never know his mother, and with the shame of knowing that someday the child might learn why.

*   *   *   *   *

The warm old quilt comforted Dolores and Frank, who sat and contemplated the future in silence. Frank was leaning on a pillow, while Dolores rested her head on his chest.

"Don't ever leave me, Frank," Dolores whispered.

"I will never leave you, 'Lores," Frank whispered back. "I will hold you 'til the end."

Frank had had to make another choice. Though he knew he could—and maybe *should*—be fighting for the city, it would leave Dolores alone to fend for herself. She was not a violent person. Her gentle nature and kind compassion were some of the things that attracted him to her many years ago.

But he could not let her go. If he were to die, (which certainly was the highest probability,) Dolores would be alone in the harshest environment the world had ever known. He was not willing to do that.

"*I will hold you 'til the end, 'Lores,*" he whispered again, closing his eyes, savoring what he was quickly realizing might be their final moments together.

Two candles illuminated the living room by the votive hands as the husband and wife of nineteen years fell asleep together on the couch.

* * * * *

Alex drove back up the road to the ranch property he and Red had originally snuck in on. He turned up to the gated entrance, opened the gate, and went in.

He passed the barn where they picked up Miguel, then passed the house that shot at him earlier. There was no shooting this time around, though.

Nearing the gate and his anticipated freedom, he noticed a bright light in the distance that seemed to emanate from the road. Sure enough, as he got closer, he could see that the United Nations had set up shop on the road.

His escape route was cut off.

He also noticed something else: A large mass of people had gathered and given themselves over to the U.N. Though Alex could not recognize anyone, he assumed the people of Beeville who chose not to fight were turning themselves in for military protection.

"*I can't believe it,*" he whispered to himself.

Before he could be spotted, he put his vehicle in reverse, executed a quick U-turn, and drove back into town.

—His last hope.

* * * * *

"Pull over!" Lance shouted, desperate for the life of the baby in his arms.

"Where?" Stephanie asked, still rattled at the cries of the newborn.

"That convenience store! I want to get a bottle and milk!"

Stephanie agreed. Perhaps it would shut the child up, as the crying was shaking her unprepared nerves—and if that would calm Lance down, too, then that was all the better.

They parked at a convenience store that seemed to have been trashed by looters.

Stephanie asked, "You think its safe?"

"It's worth a look," he said, opening the car door. "I need some milk *right now.*"

Though she was upset, his take-control attitude was turning her on again. They exited the vehicle and entered the mom and pop convenience store through the cracked glass doors. For a moment, they listened for any movement that might signal a ghoul wandering in the stillness, but all they could hear was a Muzak version of Barry Manilow's *I Can't Smile Without You* gently gliding from the speakers in the ceiling.

Glass and trash littered the floor. Though the store was a mess, there still seemed to be lots of merchandise around. Lance stood in the doorway. Outside, two cars sped by in the night.

"I see a bottle," said Stephanie.

"Get it on the way out. Milk comes first."

Stephanie walked to the coolers. Walking along the glass doors, she looked down on the bottom of one of the doors that was labeled with the price of a gallon of milk: *$3.49.*

She bent over and reached down to look for one. There was one in the back of the rack. She reached in for it, but couldn't get a hold on it. She tried again. Her fingers tapped the handle, but not enough to grab it or maneuver it forward. Tapping it again, the gallon jug refused to slide forward, and she did not want to get on the floor to reach for it.

"I can't reach it," she said.

"There's a passage to the back over here," Lance said, indicating a small passage that also led to the restrooms. Stephanie followed where his finger was indicating until she saw the passage herself.

"Okay," she said, walking to the narrow hallway. She pulled the thick plastic drapes aside.

The zombie was hidden in the darkness of the cooler, and Stephanie walked right into it. It took no time to grab her shoulders and bite into her mouth with an icy kiss of death, tearing her lips off and ripping away part of her cheek. She screamed in terror as her feet slipped out from under her and she fell to her butt.

As she screamed she noticed the '*Wet Floor*' sign and the stick figure sliding around on the floor, trying to get to her. She scrambled backwards, but the zombie fell on top of her. It bit into her neck, spraying a jet of blood onto the wall.

Another splash of crimson bathed the yellow '*Wet Floor*' sign in red as Lance shot a hole in the monster's head. The beast collapsed on Stephanie. She continued screaming, blood pooling around her head.

Lance quickly entered the cooler. His baby was shivering in his arms. He saw the gallon milk jug stuck in the rack. He picked it up, then headed back out of the cooler.

Stephanie had pushed the monster off of her and was regurgitating on the floor.

"Where did you see the baby bottle?" Lance asked.

Whimpering in anguish on the ground, she pointed at the second lane. It was a final simple gesture for the man she loved.

Lance immediately saw the bottle that was already in his line of sight.

"Lance!" cried Stephanie, clutching her throat with her palm, her voice gurgling, "Help me!"

Lance walked over and gazed down at her. He raised his gun and let a bullet fly into her skull.

She was gone.

Lance dashed down the aisle and snatched a baby bottle from the rack. He then ran out of the store, threw open the car door, and jumped inside. He locked the doors and turned the engine on.

Opening the milk, he precisely poured the white liquid into the bottle. Not a drop was missed.

Four ounces.

Lance placed the nipple of the bottle in his baby's mouth. With the instinct of an infant, the child accepted the nipple, and serenity found its way into its heart.

And for the next few moments, with the engine humming alone in the parking lot of the Mini Mart, Lance gazed into the eyes of his child and felt the love that the world had lost.

No one else in the entire world was more important to Lance now than his baby child.

The Last Day

Father O'Leary had been praying the rosary along with his new ally, Miguel. Miguel was in the back of the church where the votive candles were. Kneeling below a statue of the Virgin Mary, he prayed for his family, his friends, and begged to be allowed into the Kingdom of Heaven. The dark corner of the church was illuminated by the many candles surrounding him in a red glow.

O'Leary stood near the altar praying under the large crucifix. Painted blood dripped from the hands and feet of Jesus.

Miguel looked up at *La Virgen*. Tears had formed in her eyes. Surprised, he stumbled out of the cubicle in amazement and awe. He immediately began to recite a Hail Mary in Spanish.

As O'Leary looked upon the face of Jesus, blood began to drip from the eyes of the statue. In amazed reverence, he stood up. His hands felt moist. Looking at his hands, blood dressed the crystal rosary in red, the stigmata large and juicy.

When he looked up again, the blood was gone from the eyes of the Jesus statue. Looking at his hands, that blood had also vanished.

Looking back at the statue, the mouth of Jesus began to open. From the mouth sprung a swarm of locusts. As O'Leary looked closer, they were not just any locusts—they had the tail of a scorpion.

...Locusts came out of the smoke onto the land, and they were given the same power as scorpions of the earth.

The swarm began to envelop the church.

...During that time these people will seek death but will not find it...

The swarm attacked O'Leary, striking him with their stingers. He screamed.

Then an explosion rocked the church—*a real explosion*—shaking the sacred sanctuary to its very foundation. The stained glass windows to his left cracked and splintered. The cross of Jesus shifted violently, then flipped upside down.

O'Leary flailed about, collapsing over the first set of pews. He looked at his body.

The locusts were gone.

The devil's illusion had disappeared.

The omen was not received well. O'Leary made the sign of the cross. Mentally and spiritually prepared to smite the evil that had descended upon his town, he picked up his shotgun, grabbed a weapon for Miguel, and walked to the back of the church where Miguel was praying. He put his rosary around his neck.

Entering the back of the church, O'Leary lifted Miguel off the floor. The statue of the Virgin of Guadalupe had fallen and was smashed on the floor by the candles. Anger rose in O'Leary's heart, knowing that the Prince of Darkness was visiting his holy temple and fair city.

"*Levantate, Miguel, y vamanos,*" he said, handing Miguel the weapon. Wiping his tears, he exited the church and positioned himself behind a car, waiting to face the minions of Satan.

*   *   *   *   *

A small frontline column consisting of two armored personnel carriers began their assault on the three roadblocks. The roadblocks were populated by local militia working alongside the police. Two police blockades were leveled within minutes. The police and militia could not compete with the rocket-propelled grenade launchers the U.N. was battering their positions with. One police car with two occupants, seeing their predicament, fell back to Largent Lane.

Largent Lane was ill-prepared, with a majority of the militia men drunk despite the imminent assault.

The other blockade held fast to their position, with police and militia snipers countering the RPG attacks. But the U.N. matched the snipers with several of their own. After transitioning between two police leaders and seven dead (who rose and attacked four other people, who then had to be put down), the guerillas retreated into the woods where they repositioned themselves. The armored column advanced to Janacek Street.

The final Beeville police position was the one that was to fall back to McCann Street.

Utilizing what was reported as the best mode of defense, the defenders of Beeville positioned snipers composed of militia men and professional police snipers. The men held off the U.N.

When the U.N. soldiers went into defense mode and retreated to their two massive personnel carriers, a small contingent of militiamen charged the U.N. line, tossing Molatov cocktails at the narrow openings of the armored vehicles. Some men were able to run up to a vehicle, open the hatch, and fire into it with automatic weapons, ripping the occupants to shreds. When one defender tossed a Molotov cocktail into the vehicle, he was taken down by soldiers shooting from within the adjacent armored personnel carrier, but the damage was done. A soldier appeared from the hatch, his entire body on fire.

With the Beeville militia and police gaining a tactical—*and lucky*—advantage, the U.N. personnel carrier fired up its engine and moved in reverse. The audacious militiamen opened fire on the vehicle, tossing more cocktails at the rolling heap. One man was hit in the leg by a bullet that ricocheted off the metal. The steel behemoth then revved its engine and shifted gears, advancing forward in a desperate attempt to break the line of the militiamen.

Busting the orange and white barricades like toothpicks, the large metal vehicle rammed the two police cars lined up facing each other on the road, breaking the line of the militia. Another armored carrier pulled up beside the one on fire. Eight soldiers exited the new vehicle, all preparing a rocket launcher attack. The soldiers targeted the positions in the woods beside the road where they suspected militia snipers were basing their attacks. Once they fired several rockets into the woods, another small squad of soldiers exited the vehicle and took up tactical positions. At the same time, the other armored carrier opened the back hatch and the remnants of the squad exited and positioned themselves to return fire.

The Beeville militiamen were surrounded.

In a desperate attempt to escape, the militiamen opened fire, fighting a pointless battle on two fronts. The brave men and women of Beeville were being mowed down by the blue demons. No quarters were asked for, and none was given.

Deputies Armstrong and Ferguson made a mad dash to their cruiser, threw open the doors, and climbed inside. Armstrong started the vehicle and put it in gear, charging the metal monster in the middle of the road. He knew he had to warn the people at the next line on McCann Street. A rocket-propelled grenade flew to the charging vehicle, but Armstrong weaved just in time to send the missile smashing into the SWAT van, exploding the simple transport. Gunfire riddled the police vehicle, cracking and penetrating the windshield and catching Ferguson in the chest, mouth, and shoulder. Armstrong clipped a soldier before breaking their line and charging down the road back to the city about five miles away.

He felt a warm trickle down his neck, then reached for his ear. A large portion of his right ear had been removed, dripping blood and cartilage onto his neck and shoulder. He took a handkerchief from his back pocket and placed it on his ear to try to stop the bleeding.

Armstrong looked over at Ferguson in the seat beside him. He was dead. Armstrong knew he needed to get his body out of the car before it reanimated. Scared that the U.N. would be in pursuit, he quickly pulled over so he could push the body out and neutralize it.

Just after the car came to a complete stop, the body in the passenger seat rose up and snarled. Armstrong hadn't even had time to remove his seat belt. The zombie lunged at him. He tried to fight off the beast by pushing at its chin, but the creature bit into his fingers, removing several digits. Armstrong screamed in pain.

Making a cruel decision, he allowed his right hand to remain vulnerable to more bites as he used his left hand to awkwardly unlock his seat belt and draw the gun from its holster on his right hip. The monster bit again, removing another portion of his hand, exposing bone and tearing cartilage from the appendage. Blood splattered all over the interior of the cruiser.

Finally grabbing his gun, he placed the barrel point-blank against Ferguson's throat and pulled the trigger.

The blast disintegrated the zombie's neck, removing the head from the body. Yet the head fervently continued biting into Armstrong's hand. Armstrong swung the head against his cracked passenger side window. Three swings later, the window was busted. He flicked his arm in pain several times, using the natural forces of momentum to fling the head off what remained of his now lame hand out of the car and onto the street.

The head continued to munch on the flesh in its mouth, mocking Armstrong in the middle of the road. Small portions of devoured flesh exited out the bottom of the head from the esophagus, dripping out onto the gray asphalt in a great gooey glob.

In a spite-filled rage, Armstrong leaned out the door and unloaded his weapon on the zombie's head. Hot lead ripped the head to pieces, leaving the remains scattered on the road like a watermelon that had fallen off the back of a moving truck and busted open on the highway.

In horror, Armstrong realized that the headless body was still laying across his leg and pumping out its blood onto his uniform. In immense pain, he found it in himself to step out of the vehicle, run to the other side, and with his good hand attempt to pull the body out of the vehicle.

As he was heaving the body out of the vehicle, he lost his balance and fell to the asphalt, the headless body coming next. Blood pumped from the neck onto Armstrong's face and into his mouth. He immediately vomited in utter disgust, almost choking on his own bile as he struggled to get the body off of him.

Armstrong stood up and watched the body writhe in its death throes. Blood dripped down his neck and laced his face in a veil of blood. He pulled off his bloody shirt and tried to wipe away the blood to no avail. He threw up again, feeling a fever rising in his body.

He had to do one last thing: He had to warn the remaining people in Beeville of the approaching blue hordes.

Armstrong began to feel his muscles stiffen. He was slowly becoming dizzy. Beeville was still a five minute drive up ahead, and five more to get to McCann Street.

He entered his vehicle, awkwardly swapping magazines for his pistol before starting toward the city.

He chose not to wrap what remained of his right hand.

* * * * *

The operations started at around six in the morning, and all the blockades had fallen three hours later. The U.N. peacekeepers then began to assemble and form their own blockade. They would launch their assault at around noon. Most people in town assumed that the blockades had fallen after reports from City Hall filtered in.

"Pile that shit up!" Audrey yelled. "Put all that shit in the road!"

McCann Street had decided they were going to pile large furniture pieces on the road to prevent penetration into the city, and they spent a large part of the morning doing it. Though there were other avenues around McCann Street, the residents and a large contingent of militia men and women decided to make a stand there. Couches, recliners, mattresses, dressers, entertainment centers—anything that might prevent vehicles from passing, at least temporarily, were set out in the street. Eric was even cutting down trees with a chainsaw to create more obstacles in the road.

"We should blow up the truck," Wayne said, pointing to the truck still flipped over on the road.

"That's just in the movies," Gary told him.

That was when Armstrong's cruiser came around the corner. It plowed into a dresser, shattering it into pieces before crashing into the first house on the corner.

"Holy shit!" Audrey yelled.

Armstrong exited the vehicle. Dried blood was flaking on parts of his arm and neck. He was stumbling, his face sunken. He held a gun in his hand.

"They're coming!" he yelled. "They've got tanks! Stop them!"

"What's wrong with him?" Benny asked.

"*He's infected,*" Margie uttered.

In a surprise move, Armstrong put the gun to his head and pulled at the trigger.

No response. He hadn't released the slide after reloading.

Eric yelled, "Oh, shit—*Stop him!*"

But it was too late. Armstrong pulled the trigger again, this time removing a portion of his head. He fell to the ground.

"We knew that already," Audrey whispered. "What a douchebag."

* * * * *

By noon, the assault on Beeville proper began. Securing streets, squads worked door to door. They blasted zombies holed up in houses, and arrested people who were still holding out in their residences but not fighting. They disarmed them and zip-tied their hands behind their backs, then sat them outside their homes so they could be collected later.

Eventually, the squads arrived at McCann Street.

"*This is it*," Gary said to Wayne, positioned up the road.

Two armored personnel carriers pulled up to the street. A small gang of militiamen near the mouth of the street charged one of the carriers and pelted the vehicle with Molotov cocktails before being mowed down by automatic gunfire. One vehicle was set ablaze on the inside, setting fire to the uniforms of the soldiers within.

But one personnel carrier was able to park unscathed. The back hatch opened and a squad of soldiers exited and positioned themselves on both sides of the street. A firefight broke out between the two factions, and the militiamen were taking the brunt of the losses.

Then two more carriers pulled up, and more troops were unleashed. By this point, the fighters on McCann Street were being attacked on three sides, the U.N. having made their way to the other end of the street through the inadequately-secured back alleys to surround the guerillas.

Red ran into Lucy's house. "Lucy, we've gotta run!" he yelled. "We can't hold them much longer!"

"I'm *staying*," she said, adamantly. She was holding a short and pointed dagger in her hand.

"Are you *crazy*?"

"It's death either way. Let me do it my way, okay?"

"Please," begged Red.

"Would you get the fuck out of here?!" she yelled at him. "Go!"

Men in blue had already taken control of the street two houses down from Lucy's, and their stray bullets were splintering her front door.

Taking one last look at his lover, Red threw the door open and dashed outside.

A bullet clipped his thigh and he collapsed on the ground,

clutching the wound. Another shot took a piece out of his ribs, barely sparing a lung.

He was finding it hard to breathe. He tried to fire his machine gun, but the pain of his wounds prevented accurate aiming.

A line of dirt danced toward him as a machine gun open fire on him. It would have danced up his chest had Alex not grabbed him and dragged him to the side of Lucy's house.

Red groaned, painfully, "*Alex...*"

"What's up, Red?" Alex said, peering around the side of the house. "What do we do now?"

"You stay here, I'm getting your truck."

Finding a moment, Alex hobbled to the truck that was parked two houses up the street away from the soldiers. Bullets buzzed by his head. He reached the truck, started it up, and drove to Lucy's house as all around him milita men and women scrambled for position, retreating to the Beeville plaza.

Alex pulled up into the yard. He then saw Red in the midst of defending himself against a zombie, kicking away at the ghoul from his back. Alex rammed the beast with his vehicle. Red pulled himself up and entered from the passenger's side.

"Let's get out of here," said Red.

The elderly blue truck plowed through the wooden fence to Lucy's backyard and out the other end, running over two surprised U.N. troops, and motored up the alley.

Red grabbed a handkerchief from the glove compartment and wrapped his hand. He then gazed over at Alex, ashamed.

He had been bitten.

As the U.N. advanced forward into McCann Street, a small squad positioned themselves behind the upside-down truck. A militia man tossed a Molotov cocktail at the vehicle's exposed undercarriage and it burst into flames as it collided with the truck. The undercarriage caught fire and the vehicle exploded two seconds later, setting the troops on fire and scrambling in different directions.

"Well, shit. I guess it *could* blow," said Audrey as she and Eric retreated to the plaza.

The new friends all gathered away from the U.N. and headed toward City Hall.

* * * * *

Lucy St. Claire looked out her window and watched as small waves of blue were overtaking McCann Street. George Strait's *I Get Carried Away* began playing on the stereo, the fourth song on her custom mix-tape. An explosion resounded and she heard gunfire directly outside her window.

Slowly, and with dagger in hand, she crept back to the kitchen. She looked at the table, remembering how she seduced Billy Joe Garner there. She winced and took the small battery-powered radio off the windowsill and slowly walked to the back room.

But her own bedroom offered no solace. She looked with guilt at the bed where she had chipped away at Billy Joe's innocence. Maybe her father had been right. Maybe she was nothing but a filthy whore.

Sunlight drifted through several cracks in the boarded-up window as she began to cry, sliding down the wall of her room, the stereo continuing its song of love.

She stared at the dagger.

* * * * *

Frank and Dolores Garza held each other tight on the couch. The gunfire and explosions had scared them throughout the morning and afternoon. They had only ever left each others' arms long enough to take a quick drink of water.

The television news was painting a horrible picture of their town. The light from the television illuminated their sad embrace.

"*...Our top story today: Insurgents have captured the small south Texas town of Beeville, Texas. Twenty-three U.N. soldiers have been killed by the terrorists who attacked the U.N. contingent early this morning. Kent Mareou has more...*"

They knew the world had no idea of the truth of their situation. They held each other even tighter, but as the knock came at the door, they knew it was almost over.

"I'll never leave you, Dolores," Frank whispered.

"I love you, Frank," Dolores replied.

When the boot kicked open the door, they flinched, but offered no resistance as a small stream of blue men entered the house, yelling at them. With the metal barrels of the machine guns pointed at them, ready to fire, Frank gave Dolores a kiss.

* * * * *

Lucy flinched when her front door was kicked open. She could hear the soldiers stomping into her house. She sat beside the door, quivering, knowing that she was about to pay for her sins. She prepared herself, hiding behind the door, gripping the knife tightly in her hands, raising it above her head. She figured there was no sense attacking the heart, as they were probably wearing flakjackets.

Then she had a cruel idea.

Willie Nelson's *Angel Flying Too Close To The Ground* began. The familiar resonance of Willie's sacred guitar and his nasal delivery attracted the soldiers to the closed door of Lucy's room. She heard them gather outside in the hallway. Her body was shaking in fearful anticipation.

Then the room was booted open. Momentarily, she stood face-to-face with a machine gun barrel, but another soldier began his entrance into the room.

Without hesitation, Lucy stabbed the first soldier in the groin, piercing his blue suit. The man screamed. Blood began to stain the blue uniform at the crotch as the soldier dropped his gun and grabbed at his privates.

Lucy was a woman possessed. Her eyes seemed to be red; her screams were unearthly. She was purging her demons. Looking at the face of the soldier, all she could see was the face of her father.

Lucy penetrated the body of the man four more times in rapid succession with the might of a grim reaper, stabbing the soldier's leg twice, arm, then neck, before being mowed down by machine gun fire from the soldier's comrades.

For a moment, it was as if she was going to stand up, absorbing every metal blast that was peppering her luscious body. But it was not to be. As she was rising, the blasts busted her skull open, knocking parts of her brown hair into the air and busting an eye into goo, splashing on the wall like the blood that was flying from her body. More bullets pierced her arms, breasts, stomach, legs, and neck as she was flung onto her bed by the force of the assault. Portions of her brain dripped on her pillow. Her right leg was twisted in an awkward position, the bone shattered and the muscle contorted. Her jaw shook loose from her head and fell onto the bed. Her tongue hung out from where her jaw used to be. The piercing was still in.

Blood began to stain the comforter at odd portions where the bullets had penetrated. Her white top stained with blood, plaid skirt torn from gunfire, and knee highs now made Lucy look more like a murder victim than sexy Catholic schoolgirl.

Her sins were punished, but her tormented soul was now free from the material world.

* * * * *

Gunfire could be heard outside, muffled by the insulation of Mary Moore's house. Danger was at her doorstep. She held Timmy close.

But Timmy suddenly kicked loose. "My turtle!" he cried out, freeing himself from his mother's arms and opening the attic door.

Mary wanted to yell, but was afraid to attract attention. It was too late, at any rate. Timmy was flying down the attic ladder.

He could hear the voices outside his house and felt a small group of people approaching the front door as he dashed to his room. Foreign voices made demands as he grabbed his turtle, put it in his pocket, and headed back to the attic. Fear coursed through is veins.

He dashed up the attic ladder, then slammed the door shut. Mary knew the sound could be heard as her front door was being kicked repeatedly. She could hear the door splintering, but holding. Her plan to hide was probably foiled by her loving son.

Mary held Timmy tight in the attic as the U.N. forces kicked open the door to her house with a second attack. Somehow, Mary knew they would be found.

"Timmy," she whispered desperately, "I want you to go stand by that vent over there." She indicated the vent that exited out the backyard.

"No, mommy, *please.*"

"Timmy, you stop crying and listen to me. If they come up here, you pop that vent open and you run to City Hall and find Aunt Margie, you hear me?

"No, mommy. Don't leave me."

"If you love me, Timmy, you'd better do it. Your dad would be so proud of you."

Timmy began to whimper. Mary urged him to be quiet.

The U.N. soldiers entered her garage and noticed the boxes and other storage items upset under the attic door. They yelled at her in a foreign accent, urging her to come down.

"Timmy, I need you to go now."

"No, mommy, please."

Mary gave her son a big hug. Timmy didn't want to let go of the embrace.

Then the attic door swung open and the ladder was pulled down.

"*Go, now*," she said.

Crying, Timmy obeyed his mother. He had to be Blue Panther again.

The men yelled at his mother to come down as he made it to the vent. His mother began her descent as Timmy pushed open the grate. Men in blue were lining the alleyways. Scared, Timmy made his way along the roofline. Noticing he hadn't drawn any attention, he jumped for his swingset that was close to the roof. With youthful agility, he hit the cross bar across the top of the swingset, then grabbed for one of the swing chains. He found one, but was not able to hold the chain. He fell clumsily, being flipped on his head by the rubber swing seat. His head met the ground, drawing blood on a rock. Though the wound was not so bad, it scared him.

He wanted his mommy.

But he had to find the courage of Blue Panther again. It did not take long for him to recover and stealthily work his way out of the backyard, hiding behind trash cans and bushes and doing what his mother had told him. Having spent much of his childhood bounding across the neighbor's fences and sneaking around the neighborhood, it was not long before Timmy was on his way out of danger and toward City Hall.

Meanwhile, inside, his mother was being forcefully dragged down out of the attic. Two men were holding her at gunpoint while the others were securing the house.

One man made a comment in an accent Mary could not place. "She is very pretty, no?"

"In America, we call her a *milf*," another man replied, giving his international guest a taste of the seedy side of America.

As the other three soldiers came in, Mary knew that things were about to get worse before they were ever going to get better again. As the men shared their comments about Mary, and knowing that she was alone in the house, she realized she was going to be raped.

She cried as they dragged her into the bedroom. The soldiers kicked over children's toys and crushed Timmy's *Finding Nemo* video on the floor as they threw his mother onto the bed.

* * * * *

Gary Chapman and Wayne Crocker were headed to City Hall when they were blindsided by a large truck that totalled the passenger side of the vehicle. They tumbled around in the front seat, rattled but uninjured.

"What the fuck?" Wayne said.

Gary looked out the window and saw people exiting the other vehicle. Two large rednecks, unshaven and with dirty long hair, were standing outside, toting M-16s.

"Get down!" Gary yelled.

The rednecks started firing on the Suburban.

Wayne ducked and covered his head. Bullets danced around the interior as Gary forced open the driver's side door and he and Wayne scrambled out.

Both men armed themselves with pistols that they had tucked away in their clothing. Gary immediately fell to his belly, looking under the truck. He saw four large feet, and fired on one pair. The bullet split the leg at the ankle, shattering the bone and sending the fat man to the ground. The man fired at Gary, but only hit the back wheel. Gary sent off three more shots that ripped through the man's body and head.

Wayne had jumped out in front of the Suburban, firing wild shots at his assailant, who was firing back. One bullet caught the man in the gut as Wayne emptied his weapon. Getting to his feet, he dashed to the rear of the redneck's truck, who was firing wildly back at Wayne. The redneck did not expect Gary to rise and take out a portion of his head.

"Gary, was that you?!" Wayne yelled from behind the truck.

"It's clear, Wayne!" Gary yelled back.

Wayne stood up. "Jesus Christ. What the hell was that?"

"*Payback*," Gary said.

The U.N. army was still approaching, and the men were forced to advance to City Hall on foot.

* * * * *

Timmy dashed to a car and hid behind it. He had not seen any soldiers since clearing the old neighborhood, but he knew they were close. Gunfire and explosions resounded in the air around him. He started to whimper, scared and wondering if he would ever see his mother again.

He pulled his pet turtle from his pocket.

Nearby was a bridge where a small artificial stream ran. Timmy began to cry, as he wanted to keep his little friend, yet somehow realizing that if something were to happen to him there would be no one to take care of the turtle. He remembered his mother telling him that turtles could survive in the wild, but needed to be near water. This would be the perfect opportunity for his little friend.

Looking around for danger, he felt it was clear. He ran into the concrete waterway.

"*Goodbye my friend,*" he said, kissing the turtle on the shell. He placed it near the stream.

Still hiding in its shell, it took a moment for the reptile to poke its head out. Finally, it did. Taking in the environment cautiously, it extended its legs, dashed into the water, and floated off in the stream.

A bullet hit a piece of concrete on the bridge above Timmy's head, knocking a chunk out of the barrier. Frightened, he jumped across the small stream to the other side.

Climbing the concrete wall, Timmy saw City Hall just ahead.

The Siege of City Hall

As the first two lines of defense fell, the remaining citizens of Beeville gathered at the plaza around City Hall. Civilian snipers set up around buildings, positioned around all of the streets that entered into the plaza. The citizens spent the remainder of the day fortifying the plaza as the U.N. secured sections of the city. They figured out the strategy of the citizens easily, and were coordinating.

Mayor Lance Hickland stood in his office holding his infant son. He asked, "What's the situation?"

"They've got us surrounded," Sheriff McMurtry told him, realizing his tactical error. He had made no plan, even after being warned by Alex. Instead, he kept the original plan of gathering at City Hall. "Things are not going to be good."

"I know it," Lance said, gently rocking his napping baby in his arms.

"You should probably get to the shelter. They're going to attack," McMurtry suggested, thinking about the father and his newborn child, and at the same time remembering and missing his own son.

Lance stood silent for a moment. "What about the people?"

"If they're found, they're *dead*. They'd bomb the shelter. Maybe *you* might be spared, you know?"

Lance stood silent.

*   *   *   *   *

Early the next morning, the U.N. offensive began.

Rocket attacks penetrated the defenses of the militiamen. Stealth teams were brought in that penetrated the buildings and immobilized the militia sniper positions. Armored columns made up of armored personnel carriers were bringing more troops to the area, leveling the brave Beeville militia into nothing. Before long, the U.N. was on their way to securing the area around City Hall.

"This might be a good time for you and the baby to get in the shelter," McMurtry suggested to the mayor in his office. "I can take it from here."

Lance hugged his friend, picked up a pistol, and left the room with his baby child. Only about half of the gallon of milk remained. It was very warm at this point, having been out for quite a while.

Lance dashed through the chaotic war zone outside of City Hall. With everyone scrambling for position or dying under the heavy gunfire, Lance was ignored as he unlocked the metal door stuck flat in the ground. He heaved open the door, revealing spider-webbed stairs and small bugs running away from the sunlight. He quickly entered despite the insect infestation and slammed the door shut behind him.

In the darkness, he secured the iron bolt lock. He flicked a switch that illuminated lights along the stairs. Bugs danced on his hands and webs tickled his face. Gunfire and screams could be heard above ground.

He descended the stairway into a small room. A light switch was illuminated, triggered by the door opening. He flipped the switch. Two light bulbs were burnt out, but two were still working. They lit up the small dusty room, revealing a shelf with old canned goods, five small cots, and sealed jugs of distilled water. They would have been appealing if they weren't so old.

As the gunfire, screams, and explosions continued above ground, Lance dusted off a place to sit on one of the cots. He pulled his infant son's bottle from his pants pocket and began to feed the child, who was ready to receive the nipple, even though his eyes were resting in sleep.

* * * * *

It was a wholesale slaughter on the plaza. The steel barriers had all been struck down within minutes by precise rocket attacks, then penetrated by the armored vehicles before the soldiers began to set up positions around City Hall, picking off militia men at their leisure with little resistance.

Benny Reyes held his wife Lupe close as bullets flew around his head. She had been shot three times, and had passed away in his arms. He raised his gun to shoot her in the head when several bullets punched holes through his own neck and chest. He fell to the ground beside his wife.

Gary Chapman and Wayne Crocker used as much cover as they could to get to the steps of City Hall. Following Gary's lead, Wayne had helped cause some casualties for the men in blue.

Alex Rich brought his friend Red LaRue to City Hall. He was looking quite bad. His shirt was caked in blood and his skin was turning pale. It had been halfway to City Hall that they realized the wound was worse than they originally thought.

Margie Montemayor was falling back when someone caught her eye. It was little Timmy Moore, running with abandon through the barriers and into the plaza. They both ran over the dead bodies of the citizens of Beeville to join her daughter Gina at City Hall.
"Timmy, where's your mommy?" Margie asked as they entered the building.
"She's still at home. The men got her."
Margie shook her head. A tear formed in her eye for her friend.

Eric and Audrey Garner were effectively holding off the blue soldiers at their position, but the fall of the other barriers forced their hand. They tried to re-secure the other areas to no avail. Before they knew it, their original position was breached and they fell back to City Hall, but not before Eric was shot in the shoulder. He cried out in pain and fell to the ground.
His loving wife picked him up. "C'mon, Eric. Don't be a pussy," she said with a smile. "You're coming with me."

* * * * *

As Monsignor O'Leary and Miguel DeLaMontana were falling back to City Hall, O'Leary felt like he had been here before. He experienced a bit of *déjà vu* as they entered the building.

Deputy Anderson, wounded but still fighting, scanned the plaza around City Hall. He had covered his wound, but it was festering. People he knew, people he had put in jail, and people who were his close friends were all scattered around on the ground. He knew then that he was the last.

Armstrong, Ferguson, Tomasi—all gone.

Anderson knew *his* number was almost up, too.

He entered City Hall.

Captain Phillip Carson, U.N. Peacekeeping Mission Leader, sat in a requisitioned home on McCann Street, several blocks away from the battle at City Hall, sipping a cup of coffee. A map of the city was spread out on a table in front of him.

A soldier approached the table. He handed Carson a radio and said, "Message from the front line, sir."

Carson smiled as he listened to the message. His smile grew as he replied to the message, "All resistance overcome?" A reply confirmed the question, but stating some people were holing up in City Hall.

"Good. Refortify the blockades. We'll let them deal with their dead friends while we secure more of the town. Let them spend more ammunition. We will take them down later on tonight." The man on the other end voiced his approval. Carson handed the radio to the soldier.

"These Texans are all the same," he said, smirking. "Always thinking small buildings will protect them from invading armies."

Frank and Dolores Garza were entered into a database, given an ID card, then sent outside the blue tent toward several military transports. Both had been frightened out of their wits since their capture. Dolores whimpered, but Frank was there to hold her throughout. Now they were on their way to a FEMA center.

Someone yelled at Frank in a foreign accent and yanked him

away from Dolores. Frank looked at the man, who was indicating a line he needed to go to. It was filled with men.

Immediately, Frank knew they were going to separate him from his wife. He was not about to break his promise.

Pushing the soldier away, he ran to Dolores and held her in a tight embrace.

"What did I tell you?" asked Frank.

"That you'll never let me go," she quickly replied.

Two soldiers tried to separate them to no avail. Frank and Dolores had their arms tightly wrapped around each other and their heads on each other's shoulders. One soldier cut at Frank's hand with a knife. Frank cried out, but it was not enough to make him let go.

The soldiers stepped away from the husband and wife and raised their weapons, yelling at the two Americans in a foreign tongue.

Frank and Dolores began to weep.

"I love you, Dolores," he said.

"I love you, Frank," she replied.

The loud foreign voices yelled more in their native language.

Frank and Dolores kissed a long final kiss as the soldiers opened fire on them, bringing the husband and wife to the ground, dead.

A soldier then walked up to them and put a bullet in both of their heads.

Bowie V. Ibarra

Twilight

The afternoon was spent shooting zombies as they rose in the plaza. Once the surviving militants were secured in City Hall, it was only ten minutes later that the dead militia men and women in the plaza started to rise. Anticipating the problem, Sheriff McMurtry and several others went to the roof and began shooting the creatures in the heads. Gary and Wayne were brave enough to stand outside the building and take some down as they got closer. Before long, Gary and McMurtry both realized why the soldiers were allowing the second wave of carnage to occur.

—It forced the militia to expend their ammunition.

After about thirty minutes the second wave was neutralized, posing only a small threat to the well armed but confined militia.

Gary and Wayne walked back into the building. Like the rest of the survivors, their ammunition was seriously limited.

Sheriff McMurtry came down from the roof hatch, exiting on the third floor. He called an informal meeting in the mayor's office. Red, Eric, and Anderson were being treated on the floor of the office. McMurtry waited for the group to make it in and gave one last glance at his cell phone before beginning the meeting. He set the phone down on the desk. A television had been moved into the room, but was switched on mute as the sheriff began his speech.

"Ladies and gentlemen. It's hard to bullshit any of ya'll now, but things don't look good for us. Our original plan to use the plaza and City Hall was in regards to infection, not for an encroaching army. But all that aside, we're here now, and it looks like they might let us out alive—alive so we can join a FEMA center and wait until who knows when. But before I get into anything else, I want to apologize to someone. Alex Rich tried to warn me of this impending invasion, and I ignored him, telling my charges to utilize the same plan we've had in place from the beginning. I hope Alex will forgive me for thinking he was a liar, and I pray that ya'll will forgive me for letting you down."

"*Asshole,*" Audrey mumbled, lighting a smoke for Eric, who was nursing his wound on the floor. Margie bowed her head in disappointment, holding Timmy tight.

"I forgive you, Sheriff," spoke up Alex, letting bygones be bygones. He added, with dignity, "And I will not leave you or your people here today."

"Where's Mayor Hickland?" Wayne asked.

"The mayor has chosen to travel outside of City Hall in an effort to protect his child." A gasp came across the room, mostly by the women. McMurtry explained, "For those of you that didn't know, Evelyn was pregnant with their first child and delivered her baby after mass. I don't think the details are necessary, but Lance was given charge to his child."

Gentle mumbling and discussion ensued.

"All that aside now," McMurtry went on, "We need to know how much ammunition we have left. We also need to know who is going to stay. Make no mistake: They've come this far and done this much; I don't think they're going to let us get away with holing up in here for very long."

"Hey!" Wayne exclaimed. "Turn up the television! They're talking about our town!"

As the mute was taken off of the television, CNC news night anchor Marie Watters' voice reported.

"*...In Beeville, Texas, U.N. forces have met with fierce resistance. Vince Haile has more.*"

Footage of U.N. soldiers in Beeville played across the screen.

"Hey, that's Benny's house," Wayne said.

"*Shhhhhh,*" came the collective reply.

"Insurgents have held the little south Texas town of Beeville in a stranglehold, preventing United Nations peacekeeping forces from securing the town and its citizens. Close to forty U.N. casualties have been reported."

"Oh, poor fuckin' U.N.! They've wiped out at least two hundred of our people!" Audrey screamed, throwing a well-manicured and red-painted middle finger at the television.

Nobody bothered to tell her to be quiet.

Captain Phillip Carson's face came up on the screen.

"The insurgents are well armed and fierce. Sources have said that the leaders might be part of an Arab terrorist cell that went rogue when the outbreak occurred, but at this time, we can't know for certain."

"What a load of shit!" Gary shouted.

"Live with it, ya'll. We're terrorists now," Alex said with an *I-told-you-so* tone.

Red slowly lifted a middle finger at the televison before coughing up blood. Alex wiped the mouth.

"...The U.N. also found a stack of dead human bodies, murdered execution-style by the insurgents and burned."

McMurtry knew exactly what she was talking about and realized their own efforts to secure the city were being thrown right back in their faces.

He said, "Turn that damn thing off."

The report took the wind out of the sails of the survivors. Labeled as terrorists and insurgents to the world, a final battle was inevitable.

The sheriff took the reins back. "How much ammunition do we have?"

Everyone volunteered what ammunition they had remaining. No one had more than two full loads for their weapons. Some had less.

"*Shit,*" Gary mumbled, realizing the proverbial corner they were in. He put his hand in his pocket, pulling out the set of dice he found several days before. He threw them on the floor against the wall. Boxcars.

Margie held Timmy close. She soothingly whispered in his ear, "Timmy, you're a brave boy to come this far. I need you to do me a favor." Fear and dried tears colored the face of the child. "You need to find a good place to hide in here, okay? Can you do that?" The boy nodded in approval. "All right, go find it and then come tell me where it is." As the boy ran off, she added, "Make sure it's good!"

"Mom," said Gina, moving toward her mother. "Are we going to get out of here?"

"I don't know, baby. I don't know," her mom replied, holding her own daughter for the first time in years.

* * * * *

"Sir," said a soldier walking up to Carson's tent, "The assigned portions of the city have been secured. Soldiers are awaiting your orders."

Carson had been considering his options. An air strike would be too expensive and unnecessary. Rocket attacks would level the building. He wanted to preserve the structure and use it as his base of operations in Beeville. Since special units of the United States military were on hand, he arrogantly made his decision.

"Set up all personnel to mobilize for travel down the road to the next city. They need to depart at twenty-two hundred hours. I need the special unit sent by the U.S. military to stay along with Beta group. I will give the people in City Hall one last chance to surrender. If they don't, Beta group will engage in an operation to exterminate the insurgents and secure the building. Either way, by nightfall, we will sleep in there."

"Yes, sir."

* * * * *

"Eric, gimme a cigarette."

Eric calmly reached into his pocket and gave her a smoke. She lit it, took a puff, then coughed.

"What is this shit?"

"Kools."

"Where the fuck did you get *Kools*?"

"That's all there was, baby."

"Shit. Trading out my Marlboro Lights for Kools. Jeez, this *is* the end of the world."

"Hey, check it out," said Wayne, pointing at the television. A lone camera was focused on City Hall. "We're on TV!"

The group gathered around the television and listened closely.

"...*We will be providing live footage from Beeville as news arrives.*"

"Hey, let's hang a banner outside the window," Wayne said.

"That's a little too close to something that happened in Waco a while back," Alex replied.

"It's a good idea, though," said Audrey.

"There's some black spray paint upstairs," McMurtry volunteered. "And I think there's a tarp up there, too. You can write on that."

"Eric, are you going to be okay?"

"You know you don't need to baby me, Audrey," Eric told her, taking a long drag off a cigarette.

"Who can help me?"

"I'll go," said Wayne.

After asking McMurtry where everything was, they raced upstairs.

"Hey, look everybody," said Margie, who was looking out the window. "One of them's coming."

They all looked to see a man walking to the building with his arms raised.

"I think they want to negotiate," said McMurtry. "Well, everybody stay here. I'll handle it."

He walked to the main doors. He stayed hidden behind the rightmost door as he pulled the left one open and allowed the man two steps inside.

"I have come to offer terms for your surrender," said the man, in a British accent.

"What are they?" asked McMurtry.

"One, that you disarm yourselves now and exit the building. Two, that all of you face charges of crimes against humanity in the execution of the twenty-five people outside of this town. Three, that the people not found guilty of crimes against humanity will be entered into a FEMA camp for the duration of the state of emergency."

McMurtry thought for a moment. He knew the remaining people of Beeville were listening behind him, so he turned around to address them. "Well, what do you think?"

The silence was broken by Eric: "Tell them to fuck off! This is Beeville, Texas, and they can kiss our ass!"

Though they knew staying in the building was a futile gesture, they also knew there was no way out now.

"We'd rather die than live as slaves," Gary added.

Everyone else nodded solemnly.

McMurtry turned back to the negotiator and said, "You heard them."

"Right," he said, unfazed. He turned on his heels and exited the building.

McMurtry closed and locked the door. He turned and looked at every person in the room. He told them, "God bless you all, and God bless Texas."

As the negotiator walked back to his area, he turned around one final time to see a banner set up outside a third floor window in City Hall.

It read: *We're not Terrorists. We're Texans. Back off.*

Wayne popped open a 24-ounce can of Busch beer. He had made a point on stocking up as much as he could as he retreated on foot to City Hall. Thankful for his foresight, he took a long swig.

Wiping his mouth, he noticed Miguel and Father O'Leary sitting in the corner, concentrating, praying their rosaries.

"Padre," said Wayne, impolitely trying to get the priest's attention. "Hey, Father?"

O'Leary finished his current prayer, his fingers marking his place on the beads. Benevolently, he turned to Wayne. "Yes, my son?"

"Father, are we going to hell for killing those monsters out there?"

O'Leary shook his head gently. "No, my son. Those ghouls are no longer children of God. They are abominations, repugnant servants of Satan. Without their souls, they are the devil's puppets."

Timmy ran back down from the second floor and returned to Margie.

"I found a spot, Aunt Margie," he said.

"Very good, Timmy." She held the boy in a warm embrace. "Now I need you to be brave. I need you to go up there and hide and you need to stay there until I come get you or you think it's safe, okay?"

"Okay, Aunt Margie," said Timmy. Tears rolled down his face, and he knew Blue Panther would have to make yet another appearance. He bounded up the stairs to the second floor.

Audrey tended to her man. "This is it, huh?" she whispered. She wiped away the tear-laced mascara as she ashed her cigarette.

"Baby, don't sweat it. We kicked some major ass the past couple of days. You know you can't do something like that without your number coming up." He was as cool and collected as he'd ever been, like a punk-rock Buddha.

"We did kick some ass, though," she agreed with a smile, trying to suppress the tears that refused to hide.

"*Fuckin'-A*," he said.

Scanning the room, Eric saw Father O'Leary. He called out, "Hey, padre!" O'Leary turned with a smile. "Get your ass over here. I want to renew my vows to my wife."

Audrey beamed in surprise.

O'Leary shook his head at the humorous impudence and walked to the couple. Miguel followed closely at his side.

"No better time than now," said O'Leary. "Please take her hand."

Audrey moved to the side of Eric that was not wounded.

O'Leary read the name on his shirt, and began, "Do you, Eric, take..."

"Audrey," she chimed in.

"...Audrey as your wedded wife?"

"Fuck yeah."

O'Leary grinned at the attitude. "And do you, Audrey, take Eric as your wedded husband?"

Crying, she whimpered, "Hell yeah?"

Grinning, O'Leary stated, "Then with God's blessing, I call you man and wife."

The padre didn't need to finish, as Audrey kissed her wounded man on the lips. The gathering of people clapped in appreciation.

It was at this point that Red began to cough, convulsing violently before gaining control again. The celebration was suddenly in shock as Red—one moment looking in good shape—was now falling apart.

"This is it, man," he said, gasping for breath.

Alex held his friend. "You hang in there, Red," he told him, gripping Red's hand tight, lips quivering. Alex was surprised, feeling the cold breath of death freezing Red's blood.

"Audrey, Eric, I have something to say to you."

Surprised, the newly married couple walked toward Red.

Red coughed up blood again. "Audrey, Eric, I want you to hear me out first. Please."

Audrey shook her head in confusion. "Okay..."

Red was shivering. He stuttered, "By some strange mistake, I shot and killed your son."

Eric exclaimed, "What?!"

"Don't ask me how, but I was fooling around with Lucy St. Claire, and he snuck on the back porch of her house..." He coughed again. "He snuck up on the back porch and was jumped by one of those monsters. I didn't know why he was there. But he was bit. I shot them both. Lucy told me not to say anything. I'm sorry."

"That fuckin' whore," Audrey growled, making a fist with her hands, popping her knuckles.

"Take it easy, babe," Eric said. "This ain't a time for us to be bitching about that. He'd be cooped up with us here anyway. Maybe it was for the best."

"Fuckin' whore. I trusted that bitch," she said, holding Eric close.

"We forgive you," Eric said.

Red smiled. It faded as another coughing fit ensued. He blurted, "I'm sorry." He turned to Alex. "Hey, Alex, you remember that promise we made each other a couple days ago? I need you to do that for me."

"Not now, man. Not now."

"Goddammit, Alex. You gotta let me go," said Red. "I'm done. Shoot me in the head when I come back."

Alex refused to believe his friend was going to leave him so abruptly. He shouted, nearly in tears, "You're not dead yet, man! Fight it!"

"Let me go, Alex!" Tears began to form in his bloodshot eyes.

"Fight it!" yelled Alex at his dying comrade. "Goddammit!"

Within the dank room, a cell phone signal went off. It was the sheriff's phone, signaling a call from his son.

After coughing up some muck and listening to the old familiar tune, Red asked, "Is that the *Sanford and Son* theme?"

Everyone listened.

Sheriff McMurtry yanked the phone off the table. He turned to Red long enough to say, "*Yes*, it's the *Sanford and Son* theme." He then put the phone to his ear and said, "Hello?"

As the sheriff began to communicate with his son, Red broke

out in hysterical laughter. Alex soon joined him, as well as the rest of the room.

"Fuckin' *Sanford and Son*," said Audrey, giggling.

"Dad?" said the digital voice of his son Edgar Lane McMurtry in amazed surprise.

"Son?" he replied, "Is that you?"

"It's me!" he exclaimed in excitement.

"Oh, my God. Edgar, how are you, son?"

"Dad, I'm fine. We're still in a bunker in Germany and—"

"*Germany*? I thought you were in Kuwait?"

"We were. But when the plague broke out, they moved us here. Hey, Dad, they're airlifting us back to America tomorrow."

McMurtry could feel his son's enthusiasm. He was responding as the young child he remembered making good grades, doing good in sports, and proud of his civic work. "Tomorrow? Where to?"

"To a base in West Virginia."

"*West Virginia*? There's nothing in West Virginia."

"I guess there *is*," Edgar replied. "But I hear this is supposed to be something big. They're bringing in all different branches of the military, scientists, the whole lot. None of us grunts knows for sure yet, be we think they're doing *special training* there. I think this is a big step for me."

"Son, I'm so proud of you," McMurtry blurted.

"Listen, Dad, this place I'm going is supposed to be super-secure —and *safe*. They'll let family members in. If you can get there, I can get you in."

McMurtry paused, swallowing back a lump in his throat. He said, "Edgar, I'm sure we'll see each other again real soon, but you know how important my job is here in Beeville." He paused again, then added, "Son, I know the world's flipped on its ear, but if you don't hear from me after this, I want you to know that I love you."

"Yeah. I know, Dad. I love you, too."

"Thank you, son."

"No sweat, Dad. Listen, I gotta go. I'll call you later with the specifics, okay?"

His dad smiled, realizing that he probably was not going to get that follow-up call. "I'll be by my phone, son. I love you."

"I love you, too, Dad. Bye."

"Goodbye, son," and he hung up. Tears began to well up in the sheriff's eyes, and he started to sob.

"Hang on," said Red, coughing, "You downloaded the *Sanford and Son* theme song on your phone?"

"No," grinned McMurtry through his tears, "My son did. It was to signify when he called."

"Dude, your son *rules*," said Red with a painful smile. "Can..." He coughed up more red and black goo. Alex helped wipe his mouth. People in the room were starting to take notice of his escalating symptoms. Alex shook his head as they started to get too close. His subtext was obvious. Eric and Deputy Anderson subtly moved away from Red.

"So, is it the opening theme or the end theme?" Red asked. "Because..." He coughed up bile again. Alex caught it in a cloth. "Because there's the opening theme, and the extended version at the end of the show."

"No, it's the opening theme," McMurtry replied, regaining control of his emotions.

"Can you play the whole thing for me?"

In a sad tribute, McMurtry replied, "Of course."

Pressing a few buttons, the sheriff let the song play. As the first few chords began, Red started to laugh. Followed by Alex. Then McMurtry. Before long, the entire room was laughing.

"Man, I loved that show," Red said, slowly slumping in the corner. His eyes remained open.

Alex closed the eyes of his friend, then hugged him. After a moment he let go, placing a first and final kiss on Red's forehead.

Not wasting another second, he then sent a bullet into the forehead of his friend. Alex hung his head in sadness.

A metallic clink was heard around the building.

"What the fuck is that?" Audrey asked, heading to a window.

As she approached, a shot punched through the glass and pierced her shoulder. Her collarbone was instantly shattered. She fell to the floor in pain.

"Shit!" McMurtry yelled. Father O'Leary and Miguel ran to tend to Audrey as the sheriff barked orders. "Everyone, listen to me. They're scaling the walls to flush us out through the roof. Do as I tell you. Gary, Wayne, to the third floor! Get them coming down the portal from the roof!"

Gary and Wayne took no time to hoof it up the stairs to the third floor entrance.

"Alex, it's you and me on the second floor... Wait." Alex complied. "Margie, you and your daughter hold out here. Take care of Eric and Anderson."

"Fuck that," Eric said. "I'm not going to sit here like a bitch. Give me and my old lady something to do."

"Goddammit, Eric. You and your macho bullshit," groaned Audrey through her pain, yet ready to join her man.

"Okay. Cover the front door."

"Done," they said, hobbling to the front door.

"Father, you and your friend can cover the office door. Position yourself behind the secretary's desk."

The two Catholics made the sign of the cross and headed to the secretary's desk.

"Alex, let's go," said McMurtry, and they ran up the stairs to the second floor.

Gary and Wayne made it to the third floor just in time to have a flashbang explode in their faces. They both screamed in pain and were temporarily blinded.

As they were regaining their senses, gunfire erupted all around them. Gary was shot in the shoulder, and Wayne was hit in the stomach. They fell backwards into the stairway, stumbling painfully down to the second floor.

The explosion of the flashbang surprised Alex and McMurtry as they made it to the second floor. They watched Gary and Wayne stumble down the stairs.

"*Shit,*" McMurtry breathed, helping the men. "They're clearing the third floor. They'll be here any second. Get ready."

In a small corner of an office on the second floor, Timmy shivered in fear. He could hear the desperation in the men's voices.

Alex searched his mind for an advantage. Then it hit him. "Sheriff, you remember that canister I found?"

It didn't take the sheriff a moment to know what Alex was getting at. "Help them, I'll get it."

Alex went to Gary and Wayne as they fell to the floor. McMurtry dashed into the city clerk's office.

"I ain't done," Gary said, shouldering his weapon towards the stairway. As they waited for the sheriff, an instinct drove Gary to fire his weapon. It was as if he could smell the enemy. He hit a U.N. soldier that was about to toss another flashbang onto their floor. The soldier collapsed and fell near the flashbang. The exploding device tore the soldier's face off, busting his eyes like grapes and splitting his eardrums. The soldier, a mangled remnant of a man, screamed in pain.

"*Goddamn right*," Gary muttered bitterly.

McMurtry exited the clerk's office, holding the mysterious canister. He mumbled, "I'm not too sure about this."

Alex grabbed the device from the sheriff. He said, "It might be the only advantage we have."

He pulled the pin.

A thick cloud of gas swiftly emanated from the canister like a bug bomb, blinding Alex and McMurtry. The gas was violently shoved up their noses as Alex tossed the canister at the stairway. Their nostrils were already burning.

A soldier on the roof, monitoring the activity within the building using a small electric device, sent out an urgent message as new information danced across the screen regarding the gas.

Before the soldiers had a chance to infiltrate the second floor, they threw on their gas masks and retreated back to the portal in the roof. They scampered up and out in a panic.

The second floor of the building was quickly enveloped in the thick gas. A slimy buildup began to cake the walls. Alex, Gary, Wayne, and McMurtry were quickly immersed in the thick of the gas. The concoction burned their nostrils and throats, suffocating them as they collapsed on the floor, writhing in pain.

The gas quickly infiltrated the room Timmy was hiding in and penetrated it. Timmy quickly started gagging. Hoping for solace outside of his hiding place, he only found more gas that choked and burned his nostrils. He slowly began to suffocate in intense torment.

The air conditioning and ventilation system dispersed the gas swiftly around the building, and the canister showed no sign of stopping, incessantly spitting its toxic load into City Hall.

Margie, Gina, and Anderson detected the smell.

"What's that?" Margie asked, immediately coughing.

"Don't know," Anderson replied. He looked around as the gas began to fill the room. "It's the vents!" he shouted. "It's coming from the vents!"

Margie desperately tried to cover the vent, but realized there were three more that needed to be secured. Her eyes were itching badly. The gas was insidious, filling the room within seconds and drifting into the hallway.

O'Leary began to inhale it, and it quickly burned his nostrils. Miguel began to inhale it, too. Both started scouring for the source.

"What the fuck?" Audrey asked, looking back at her allies, who were choking in pain.

"Fuckin' shit," Eric growled. "They're using gas against us."

"Motherfuckers," added Audrey.

The gas began to waft in their area.

"We can't go out like this," Eric said to her, standing up from behind the large leather couch. "We gotta rush 'em."

The gas filled the room around them.

"Let's do—" but Audrey could not finish her sentence, as the gas had already enveloped her and her husband. They inhaled it, and began painfully coughing.

Audrey muttered, *Fuckin' douchebags,* as the gas overtook them. They both fell to the floor. Their cigarettes danced across the floor until they came to a rolling stop, the cherries still lit.

The gas canister caked the walls and the bodies in jelly-like goo. The bodies were twisted grotesquely on the floor. White goo filled their nostrils and covered their clothes and flesh.

As the gas danced in the air in the confines of City Hall and began caking every wall in greasy slime, it started drifting to the floor with lingering fingers. The thick mist caressed Audrey and Eric's discarded cigarettes.

And it only took an instant for the smoldering cherries to ignite the flammable fumes.

A huge fireball swirled and churned around the cigarettes, quickly bursting through the first floor, searing and setting ablaze all furniture and the dying bodies of the last valiant warriors of Beeville. With the gas being thickest on the second floor, the windows burst out with flames as the second floor and the bodies lying in their death throes were enveloped in fire. The third floor followed suit, set ablaze by the gas and residue on the walls, floor, and ceiling.

City Hall was now a furnace.

The soldiers were retreating away from the building as it burst into flames. Fire licked the walls along the outside through the windows.

* * * * *

Captain Phillip Carson received a communication from the squad: *Mission complete by default.*

He smiled and watched the building burn.

His final order to the elite squad was to raise a flag. Moments after the command, the Texas flag was lowered. In the glow of the burning City Hall, the United Nations flag was raised as the interior of City Hall was reduced to charred wood.

Beeville had fallen.

Revelation

The bright moon, glowing in full, bathed Beeville in its celestial feminine glow.

Triumphant, Captain Phillip Carson established a small base of operations by the now smoking hulk of Beeville City Hall, consisting of a circle of four tents and a skeleton crew of men. He ordered his subordinates to gather all the corpses and pile them on the other side of the building.

A large set of floodlights was set up near the four tents. Inside, two other subordinates were resting away the night. One tent was set up for the four guards who were assigned to protect the officers, since the majority of the force was already sent on down the road. Only one guard stood watch over the secured city.

Carson sat in a lawn chair outside his tent, gazing at the moon and drinking a glass of whiskey.

Another city conquered by his command.

He felt fantastic.

A guard emerged from the communications tent and timidly approached Carson.

"What is it?" Carson arrogantly and impatiently asked.

"Sir. General Mutumba has sent word that once the mission to Corpus Christi is completed, you will receive a promotion."

Carson closed his eyes and let the statement sink in. He smiled.

The guard went on, "He also said that they are currently working on plans to implement your strategy for forces around the world. They see your work here as a complete and total success."

Relaxed, Carson smiled. He had never felt so proud. He finally proved to the incompetent officers above him that he was, indeed, a wise and capable leader. "Anything else?"

"No, sir."

"Dismissed."

The soldier saluted, thankful. He was ready to return to his interrupted slumber.

Katy Russell, the last surviving citizen of Three Rivers, peeked out of Carson's tent. She was barefoot and wearing only her thin blue belly shirt, displaying a glistening piercing in her navel, and a skimpy white thong. Once she saw the coast was clear, she exited the tent and sauntered over to him.

She hid her anxiety with a forced smile as she leaned over and kissed him on the cheek. She whispered, *"Let's finish our business and I'll be on my way."*

Though she was the perfect physical specimen of the white race, this time he mostly ignored her. He was aroused more by his conquest than the lascivious sellout.

Katy silently re-entered the tent.

Carson took another swig from his glass of whiskey.

Suddenly, in the distance, he heard the clanging rattle of metal on metal. He stood up and shouldered his rifle.

Then, to his amazement, he watched a metal hatch open in the ground outside City Hall. He peered at the opening through the scope on his rifle, anticipating a sneak attack. He released the safety.

He watched through the scope as Mayor Lance Hickland climbed out of the hole, carrying an infant child in his arms. The mayor looked around for a moment, then caught sight of Carson and the rifle he had aimed at him.

The mayor stood, helpless and frozen in place except for his arms, which continued gently rocking the baby.

Carson stared at the man in his crosshairs. Then he situated the crosshairs on the baby, holding them there for several seconds.

The baby was sleeping, oblivious.

Carson lowered his rifle and clicked the safety back into place.

Though he made no signal to Mayor Hickland, the undertone was clear enough.

Mayor Lance Hickland and the infant in his arms were *free to go.*

The mayor turned and ran with his infant into a dark street of Beeville, the sound of his footsteps colliding with the asphalt slowly growing fainter and fainter until they were heard no more.

Satisfied, Carson put his weapon down and, after taking a last sip of whiskey, entered his tent.

Katy Russell was waiting for him, laying on the cot and smiling. She modestly held a blue blanket across her chest, keeping herself covered.

Carson walked in and pulled the tent flaps closed. He lit a kerosene lamp, then went to a small CD player and selected a song.

A Chopin nocturne danced gently from the speakers.

The soothing, yet ominous piece filled the air as Carson went to Katy Russell and used his arms to guide her into a different position. She was now bent over across the cot, her perfectly-proportioned thonged posterior up in the air. He violently smacked her ass with the palm of his hand.

He asked, "Is this how I like it?"

She wanted to say no, but instead nodded in silent approval.

Carson grinned. The girl was a naïve opportunist, making herself a spoil of war. But she was in for more than she bargained for. She was about to be put in her place.

He ripped her thong off with a violent yank, tearing the fabric so it would never be usable again. He pulled his pants down to his ankles.

Then he ravished her.

The music seeped from the canvas tent and flowed gently across the plaza, dancing through the broken windows of City Hall.

Within the scorched tomb, the bodies of the freedom fighters lay burned beyond recognition. The bodies had been fricasseed, but not totally consumed by flames. Eyeballs, though burned, remained open on the corpses, the slimy residue perhaps protecting the optical nerves. The bodies were burned black, and though the skin was burned through and through, the muscles remained.

On the second floor, a torso twitched.

On the first floor, a leg moved.

Below the open door of a small cabinet, a small human figure began to rise.

In the office of the mayor, two bodies slowly and painfully rose.

In the hallway leading to the office, four bodies found their feet and stood upon them.

The burned and smoldering bodies of the men and women who valiantly tried to defend their fair city had risen up again, on the last day.

On the second floor, the five bodies, including the small child, shuffled slowly to the stairs.

As if guided by a sinister evil, the bodies somehow began to congregate in the mayor's office, perhaps remembering their final moments. The group of creatures gathered together, connected by a kind of psychic bond. Though they somehow still felt the pain of their burned bodies, they repressed the urge to resonate with their misery.

Without words, they worked their way to the front doors, marching together in a unified front. They gently pushed the front doors open.

The sentry positioned outside heard the noise, but ignored it, placing the blame on the soft breeze blowing through the plaza. He went back to his Playstation portable, content in the fact that the city was secured. He should know. He was a part of it.

Chopin continued to caress the night air.

The charred group of risen insurgents—twelve in all—stealthily walked down the steps of City Hall. They gazed at the blue tents in their sight line. Though their vision was blurry, their motivation was clear. They segregated, choosing tents indiscriminately, and approached them.

Within moments, they all stood in front of the tents. With the soldiers asleep inside, no one took notice of the malevolent shadows cast over the canvas flaps by the floodlights.

It was a symphonic coordination, with the beasts outside the tents as if preparing themselves. And then, as if a whistle had been blown, the ghouls entered the tents simultaneously.

Two monsters snuck in on an officer and bit into his neck and legs. The man screamed in terror as flesh was torn away from his body, munched on by the burned remains of his enemies.

Two more ghouls entered a tent and were met with gunfire, only to grab the man and bite into his skull and wrist. The man cried out as his hand was bitten and torn away from his body.

Yet two more zombies, one of them small, entered a tent and attacked the two soldiers within. The small monster attacked the neck of the sleeping soldier while the other went for the face. Blood contrasted their burnt and disfigured flesh.

Carson was still on top of Katy Russell, their deviant intercourse causing her to breathe through gritted teeth, when the first beast entered their tent. It grabbed Carson by the shoulders and pulled him away. Katy turned and looked over her shoulder upon feeling Carson's withdrawal, then opened her mouth and screamed. Monsters replaced Carson's position on top of her, but they penetrated with their teeth, tearing through her arms and back.

Carson reached for the pistol next to the CD player, but was attacked by three of the zombies, who quickly took a bite out of his chest, head, and shoulder. Katy Russell suffered a similar fate, with the remaining two taking a large chunk out of her neck and breasts and biting her navel piercing directly out of her skin.

The sentry, suddenly sensing being totally alone, paused his videogame and approached the tents.

In the first tent, the man was being disemboweled. A long cord dangled from the mouth of the burnt ghoul as he munched on the fleshy digestive tract. The other creature was tearing the remains off of the man's foot.

In the second tent, a creature used a pistol to crack open the soldier's head and dig into his skull for his brains. The gun had discharged once, busting a hole through the monster's chest, but it continued eating, unfazed. The other zombie was content to sit and devour the hand it had just separated from the body, crunching on the bones.

In the third tent, one soldier stumbled from his cot as the small zombie was clawing into his neck, tearing at innards and munching on flesh. Blood squirted from the artery onto the blue canvas. The other soldier could not escape the literal death grip of the other ghoul, and submitted shortly after the monster gouged his eyes and bit into his face.

The soldier ran to his commanding officer's tent and threw open the tent flap. Before his eyes, his commander and his lover were being consumed. A large portion of flesh had been removed from Captain Carson's chest, and the zombie was already digging into his ribcage for the heart. Another had already cracked open his skull and was eating his brains directly out of his head. Another was yanking at his arm, trying to pull it loose from the shoulder so it could be more easily devoured.

Katy Russell was lying on the ground, naked, caked in blood, and being consumed. Only a single breast remained as the zombie devoured the first fleshy breast with gusto. The other ghoul was trying to twist her head off at the neck after consuming everything down to the spine.

The soldier opened fire, taking down two zombies before one of the other creatures lunged at him and chomped into his neck, ending his military career and his life.

The screams of the dying faded out under the full moon. A coyote howled in the distant woods as the zombies devoured the soldiers. The ghouls, free to express their pain, howled with the wild beast. Their cries echoed across the abandoned city, calling forth any other zombies that might be in Beeville.

As the ghouls devoured the bodies of their adversaries, one thing —though debatable—was apparent:

Satan made good on a promise from God.

While their overconfident leader was being devoured in an orgy of blood, a large contingent of United Nations peacekeepers were hours away from their next destination. Following what was to be their final order, the soldiers continued on, bathed in the cold radiance of the moon. Under that malevolent light they marched, determined to carry out their orders and secure America somewhere down the road.

3:28 a.m.
Sunday, July 30th, 2006
Kyle, in the republic of Texas

HUNGRY FOR MORE?

Join the frenzy...

A bizarre plague of the walking dead...

A nation desperate for survival...

It could be the end of the world.

DOWN the ROAD

A Zombie Horror Story

by Bowie V. Ibarra

Around the globe, the dead are rising to devour the living. Hospitals are overrun and martial law has been declared. The streets are in chaos. Society is disintegrating.

George Zaragosa is a young school teacher living in the shadow of his fiancee's unsolved murder. Now he just wants to go home to his family. He has made the journey before, traveling from Austin to San Uvalde. It is usually a short drive. But he knows this time is going to be different.

Along the way, George will have to negotiate military roadblocks, FEMA camps and street thugs, not to mention hordes of the living dead. He is determined to make it home, but only one thing is certain: his trip down the road will be a journey like no other.

ISBN# 0-9765559-8-0

www.permutedpress.com

Killing
zombies...

...with
<u>attitude.</u>

www.twilightofthedead.com

THE MORNINGSTAR STRAIN
PLAGUE OF THE DEAD
A ZOMBIE NOVEL BY Z A RECHT

The end begins with a viral outbreak unlike anything mankind has ever encountered before. The infected are subject to delirium, fever, a dramatic increase in violent behavior, and a one-hundred percent mortality rate...

Death.

But it doesn't end there.
The victims return from death to walk the earth.

When a massive military operation fails to contain the plague of the living dead, it escalates into a global pandemic. In one fell swoop, the necessities of life become much more basic. Gone are the petty everyday concerns. Gone are the amenities of civilized life.

Yet a single law of nature remains:
Live, or die. Kill, or be killed.

The Morningstar Saga has begun...

www.permutedpress.com
www.themorningstarsaga.com

Printed in the United States
216922BV00005B/56/A